Saltaire

HAZEL JACKS

Published by Hazel Jacks

Editing: Dawn Alexander at Evident Ink and James Gallagher at Castle Walls Editing

Proofreading: Elaine York at Allusion Publishing and Marla Esposito at Proofing Style

Cover Design and Formatting: Mary at Books and Moods

To N & M. Thank you for letting me give this a try.

Playlist

"Mr. Brightside" – The Killers

"Konstantine" – Something Corporate

"Hit or Miss" – New Found Glory

"The Boys of Summer" – Don Henley

"Here's to the Night" – Eve 6

"Thong Song" – Sisqó

"Back to California" – Sugarcult

"In Too Deep" – Sum 41

"Seasons" – Good Charlotte

"In This Diary" – The Ataris

"I'd Do Anything" – Simple Plan

"One Year, Six Months" – Yellowcard

"Suspension" – Mae

"I Wanna Dance with Somebody" – Whitney Houston

"Fight for Your Right" – Beastie Boys

"The Brilliant Dance" – Dashboard Confessional

"Playing Favorites" – The Starting Line

"You're So Last Summer" – Taking Back Sunday

"What's the point of thinking about how it's going to end when it's just the beginning?"
Judy Blume,
Summer Sisters

CHAPTER 1

Raegan

"**T**his is the summer of us—sun, beach, and boys! I know we only graduated a week ago, but I feel more grown-up already. You know we're practically college girls now."

Lily has been in one of her whimsical, nonstop-talking moods since we started our annual summer pilgrimage from New York City to Fire Island. For as long as I can remember, we've always arrived the Saturday before Memorial Day and headed back to the city the day after Labor Day, on what the locals like to call Tumbleweed Tuesday.

I roll down the Town Car's window and breathe in the hot and muggy suburban air as we approach the ferry terminal in Bay Shore.

Lily leans over and whispers in my ear so Remi, our driver, doesn't hear. "I know you're still going all Virgin Mary on me and saving yourself for that special someone, but I need to expand my sexual knowledge. I refuse to leave for college and only have experience with immature high school boys."

She takes a bite of crunchy Cheetos and seductively licks the orange powder off her fingers, making her point all too clear. Lily is one of those people who possesses natural beauty. She is stunning. Her honey-blonde hair is pulled back into a full ponytail, a few wisps framing her indigo-blue eyes. She has perfect skin and never has to wear foundation to cover up zits.

"I'm not *all* Virgin Mary," I protest before I roll my window up and pop a Cheeto in my mouth.

Lily rolls her eyes and gives me her I-don't-give-a-shit look.

"You are still a virgin. So, therefore, I must keep calling you Virgin Mary." She sticks her orange powder-coated tongue out at me.

Lily has always been more outgoing, dragging me along on her adventures. She's been trying to get me to expand my "sexual prowess" and get more experience. I'm hoping this summer will be my opportunity to do more than just kiss a guy before Lily and I leave for UC Berkeley together in August.

Thinking about it makes me anxious because I don't want to hook up with just any guy. I want it to be special, to mean something.

"All right, ladies. Here we are." Remi puts the car in park, then twists to look over his shoulder at us in a fatherly manner.

"Go to the cashier and purchase your ferry tickets to Ocean Beach. I'll take your bags out of the trunk and bring them to you."

Lily slides out of the car, jumping up and down in the gravel parking lot in her pleated skirt and teal tube top. "Remi! You are the best!"

My wild but loving best friend is all leg, and with her four-inch wedges, she stands just over six feet tall, a stark comparison to my meager five feet two inches.

"Miss Raegan, you'd better be on your best behavior this summer. I don't want to hear through the grapevine that you're causing a ruckus on the island." Remi pulls me into a bear hug, dragging my feet off the ground.

Remi has been a driver for my uncle Rhett since before I was born. Over the past few years, his role has shifted, becoming my personal driver, taking me to and from school and after-school activities, and driving me around the city on weekends to hang out with Lily and our other friends from school. Though I know Remi secretly shares the ongoing details of my "back seat" discussions with Uncle Rhett, I see Remi as family—he's another uncle.

"Remi, it's me. If you need to worry about anyone, worry about Lily." I laugh as he drops me back to the ground.

"Jed will be coming to the island in a few days. I'm going to tell him to keep his eyes on you both." Remi gives us his much-practiced dad eyes that say, "Don't even try."

Cue dramatic eye roll.

"I can't wait." The last thing I need is my protective older brother, Jed, keeping an eye on me. Ever since I turned sixteen, almost two years ago, it's become his personal mission to take on the role my dad walked away from after I was born. Jed does everything in his power to ensure I'll never have a serious boyfriend. The few times I've actually been out on a date, Jed interferes and scares the guy off shortly after.

He's a real cockblock.

Lily and I wave to Remi as he pulls away, leaving us with our suitcases and summer anticipation in the Long Island sun. "Eeeek!" Lily squeals. "I thought he'd never leave!"

Lily pulls a water bottle from her bag, unscrews the cap, and brings it to her mouth. She swallows a mouthful and hands me the bottle, her big blue eyes twinkling mischievously.

"What's this?" I'm immediately suspicious, having fallen victim to Lily's alcohol-in-the-water-bottle trick in the past. So I give it a sniff. My nose burns from the potent alcohol vapors.

"Just drink it! Let's get the party started!" She draws out the *ty* in *party*, making it sound extra fun.

I adore Lily's positive outlook on life. Always the optimist, looking for the fun in each moment. I eye her as I take a tiny sip. The clear liquid touches my tongue, and I choke on the fumes before I can swallow. I spit the contents on the ground, then wipe my mouth.

"Lily, what the hell? This is straight vodka. You couldn't even mix it with something?" I don't even know why I'm trying to act surprised. I really shouldn't be.

"What would be the fun in that?" Lily laughs, fingering her ponytail over her shoulder.

"Oh, I don't know. It may taste better, and I would actually be able to tolerate it? Plus, I don't want to show up at Uncle Rhett's drunk. Remember what happened on New Year's Eve? He'll ground us for the entire summer if he even suspects we're drunk again." I hold the water bottle back out to her in protest.

"We have plenty of time to sober up before we have to be at his house. Just take a few sips," Lily demands, pushing my arm back.

Knowing she will win, because she is Lily Hart, the girl who always wins, I roll my eyes and take another small sip.

It can't hurt to let loose a little and have some fun on our way to the island.

I pop a few Cheetos in my mouth to cover up the vodka taste, and I suck the powder off my fingers.

The line to board the ferry finally begins to move. The vodka warms my veins, and I let out a silly laugh as I walk with Lily up the boat ramp. We eagerly hand our suitcases and tickets to the deckhand and walk up the stairs to the ferry's top deck. It will be scorching hot in the sun, but to have a view when we arrive at Ocean Beach makes it bearable.

I can picture the oversized steel utility carts and wagons locked up on the dock, waiting for their owners to load them with baggage before dragging them off to their houses. I picture the handfuls of children running around in their swimsuits, much as I did when I was younger, licking ice cream off cones purchased from the small shop on the dock. I picture the countless bicycles lined up outside Shipwreck, where blue umbrellas provide shade for patrons enjoying an outside lunch. I picture sunsets from the dock, the sky bright orange, turning to red before casting purples as the sun dips below the horizon.

Lily takes a seat on a bench two rows behind the wheelhouse. I follow closely behind, brushing away tiny pebbles of sand left behind from previous passengers before slipping into the seat next to her. She giggles and hands me the water bottle. I take another quick swig, trying to maneuver the vodka past my tongue and to the back of my throat without burning my mouth. I fail, and my eyes begin to sting. I could breathe fire, but all I end up doing is choking out a few coughs.

After I catch my breath, I look ahead at the window-enclosed wheelhouse and see a guy, maybe in his twenties, at the helm, looking in our direction.

He's tan and tall with dark-brown hair and sun-kissed golden highlights, tousled and grown out, curls falling over his forehead and past his ears. His jawline is defined, with stubble on his cheeks and chin, and his nose is peppered with soft freckles. I can't see the color of his eyes, or where exactly he's looking, because they are hidden behind a pair of Wayfarers.

His Islander Ferry shirt has only the bottom three buttons clasped. I can't decide if I think it's hot or cheesy, like he knows how good he looks and has no shame letting his bare chest glisten in the midday sun. He's sporting cargo shorts, and his right arm is covered in a tattoo sleeve, adding a bad-boy vibe.

I immediately feel ten degrees warmer, and I'm certain it's not the vodka.

He is the most attractive guy I've ever seen. My heart begins to beat faster, and a knot forms in my stomach.

My eyes stay locked on him, and I whisper, "Lily."

I'm trying not to let my mouth gape, wanting to appear stealthy, but after all those sips of vodka, I don't know how suave I seem.

This guy is most definitely looking at us, and a big grin appears on his face as he folds his arms across his chest and nods in our direction. I feel my cheeks flush red as he turns back toward the helm, reaches up, and pulls the radio down.

"This is the Islander Ferry heading to Ocean Beach. It's a beautiful day. Enjoy the sun, and we'll get you to the island shortly."

He tugs on the air horn once, then moves some gears and pushes buttons on the dash. The motor lets out a loud rumble and vibrates at our feet as the ferry pulls away from the dock, signaling that the voyage to Fire Island has begun.

I look out over the Great South Bay as the ferry travels away from the south shore of Long Island toward the thin strip of land that marries with the Atlantic Ocean. Back in the car with Remi, I had pulled my hair up into a messy bun, anticipating this exact moment when the wind would blow gusts against my face and carry my curly hair into another dimension. I inhale the salty air as Lily's ponytail dances around in the breeze. I need to make my last summer on Fire Island, before I become an adult and move away from home, the best summer yet.

Lily and I spend the thirty-minute ride passing the water bottle back and forth, taking little sips while ogling Mr. Gorgeous I-Wanna-Get-in-Your-Pants Captain.

He occasionally turns back and looks our way but focuses on the water for most of the journey. It's a given that Lily will be the one to snag him this summer, because I'm sure he has a type, and that type is Lily—it's always Lily. I'm not mad about it. It's just a fact I already know. Also, I'm pretty sure Lily winked at him, which, according to her rules, establishes her as the interested party. I'm totally okay with that. I haven't even made it to the island yet, and I have all summer to find a boy—or two.

I look out at my favorite place in the entire world as Mr. Sexy Ferry Captain slowly pulls the ferry up against the dock at Ocean Beach. I have always looked forward to my summers on the island. Even with the vodka coursing through my body, the air out here feels lighter, so much less oppressive than the stuffy city atmosphere. The distinct bouquet of salt water and deep-fried onion rings from Shipwreck mingles in the air. I look around at the other passengers and see lightness and excitement as the mainland's day-to-day grind fades away. When you come here, you come to disconnect.

Lily and I already discussed that we'll stop for a soda at the market on our walk to Uncle Rhett's house. We should be sober by the time we arrive, so we won't get caught with vodka on our breaths.

Lily jumps out of her seat before the ferry is even fully tied up. I know what's on her mind. She's going in for the kill with the captain.

"Let's do this." Lily gives herself a little pep talk and tucks both thumbs under the elastic of her tube top, pulling it up. She runs her hands down her skirt to flatten it out. Straightening her back, Lily holds herself with the utmost self-assurance. You would never know from her brash outer exterior, but deep down, Lily is the most genuine person I know. Sure, she's a bona fide trust-fund kid, and her parents moved halfway across the world so her dad could take a job as a diplomat in Istanbul. So she's been raised by hired staff for the past three years, but she cares deeply for those she loves. Her brazenness is a shield to protect her from being hurt like she was after her parents left.

I grab my purse and head toward the stairwell, careful to make sure I appear normal, and not tipsy, as I walk off the ferry. I keep my head down as I get closer to the stairwell, where Mr. Could I Be Any Sexier? stands.

As we approach, I overhear him telling the other passengers, "Thank you. Enjoy your stay on the island. Watch your step going down."

My hands are sweating, and my heart is beating rapidly as I get closer to him.

Crap. Maybe I am drunk.

Lily's sultry voice echoes, "Thanks, Captain. Great driving."

He chuckles. "I technically don't drive the ferry. I steer it."

"Well, you can drive or steer me anytime. I'll take it any way you want to give it."

I can't see her face, but I guarantee Lily is licking her lips while she looks him straight in the eyes and shimmies her shoulders. She exudes more confidence than a peacock displaying its mating feathers.

My mouth pinches shut at her words because I don't want to laugh too loud. This is Lily. No filter and no shame.

I look up, and to my surprise, his eyes are not on Lily. He's staring directly at me through his Wayfarers. I stop breathing, but my heart rate speeds up, and my palms instantly get clammy. I glance to his chest and see *Penn* is embroidered in cursive on his button-up shirt.

Penn, what a unique name.

Before another thought can cross my mind, I slip and tumble the entire stairwell to the ferry's lower deck. I hit the bottom of the stairs with a blow to my head. Lying on the ground, all I hear is Lily's voice screaming, "Oh my God! Oh my God! Raegan!"

I'm on my back, and I slowly open my eyes. The top of my head throbs. I blink a few times to try to rouse myself. Captain Penn is hovering above me, his Wayfarers off, smoky gray eyes looking directly into mine.

This is for sure a dream.

"Hey there." He smirks. Only half his mouth tilts up. "You took quite the spill and bumped your head. Do you know where you are?"

Too shocked from the fall, or maybe from the unsettled vodka in my stomach, or from the heat radiating off Penn's hands, which are lightly holding my shoulders, I don't speak. I barely nod.

"Let's move over here and out of the way so the rest of the passengers can get off and I can examine you." He gestures to an empty area on the bottom deck of the ferry.

Examine me? Oh my God. Kill me now.

Embarrassed, I attempt to sit up and scoot on my butt to the area Penn pointed out, but blood is dripping down my knees, and I'm disoriented. Then, suddenly, I'm acutely aware of the whole situation, especially when Penn wraps his hands under my armpits and helps me, adding further insult to injury.

"There we go." Penn sits behind me, my back resting against his chest. My stomach knots with a strange eagerness from his touch. Fire seems to spread across my back where I'm lying against what I can only assume are his rock-hard abs. I quickly determine the feeling in my stomach can't be from the fall or the vodka—there's an electrical current running through Penn and into me.

"Raegan! Girl. What the hell happened?" Lily snaps me out of my daydream and gets in my face to examine me, as if she's a qualified doctor.

"Good thing this fearless captain is here." She winks and tilts her head toward Penn, not caring at how obvious she's being.

I widen my eyes at Lily, using them to say, "Stop talking," but Lily proceeds with her assessment.

"I mean, one second you were walking perfectly fine—next thing I know, you're tumbling down the stairs. What if you have a concussion? Let me see your eyes. Captain, do you have a flashlight? I need to examine my girl's pupils to see if they are dilated. Do you have a doctor on board?"

"Lily," I interject through gritted teeth. She stops, finally taking a breath and pausing. "I'm fine. My head hurts a little, and the blood on my knees looks worse than it feels. I just want to get off this ferry and head to the house."

"You fell pretty hard. You should probably sit for just a little longer. Your chatty friend is right. You may have a concussion." Penn slides his sturdy body out from behind me and looks into my eyes.

I think I might vomit from humiliation.

No sooner than I think it, my stomach churns, and a vodka-Cheeto mixture rolls up my throat and out of my mouth. In a moment of panic, I manage to turn my head and barf most of the burning orange liquid down the side of the ferry and into the water.

Thank God I didn't barf on him.

Mortified, I cover my mouth with my hands and freeze.

"Girl, I know you're a lightweight and all, but come on. You didn't even have that much vodka." Lily gives a sarcastic head shake.

"I don't think it's the vodka. I think your friend here needs to be examined by a doctor. Throwing up after a head injury can be a sign of concussion," Penn informs us.

He's authoritative, but not arrogant.

I don't know why I think his command is so *hot*. I must have hit my head hard, because I can't believe I'm gawking at him while I'm in this state.

"The doctor is just two blocks from here. My shift is over, so I can take you there now."

Penn scoops me up, one arm secure behind my back and his other arm holding my legs. I open my mouth to tell him that I can walk and he doesn't need to carry me, but I buzz at his touch, and the words don't come out.

His scent is salty and manly, wafting into my nose, consuming every brain cell I have left after the fall.

"Wrap your arms around my neck."

I freeze, having never embraced a guy quite like this before.

Noticing my obvious pause, Penn follows with, "I don't bite." He gives me an adorable lopsided grin.

I wrap my arms around his neck, as told, while he takes long strides off the ferry and onto the dock.

I'm somehow able to hold my throw-up breath the entire way to the doctor's house, embarrassed beyond belief.

CHAPTER 2

Penn

I scoop Raegan into my arms, like a princess who needs to be saved, and carry her to Dr. Smith's house in Ocean Beach.

Her knees are torn up, and blood drips down both legs, staining my shirt and shorts, but I don't give a shit. I'm entirely engulfed by the fruity smell of her hair.

It's all I can do to resist the urge to bury my nose in her messy bun and breathe her in. I also can't help but notice she's wearing a New Found Glory T-shirt, one of my favorite bands.

Pop-punk, emo girl. I like this.

I know, without a doubt, just from her T-shirt and cute appearance, that she and I will hit it off.

I carry her into the house that seconds as Dr. Smith's office, and the nurse takes her back to the examination room. Lily stayed back at the dock to collect her and Raegan's bags from the ferry, so I'm alone in the empty waiting room with the biggest grin, thinking of how these girls are quite the pair and have made my day so refreshing.

I first saw Lily in the parking lot, back in Bay Shore. I was sitting in the ferry administrative office, a half-played solitaire game on the computer screen, strumming on one of my old guitars that I keep there for moments when inspiration hits. I was trying to work through the bridge chords for a song I've been stuck on writing for months when I looked out the office window and saw Lily with her long, toned, tan legs. She was jumping and dancing around like a teenage girl at a Backstreet Boys concert, kicking up gravel and dust.

Lily reminds me of many of the chicks who come to Fire Island for the summer—these rich cougars and trust-fund college girls come for a week, looking for a hookup, and I never have to see them again. It's perfect for my lifestyle. I don't want to be held down by anyone or anything. Historically, I'll shamelessly admit, I've been known to let almost any willing chick blow me, but I find myself becoming pickier as I get older.

Plus, my older brother, Chase, thinks I'm a man whore, so I made him a stupid bet over poker one night that I will lie low this summer and have only one girl per month. For each month that I have only one consistent hookup, he'll pay me a hundred bucks, and if I lose, I'll owe him a hundred bucks for that month. I don't care about the money, but I'm fiercely competitive, so there's no way in hell he's going to win.

I swear, though, I don't go looking for these chicks. They gravitate toward me. Something about being a local and working on the ferries turns women on, and I don't have to try hard at all.

Chicks like boats, and boats are what I know.

My dad has owned the Islander Ferry company going on thirty years now, so I grew up on these docks and boats. Once I turned fourteen, Dad gave me a job, and I worked my way up the ranks from deckhand to mate. Finally, a few summers ago, I became captain.

And with the exception of the stairs incident, today is just like every other summer day on Fire Island. Tourists flocking to the island, skimpy bikinis, random house parties—and the laid-back environment makes it the ultimate bachelor paradise.

You'd think summer would be my favorite season on Fire Island, but I prefer spring, once the snow has melted and life slowly picks back up. It's quiet; the deer are plentiful; the pathway streets are not congested with people walking and biking. It's just the locals. Only a few hundred of us live on the island year-round, and we are a small, tight-knit community.

Since it's Memorial Day weekend, the official start to Fire Island season, the ferries have been running back and forth at almost full capacity, shuttling the thousands of people who will flood the towns and villages this summer. These people will sit around on the beach and clog up the restaurants and streets. I should be appreciative, as they pay the bills, but the atmosphere changes here during summer. It's a far cry from the quiet solitude of fall, winter, and spring.

But it was Raegan in the parking lot who captured me from the moment I saw her. Casual and petite, probably not even a hundred pounds soaking wet. I watched her get out of the Town Car and hug the driver. I've been dealing with filthy-rich, snobby New York City kids for years now, and I can tell just from their car that these girls, or rather their parents, are dripping in money. And hugging your driver is not something I've ever seen these rich girls do.

Raegan held my attention the entire ferry ride from Bay Shore to Ocean Beach. I stole as many glances as I could from the helm, and had to tame down the dirty thoughts going through my mind each time I caught her staring at me while she passed a water bottle, obviously filled with alcohol, back and forth with Lily.

Her hair, all tied up on top of her head, looks sexy as hell. I wonder what it would feel like to pull the elastic out and run my fingers through her waves while she's in the precarious sex position I've always wanted to try with a short girl. I bet she's a firecracker in bed.

Chase is for sure going to lose our bet this month because Raegan is going to be mine for the next four weeks. Easy hundred coming right into my pocket.

I also like how she's dressed so casually for coming to the island, in just a T-shirt, jean shorts, and beat-up Chuck Taylors. I like the laid-back Raegan look.

It was when I heard her infectious laugh, halfway through the ferry ride, that I knew I needed to talk to her. I sneaked another glance her way as she threw her head back and laughed at something Lily said. The smile that crossed her face when she pulled her head back up hit me hard, because at that moment I didn't see a girl I just wanted to fuck—I saw a girl I wanted to spend time with and get to know.

I am a little surprised I've not seen Raegan or Lily around the island before today. There's no way I'd ever forget those piercing green eyes on Raegan, and I sure would have a difficult time not remembering someone as outgoing as Lily.

A creaking sound saves me from my thoughts as Lily waltzes through the front door, a beaming smile plastered across her face. I need to break it to Lily that it's her friend I want, not her. Lily has a little too much energy for me. It radiates from her core, and her body language screams, "I'm a good time!" I don't doubt this, but Lily will be better for someone like my buddy and roommate, Theo. They are both extreme extroverts, and I'm sure Theo would love to indulge Lily's appetite. They'll either be an epic love story or an absolute train wreck.

Lily struts my way and sits in the chair next to me. "You're so sweet. You didn't have to bring Raegan here. I could've done it. We know Ocean Beach like the back of our hands. I've been spending summers on the island with her family for a long time now. You might as well call us locals."

"Will you girls be here all summer?" Curiosity oozes from my pores.

Lily pulls out her ponytail and shakes her hair before gathering it between her fingers and redoing the ponytail as she responds, "Mostly.

This summer we're leaving early 'cause we start college in California in August."

Perfect. The entire summer is much longer than necessary. I just need a month so Chase can pay me my hundred bucks. Then she'll head off for college, and I'll be done with her, no strings attached, just the way I like it.

Lily keeps going and going, name-dropping rich people who own houses out here and the handful of bars and restaurants on the island. She's like an Energizer bunny. I smile, not because I'm attracted to her, but because she doesn't know how to stop talking. Guaranteed, I know this island a hundred times better than she does, but I let her keep talking, hoping she'll spill some vital information to help me land Raegan.

"So, Captain Penn, are you all work and no play, or a work hard, play hard kind of guy?"

I have to hand it to Lily. She's resilient. I've given no indication that I'm remotely interested in her, and yet she keeps trying.

"Guess you could say I'm a little of both. I work the ferries and spend the rest of my time at the beach and hanging out with my buddies." I purposely don't tell her that I write music. It's too personal, something reserved for only close friends and family, of which we are neither.

"Buddies, huh? Will they be arriving on the island soon? There's a great restaurant in Ocean Beach called Shipwreck. We should meet up there sometime for a drink. Do you know where Shipwreck is?" she asks in authentic sincerity.

"You really don't think I'm a local, do you?" I jokingly taunt. "Of course I know Shipwreck. I live out in Kismet with three other guys, and none of us cook, so whenever we're in Ocean Beach, we eat there. They make a great rocket fuel. The best blend of coconut milk, pineapple, amaretto, and 151 you can find."

The last time I took a girl to Shipwreck to drink rocket fuel, she got absolutely shit-faced off only one. I had to drop her back off at her rental house because she was sloppy drunk, and it wouldn't have been right to still hook up with her.

"Well, we'll have to have a rocket fuel with you sometime. We got our fake IDs ready," Lily overzealously informs me. I'm sure neither Lily nor Raegan could handle one rocket fuel either.

"Do you now? How old are you girls?" I cross my fingers.

Please be eighteen.

"I'm eighteen, and Raegan is seventeen. Her birthday is in a month. How old are you?"

Damn. Raegan is only seventeen.

"I'm twenty-three."

Six years older than Raegan, that's a big gap. I've been meticulous about never making the mistake of sleeping with, or even messing around with, an underage girl. I'll have to remind my dick to stay in my pants for another month because I'm not sure I'll be able to stay away from Raegan before she turns eighteen, even if it's just to smell her apple and raspberry hair some more.

"So how do you know Raegan?" I ask, feeling slightly pathetic that I'm gathering my own intel on Raegan, since Lily seems preoccupied only with wanting to get drunk and hook up.

"Oh, we go way back—all the way to first grade. You see, there was this boy Troy and one day he put rubber cement in Raegan's hair during art time. I saw him do it, and our teacher couldn't get it out—it was this big sticky bird's nest." Lily gestures with her hands, creating an aura of space above her head, scrunching her face into a look of disgust. "Raegan had to get her hair cut super short, and kids started calling her the 'glue-hair girl.' So I got her the vengeance she deserved, and I superglued Troy to his chair a few weeks later. The custodian had to come into the classroom and literally rip him out of his pants. Troy never messed with Raegan again, and she and I became instant best friends."

"You did not." I laugh. Clearly, Lily has balls, even as a six-year-old.

My laughing pauses as movement catches in the corner of my eye. Raegan walks out from the back room, the blood somewhat cleaned from her legs and her knees covered in extra-large Band-Aids. She's holding an ice pack to the back of her head, and she couldn't be any more enchanting.

"I may or may not have a concussion, so to be on the safe side, the doctor wants me to take it easy and stay in bed for the next twenty-four hours."

Raegan looks at Lily as she speaks, but I know she sees me sitting right next to her friend. It's almost like she's pretending I'm not here. Her eyes slowly shift toward mine, and I give her my best panty-dropping smile, then watch her cheeks blush red.

I like that I have this effect on you, Raegan.

"Oh, hey. Um. You didn't have to stay." She looks at me nervously. This girl has brought entertainment to my day, and I want to hook up with her. But there is also a part of me that is concerned about her head, and I stayed here because I sincerely want to make sure she's okay.

"I told him the same thing already," Lily informs Raegan, still looking at me.

"I don't mind. You're not interrupting anything." I give Raegan a polite smile. All that's waiting for me at home are the guys, ready to start a card game before hitting up the Sundowner later tonight. The guys can wait. Being here is much more exciting.

"I'm sorry you hurt your head, and I'm so bummed you have to stay in bed." Lily pouts, sticking out her bottom lip. "What about the summer kickoff party in Kismet tonight? You can't miss it."

No. You can't miss it. I'll be at that party too.

"I'll be okay. You should still go. My head hurts really bad, so I just want to get to Uncle Rhett's and lie down." Raegan pauses, then adds, "What happened to our bags?"

"I called Uncle Rhett and told him about you falling down the stairs. I had to beg him not to come here. I didn't want him to get suspicious with the vodka and all, so I told him this is part of letting us grow up, and I reminded him that we'll be going off to college soon. It took a little convincing, but he agreed."

"Yeah, the doctor is apparently friends with Uncle Rhett. He said they talked on the phone, and Uncle Rhett gave his verbal consent to treat me," Raegan says.

Lily leans closer to Raegan and lowers her voice so the nurse in the other room won't overhear. "Does the doctor know you were drinking?"

"No. That guy is so old, he has no clue." Raegan pauses and adds, "Thank God. The last thing we need is Uncle Rhett knowing we've been drinking. We'd for sure be grounded the entire summer."

"That would be no fun," I interject, like an idiot. Raegan turns toward me and crooks her head with a slight smirk, like she's surprised to see I'm still here.

"Thanks for your help. Sorry about the throw up, and the blood." Raegan gestures to my bloody clothes. "Can I wash them for you or something? I mean, I don't need them right now, 'cause then you'd have nothing to wear."

Her face is crimson and I just smile, wholly engrossed with her.

"I guess I could pick them up from you and wash them, then return them. Or is that weird? I could just buy you some new clothes. Oh my God, how about I just give you some cash and you can buy new clothes?" She spews words without thought, and I find it irresistible and endearing. She's cute when she's flustered.

I let her continue before I reach out and gently touch her shoulder and give her a grin. "I'm glad I was able to help today. I hope your head feels better soon. Don't worry about my clothes. I can wash them, and they'll be good as new." I remove my hand, waiting for her to respond, but she doesn't.

She looks uncomfortable or embarrassed, or maybe a mixture of both, so I quickly follow up. "You girls sound like you have things under control, so I'll get going." I point my thumbs toward the door and look at Raegan. "I'm glad you're going to be okay." I give her a wink for good measure. "Oh, and please don't sue the ferry company." I smirk. Joking, yet serious.

I point to Raegan's T-shirt. "Did you know New Found Glory will be playing at Jones Beach tomorrow night, and Something Corporate is opening? I'm going with my roommates, and we have extra tickets. You girls should join us. It's gonna be fun."

I'm not breaking my must-be-eighteen rule if I hang out with her in a group, right? Plus, she's almost eighteen, so maybe there's room to bend the rule a little? A kiss or two wouldn't hurt anyone.

"Oh, um. Yeah, maybe." Raegan stumbles for her words.

"We'd love to join you," Lily confidently assures me. "But I don't like those bands, so you better have a single friend available for me." Lily holds her pinkie out to me. I laugh. I'm pretty sure I haven't made a pinkie promise since elementary school, but I'm happy she's finally connecting the dots that I'm into Raegan. Her hating pop-punk music is even more confirmation that Theo will be perfect for her because he loathes it as well.

I extend my pinkie to Lily and interlock with hers. "I pinkie promise. Meet us at the Sundowner in Kismet at four tomorrow evening."

I release my pinkie from Lily and give Raegan one last smile before I walk out of Dr. Smith's, eager for what this next month may hold.

CHAPTER 3

Raegan

U ncle Rhett bought his first house in Ocean Beach in the early eighties, and it has been my family's tradition to spend summers on the island ever since. Uncle Rhett is always looking for his next investment opportunity, buying a new place on the island every few years.

This one has to be the best yet. It's newly remodeled, with five bedrooms and the huge bonus—a pool. The house sits on the bay side of the island and has a private dock. The house is unique, as there aren't many this size with a pool in this location.

Standing in the foyer, I decide it's one of the nicest houses I've ever seen in Ocean Beach. Modern and beautiful, Uncle Rhett must have spent a ridiculous amount on the remodel.

When Lily called Uncle Rhett earlier today to tell him about my fall down the stairs, he mentioned that he and his girlfriend, Finn, were invited to dinner at their friend's house in Cherry Grove. Uncle Rhett wanted to make sure Lily and I would be okay on our own for dinner tonight, and Lily assured him we didn't mind one bit. Their last-minute dinner plans worked exceedingly in our favor because with them out of the house, there was no chance of getting caught with vodka on our breath when we arrived.

One of the things I enjoy most about summers on the island, and another advantage to our arrival at the house this evening, is Uncle Rhett does not keep a staff. On the island, Uncle Rhett has only one housekeeper who stops by once a day to clean and do small amounts of cooking and shopping, but mostly each person takes care of themselves.

Lily and I find our room with the two twin beds upstairs. Lily chooses the bed closer to our private bathroom and gives me the one closer to the bay window because she knows I enjoy sitting in the sun and reading.

I take a quick shower in our enormous marble bathroom to wash off the throw up and blood from my fall; then I sit in bed while Lily unpacks all our clothes and toiletries. My body is torn apart from those ferry stairs, and my head still hurts. I'm not sure how I didn't get a gash on my face, just the big bump on the back of my head.

I manage to doze off for a bit and wake up later in the evening, when Lily brings me leftover lasagna, Finn's homemade specialty. Lily is ready for the beach party, her hair freshly blown dry. A light dusting of shadow accentuates her aquamarine eyes, and her little summer dress is tight and short, just the way she likes it.

"How are you feeling?" She walks over and sits on the edge of my bed, her face etched with concern as she ever so lightly touches my leg and frowns.

"A little better. My head doesn't hurt as much as it did earlier." I remove the now-room-temperature ice pack from the back of my head.

"I'm glad you're feeling better. Are you sure you don't want me to stay in with you tonight?"

"Totally. Go out and have fun. I'm going to eat this lasagna and then go back to sleep." I know Lily has been looking forward to this summer kickoff party for a while now. A few friends from our prep school will be there, and I know she wouldn't want to miss it. Also, I want to make sure I feel a hundred percent for the concert tomorrow.

I still can't believe Penn invited me and Lily to join him and his friends at the concert. He's older and so hot. I'm a queasy mixture of apprehension and excitement for what is to come.

"I'll stay here until Uncle Rhett gets home. I don't want to leave you alone, just in case something happens."

"Thanks, Lil." I smile at her.

"How do I look?" Lily stands up and twirls in the center of the room. "I need to find a good hookup tonight. I'd love a college guy, but—" The sound of the front door closing cuts Lily off, and her eyes go big.

"They're home," we both say in unison and laugh.

Lily calls that our best friend telepathic power. Finishing each other's thoughts and saying the same thing simultaneously. She thinks we were twin sisters in a previous life.

"I'll give them an update before I head out." Lily blows me a kiss and does one more twirl before heading downstairs.

I finish the lasagna and place the empty plate and fork on the dresser next to my bed just as there is a knock at my door.

"Come in."

Uncle Rhett cracks the door open and pokes his salt-and-pepper head in. "Raebird."

Uncle Rhett is the only one who calls me *Raebird*. It's been his nickname for me since I was little. I was obsessed with the pigeons in Central Park, and while other kids would run around on the playground or swing, I'd be trying to catch a pigeon so I could take it home and keep it as a pet—and that's how the name *Raebird* came to be.

"How are you doing, sweetie? Dr. Smith called me after you left his office and told me you need to take it easy until tomorrow afternoon. Are you feeling okay? He said you took quite a spill and banged up your legs pretty bad."

"I'm better than I was earlier. My head still hurts a little, but the ibuprofen and sleep are helping." I'm also relieved I was able to shower, so he doesn't smell any remainder of the vodka.

"I was distressed thinking about you, and the only reason I didn't go down to Dr. Smith's was because Lily told me you girls need some space to be more independent. You know your safety and well-being will always be my first priority, even when you move across the country for college." Uncle Rhett takes a seat at the foot of the bed, running his palms down his Tommy Bahama button-up to ensure it doesn't wrinkle, and squeezes my foot through the comforter.

"Of course I know that." I smile back at him.

"Dr. Smith mentioned a young man brought you into the office." His eyes fix on me.

Uncle Rhett and I have always been close—as close as an uncle and niece can be, but I do keep some secrets, and I feel a little guilty for lying, because I'm not planning on telling him just how attracted I am to Penn. Maybe it's not lying, just omitting, but still, I feel guilty.

I choose my words carefully and tell Uncle Rhett a condensed and nonsexual version of Lily and me meeting Penn on the ferry. At the end of my story, I casually tell him, "He invited Lily and me to Jones Beach tomorrow night to go to a concert. Two of my favorite bands will be there."

I can't believe I didn't know about the show because I stay on top of the pop-punk concert circuit in New York City, but I've never been to a performance at Jones Beach, so this one wasn't on my radar.

"I don't love the idea that Penn is older than you girls, but I know of him, and I do personally know his dad. So I guess you can go to the concert. We'll go over all the rules tomorrow when Lily is home." He eyes me knowingly and uses the authoritative voice that I always imagine him using at work when he's bossing people around.

"Thank you!" That was not the answer I thought he was going to give. But over the past few years, when Uncle Rhett is on the island, he is much more carefree and relaxed than when he's working twenty-four seven in New York City. Perhaps that's why he's in agreement?

"Sorry we weren't here when you arrived tonight. We got a last-minute invite to our friend's house and figured we should go since you weren't going to be home immediately. We're trying to respect that you and Lily don't need us hovering the entire time you're here. I don't want you to think I'm too overbearing, but also don't want you thinking you aren't cared for and loved."

"You're the coolest uncle in the world. I could never think that." I smile.

Unlike ninety-five percent of the kids at my prep school, I wasn't born a trust-fund kid. My dad walked away from my mother, Jed, and me shortly after I was born. He never paid child support or wanted to be a part of my life.

Not having my dad around growing up never bothered me because Uncle Rhett has been my father figure and filled my dad's shoes tenfold, teaching me how to ride a bike, taking me to the zoo, and showing me how to balance a checkbook and create a budget—yes, even as wealthy as he is, Uncle Rhett made sure to teach me practical, everyday skills.

After my dad left, Uncle Rhett moved us into his twelve-thousand-square-foot townhouse on the Upper East Side. It took a lot for my mother to go to Uncle Rhett and admit she needed help, but after he moved us in, she refused any more handouts and wouldn't let Uncle Rhett give her a monthly allowance. So he hired her as his chief of staff, and now she manages all of Uncle Rhett's employees at his multitude of properties.

Uncle Rhett has given both Jed and me countless luxuries—

private prep school, private chefs, private drivers, personal shoppers, housemaids, butlers—the list goes on and on. He and Finn have been together for ten years, but they've never settled down, gotten married, or had kids. They are both married to work. So Jed and I have secured the position as children to them. Through the years, Uncle Rhett has taught me how to be generous with all the luxuries we've been given. He has the kindest heart.

"I still can't believe you're going off to college. Are you sure you don't want to come work for me after graduation?" This is at least the fifth time he's brought this topic up, and I'm not going to change my mind. I need to start doing things for myself, and I can't always have Uncle Rhett on the sideline, throwing me the ball and helping me move up the field.

"I'm still sure."

My mother decided years ago that I'll be going to college pre-law, majoring in political science, and then I'll head off to law school and become a family lawyer, specializing in divorce so I can help women not end up with zero child support or alimony, like she did.

I don't remember my dad leaving because I was so young, but Jed does, and he's told me that our mother struggled for years to come to grips with our dad walking away and leaving her with nothing. I feel bad that my mother went through such a difficult time, but it doesn't mean I want to make a career out of saving other women from the same situation.

Law is not my dream. I don't know what my dream job is, but I'm going along with law because it appeases my mother, and at least I know I'll make good money once I start working.

"Well. It was worth another try." Uncle Rhett smiles. "If I've learned anything about you, Raebird, it's that when you put your mind to something, you achieve it. Ms. Valedictorian."

I give him a humble smile. On the first day of my freshman year at prep school, Lily casually commented that I'm nerdy enough to graduate top of our class. The thought stuck with me for the first few months of school, but it became my graduation goal after getting straight As first semester, even with AP classes.

"But I want to ensure you don't put too much pressure on yourself. College is supposed to be fun too. A time to figure life out."

"You're worried I won't have fun at college? Did you forget I'm going to be roommates with Lily?" I laugh. Lily has been ready for college for years. She already knows what sorority we'll rush, has researched bars in the area that hopefully accept fake IDs, and she's been slowly stocking my closet with what she calls "college appropriate" dress wear. According to her, my current wardrobe is too PG and not enough PG-13. I like my style—it's comfortable and casual.

Why pretend to be someone I'm not?

Uncle Rhett laughs back. "Oh no, my dear, I have not forgotten that Lily will be there trying to distract you with parties, boys, and God knows what else." He gazes up to the ceiling as he places his hands palm to palm and lifts a request to the heavens, shaking his head back and forth.

"I'm going to be just fine. I'll help keep Lily in line too."

Uncle Rhett opens his mouth to say something but nothing comes out. He shifts his body on the bed and turns to face me better. He swallows a breath and proceeds, "You're ..." He pauses. "You're ... using protection, right? With boys?"

"Ew. Oh my God. No! We are not talking about this." I bury my head in my hands, willing this conversation to stop.

"We need to talk about this. You have your entire life ahead of you, and an unexpected pregnancy would indisputably throw a wrench in your plans."

I feel my face go hot in embarrassment. I'm not the girl in this summer house he should be talking to about sex. He needs to be having this conversation with Lily, not me. I've made out with a few boys at school, but I am nowhere close to having the experience of Lily. She lost her virginity in ninth grade to the first guy who asked her to be his girlfriend.

"We're being safe." There. Simple and to the point, plus with that response, I don't have to admit to my uncle, who thinks I'm having sex, that I'm actually a virgin. How mortifying.

"You know, the day your mom showed up on my doorstep with you and Jed, I had no clue what to do with children? I'd never spent any time around babies, and yet the moment you moved in my heart melted, and I can't imagine my life without you, or Jed, in it. I'm so proud of you. I know you're going to be an incredible lawyer. I know you're planning on going into family law, but maybe one day you'll want to do real estate law, and you can come work for me?"

"Ha! You just want to find any way for me to work for you, huh? Maybe one day, but real estate law isn't really my interest." I scrunch my nose in distaste at the thought of law altogether.

"Raebird, come on. Help your uncle out. I'm not dealing well knowing you won't be around for Sunday-night dinners, or to join me on my weekend trips to Newport to check on the estates."

"I'm not dying, just moving away for a while. I'll be back for visits. There's winter break, spring break, and you know I'll always be back for summers on the island. This place is such a huge part of my life. I may not be able to spend all summer out here once college starts, but hopefully I can do a month or so." I reach my hand to his, feeling like our roles have shifted and I've become the adult.

"I'm going to miss you so much." He takes my hand in his. "I love you." His voice is soft, and he may be holding back a tear or two.

"I love you too."

Moments like this with Uncle Rhett are priceless. Even though he, too, travels as much as my mother, he always finds the time to make me feel important and an essential part of his life.

"Are you finished with this?" Uncle Rhett stands up and grabs the plate off my dresser.

"I am. Finn's lasagna was so good tonight." I rub my belly enthusiastically.

"I'll be sure to let her know. She had a little too much wine tonight and is already asleep in bed." He tightens his lips as if he's said too much, and we both laugh.

"Good night, sweetheart. Get some sleep. Finn and I will be on the beach most of tomorrow, with some friends, but if you're feeling up to it, you should come and get some sun with us." He leans down and kisses the top of my head.

"We'll see what time Lily wakes up."

"Ah, yes, our Lily, the girl who can sleep an entire day away. We'll be in our usual spot if you decide to come."

"Okay."

"But"—he points his finger at me—"we'll be back before you girls head off to the concert."

I smile and nod.

"Want me to turn the light off?"

"Please."

Darkness takes over the room as Uncle Rhett flips the switch and closes the door. I pull the covers over my body and lie my head on the pillow.

Somehow between the throbbing in my head and the pulsating in my knees and shins sleep pulls me in, but I don't allow it to consume me completely, not without a quick thought of Penn's gorgeous face and how excited, yet nervous, I am for the concert tomorrow night.

CHAPTER 4

Raegan

Sunlight shines through the bay window, waking me in the late morning. My head pain has subsided, but my legs ache and feel like they've been run over by a semitruck. I let out a moan of pain as I move to get out of bed to go to the bathroom to clean up.

I walk by Lily, facedown in her bed, arms and legs spread out in a wide *X*. Who knows what time she finally got home last night. I was in such a deep sleep I didn't hear her come in.

I emerge from the bathroom, freshly showered, all bandages removed from my knees and legs, my hair wrapped in a towel on top of my head, in my fuzzy polka-dot bathrobe, to find Lily awake in bed.

"I've been waiting to give you all the details from last night!" Lily shakes her braless chest in her little tank top. "Holy shit! Your legs!" Lily's mouth drops open as she points below the bottom of the bathrobe to my legs, which are covered in black-and-blue bruises.

"I know. They are so sore. I just took another ibuprofen, so hopefully that will kick in soon." It's already past lunchtime, so I don't think I'll be heading down to the beach to hang with Uncle Rhett and Finn today. I make myself comfortable on top of Lily's bed, letting my bathrobe bunch around me, careful not to let my sensitive legs hit anything—the abrasions are healing, but need some fresh air to accelerate the process.

"You are not going to believe what happened last night!" Lily squeals and begins to give me the play-by-play of the beach party.

Of course she met a guy. His name is Theo, and she is apparently going to marry him and have five kids.

Oh, Lily. She loves hard and gives it her all. One thing I admire about her, though, is that she doesn't fall hard. I know this Theo guy won't work out, but it will never faze Lily. She'll just say good riddance and move on like it never happened.

"Holy crap." Lily looks over at the clock in the bedroom. "We've been talking for too long. I still have so much more to tell you, but let me shower and then I'll give you the rest of the story." Lily jumps out of bed and dances her way into the bathroom.

I put my favorite mixed CD in the stereo and push play. The Killers' "Mr. Brightside" begins to blast from the speakers. I walk over, open the balcony door, and step out into the hot, humid day. I look out over the Great South Bay and take a moment to pause, recognizing how fortunate I am for the life I've been given. But even so, I'm looking forward to college. I'm ready to be more self-reliant and start doing things for myself.

The air is sticky, so I head back inside and blow-dry, then add soft curls to my hair.

I walk into the closet and attempt to find something to wear. I can play it safe and go with one of my day-to-day outfits, but there's a stirring in my head telling me I should find something a little cuter, maybe even sexier, to wear. I decide, for sure, I'm going to wear cutoff shorts—that's nonnegotiable. I quickly pull on a pair, along with my bra and a camisole. I take a few *fancy* tank tops off their hangers and bring them to my bed so I can get Lily's opinion.

The anticipation of tonight continues to build, a faint queasiness settling at the bottom of my stomach. I've never been out with a guy like this before, and I have no clue what I'm doing. I run through different scenarios, overanalyzing everything that could happen tonight.

Lily emerges from the bathroom in her bathrobe, along with a puff of hot steam. We have only an hour and a half before we need to leave to catch the ferry to Kismet to meet Penn and his friends for the concert. We could walk to Kismet, but the heat is a total killer today, and by the time we get there we'll be a sweaty mess, so we must abide to the ferry schedule.

"Hair is on point. Shorts are cute. We need to figure out the top," she tells me as she moves her body to the beat and dances over to the closet.

I laugh at Lily.

Always so enthusiastic about life.

"I'm nervous about tonight," I admit to Lily.

"Don't be. It's going to be so much fun. Theo's going to be there too." Lily throws a dress over her head and looks in the floor-length mirror hanging on the closet door.

"He is? Does he know Penn?"

"You mean Mr. Penn Wells?" Lily smirks at me, then looks back in the mirror and frowns before she takes the dress off, not feeling the vibe of it.

"Wells?"

"Yup. *Wells* is his last name. Theo knows him. Actually, they're roommates, and I met his other roommates too—Chase and Eamon. Chase is his brother, but—semantics." Lily waves her arms around like the seagull from *Little Mermaid* and turns back into the closet. "Let me give you the lowdown." She flips through dress options in the closet.

I throw a pillow her way. "You've told me all about all the fun *you* had last night, but you left out the fact that Theo is friends with Penn."

Lily busts out laughing and turns to me. "Do you know how hard it was for me not to wake up at the ass crack of dawn and tell you? I wanted to drag it out, ya know, *really* make it worth the wait." She throws her head back carelessly and laughs.

"I hate you," I tease and turn down the music, giving Lily my full attention. "Tell me everything."

"Okay. So Theo said Penn got home from work yesterday, obviously after he met us and took you to the doctor's, locked himself in his room, and stayed in there playing his piano. I guess he writes songs and music."

He's a songwriter? God, this guy is a ten in looks, and musically talented? Can he be any more perfect?

"And guess what?" Lily pauses, waiting for me to guess.

"I don't know. Just get on with the story." I need details. Thoughts of Penn have been taking up space in my head all day, and I greedily want to know everything Theo told Lily.

"Penn never showed up to the beach last night, and Theo told me he never misses a party, so I think you were maybe on his mind too." She pulls another dress out of the closet and throws it over her bra and thong. After taking a glance in the mirror, she nods in satisfaction.

"Yeahhhh, right. Sure. There's no way I'm the one occupying his mind." I can't be. I'm never *that* girl.

"How many times do I have to tell you how f-ing amazing you are? You've got it all. Smart as hell. You are heading to UC Berkeley at the end of summer on a full-ride academic scholarship. You're passionate, caring, and thoughtful. Yeah, you listen to that horrible cry-me-a-river music that I tolerate only because I love you, but we can overlook that. Your face is gorgeous. Your body is banging. You just need to show a little more skin and stop wearing those plain-Jane T-shirts all the time. Tonight, you wear this!"

Lily emerges from our shared closet with one of her silky halter crop tops that makes the tanks I pulled out earlier look like they are meant for an eight-year-old. This top is definitely on the *sexier* end of the spectrum. I'm just not sure it's something I can pull off.

"Lil, that's just not me." I shake my head.

"VM." She drags out the enunciation of each letter.

"What the hell is VM?"

"Virgin Mary. Raegan, listen to me. If you want to get laid this summer before we go to college, then it's time to let your belly button show off in more than just a bikini." Lily gestures with her hands up and down my body.

"I don't know, Lil. I don't think Uncle Rhett—or Jed, for that matter—would like me wearing this." Ugh. Jed. I haven't even given thought to what he will think about me hanging out with a guy who is his age.

"Jed isn't even on the island yet, so you don't need to worry about him having an opinion about it, and Uncle Rhett, seriously, when are you going to learn that all you need to do is put on the charm, and he'll melt in your hands like M&M's?"

As if on cue, Uncle Rhett's rhythmic knock is at our door.

"Come in," Lily and I both say in unison, then smile at each other. *BFF twin telepathy.*

A sunburned Uncle Rhett comes into our room, with Finn following closely behind. "Raebird. Lily." He acknowledges both of us with a tilt of his head, in a different, freshly pressed Tommy Bahama shirt.

"How are you girls doing? Is your head feeling better?" He looks down at my legs, sees the blackish-blue bruises, and makes a concerned face. "Ouch."

"I'm all right. I'm feeling much better. It looks worse than it feels," I lie. But I don't want them worrying about me or possibly telling me that I can't go to the concert tonight.

"I'm ah-mazing. I met a boy last night." Lily throws both arms in the air like a cheerleader.

"Of course you did." Finn laughs. "When do you not have a boy chasing after you?"

"Well, pretty much—never, I guess." Lily shrugs and pouts her lips out.

"Okay." Uncle Rhett clears his throat before proceeding, "So we are here to talk about this concert out on Jones Beach tonight."

Lily and I nod and remain silent, waiting for the list of rules we'll need to follow.

"I know you girls already know the house policies, but I will remind you again. No drugs. No shenanigans. No drinking. And no boys allowed in this bedroom." He looks Lily right in her eyes, and she pinches her lip to hold back a smile. Uncle Rhett tries his best to rein Lily in by setting boundaries, but Lily doesn't do too well with restrictions.

"Cross my heart and hope to die." Lily makes an *X* across her heart, but her other hand is behind her back, pointer and middle finger crossed.

Liar, liar, pants on fire.

"Yeah, yeah, yeah. I remember hearing this all before, Ms. Hart. Don't think I'm not aware that you came in after three a.m. last night— or this morning, I should say." Uncle Rhett gives Lily a stern, but caring, look.

Lily doesn't officially live with us during the school year, but she and I spend enough time together that Uncle Rhett has taken on a fatherly role within Lily's life, too, and when she's here on the island with us, she's just as much family as I am.

"I can call Abril, and she can be on the next ferry here if you two don't follow the rules. Though I can't imagine she'll be delighted doing so, since she's been looking forward to having this summer off."

Abril. My nanny, for lack of a better term. It's silly to call her that as a seventeen-year-old, but she's been my primary caregiver since I was six months old. Because my mother traveled so often for work while I was growing up, it's always been Abril attending my parent-teacher conferences and disciplining me when I break curfew, due to Lily. It was Abril who took me to buy my first bra, and who taught me about periods and sex. Abril has always been there for the big moments, unlike my mother, who missed almost every important milestone in my life.

Honestly, though, my mother is intense, overbearing, and domineering. She is a lot to handle at once, and I'm grateful for the periods in which we are separated. She's easiest to digest when taken in small doses.

"We'll follow them, Uncle Rhett. You have my word," I say, somewhat honestly.

Lily and I have never done drugs and are generally pretty conservative in the shenanigan department. We've been dabbling with alcohol since the start of this past school year and have been what we think is responsible about it, and that just leaves the whole boy situation. He did say "in this bedroom" and didn't mention any other bedrooms, so technically I don't think we will break that rule, because we won't bring any boys back to this house.

"Thanks, Raebird. I hope I don't regret this, but since you'll both be leaving for college at the end of summer, I'm going to extend your curfew, because it's not like I'll be around to dish out curfews when you're on the West Coast." He pauses, and I swear his eyes get misty at the thought of us leaving. "One a.m. and not a minute later. Farthest west you are allowed to go without prior permission is the lighthouse, and farthest east is Sunken Forest. Keep those cell phones on you at all times, and call the house if anything comes up."

At the beginning of my senior year, Uncle Rhett got me a Razr flip phone to use for emergencies. It's meant to be used to contact him, or Abril, if I need something. I find the cell phone far more convenient than the pager I used to have, but I rarely use it and seldom remember to keep it charged—or bring it with me when I leave the house.

Lily throws her arms around Uncle Rhett. "Thank you, Uncle R! You're the best! I promise we'll follow the rules."

"Thanks." I lean into the two of them, and we share a group hug.

"Please be careful tonight at the concert. Don't take a drink from anyone you don't know, and be aware of your surroundings at all times." He pauses and looks at Lily. "Is this what you are wearing?"

Lily gives him a big white smile, and he shakes his head, knowing there is no use in pressing the matter further. This must be what Lily means by melting M&M's.

"Have fun tonight, girls," Finn chimes in, and gives us both a hug. "We're so happy you are here with us this summer."

Uncle Rhett walks out the door, and just before Finn turns to follow after him, she eyes the halter crop top Lily laid on my bed. Looking at me with her ocean-blue eyes, she asks, "Are you wearing that tonight?"

Before I can answer, Lily jumps in, "Why, Finn, I'm so glad you asked. Yes, Raegan is going to wear that tonight. She's so short the crop barely shows her belly button. The color will highlight her eyes, and it's not too slutty. Can you feel me?"

Finn drops her head, and her short bob of ashy-brown hair swings at her chin as she gives it a little shake, smirking. "You girls are stunning on the outside and the inside. Don't ever let anyone try to tell you differently. But, Raegan, if you wear that shirt, you need to pair it with these earrings." Finn walks over to our vanity and grabs a pair of gold hoop earrings belonging to Lily. "These will frame your beautiful face just perfectly."

Finn has always been the classiest woman I know, in both looks and personality. That's why Uncle Rhett loves her so much. She's subtle and understated, and she has an eye for design and trends. She is one of the most sought-after event planners in Manhattan, so any advice Finn gives for style, I'll follow without question.

"Thanks, Finn. I'm so fortunate you've stuck around all these years, and we haven't scared you off yet." I lean in to give her one more hug. For all intents and purposes, Finn is my aunt. Though she and Uncle Rhett are not married, she's also family.

She hugs me back. "You girls are like daughters to me. I'm always here if you ever need anything."

"We know. Thank you."

Finn walks out, leaving Lily and me to finish getting ready for the concert.

CHAPTER 5

Penn

I got home from the doctor's office yesterday and told the guys about what happened on the ferry and how I invited Raegan and Lily to join us at the concert. They gave me shit because that's what they do best—making kissy-faces and being immature about the entire situation. Why I still choose to spend time with these jackasses is beyond me.

I then proceeded to lock myself away in my bedroom. I finally felt inspired, and I managed to finish composing a halfway decent song, motivated by a petite, punk-pop-loving seventeen-year-old.

Raegan has been all I can think about for these past twenty-four hours, and I can't have her, at least not for another month. She is stunning in an understated and confident way, but there's something more about her that's drawing me in. Something I've never felt before. Maybe it's her personality. She comes off a bit shy, pulling her eyes away from mine each time they meet, but she also carries this sense of intuition and awareness, like she knew what I was feeling without me even saying anything. I couldn't let our moment yesterday pass without inviting her to the concert. I have this strange desire to know more of what makes her Raegan.

After Theo finally woke up today, he told me about last night's

party and how he ended up meeting Lily. He said they messed around and I pieced together that she and her best friend were the two I met earlier in the day. I'm not shocked by this at all—in fact, I'm pretty sure I called it.

However, I am shocked to find out Raegan is Jed Cline's younger sister. He's a pretty cool guy, not like all those other Wall Street douchebags. Jed's ripped and fights in amateur MMA competitions. I'm pretty sure he could double as a bodyguard or personal security. Jed and I used to run in the same crowd during the summers when we were younger, but I haven't hung out with him on the island for several years now. He knows I like to occupy my time with many different women.

I doubt he'd be pleased to know the indecent thoughts I've been having about his sister. He'd probably beat the shit out of me, then cut off my balls.

I also know Raegan's uncle. Well, I don't know him personally. But you'd have to live under a rock to not know who Rhett Kellerman is. Influential and highly respected, he is one of the wealthiest men on Fire Island, owning a substantial number of properties here, in Manhattan, and all around the world.

Theo and I are kicking back with a beer at the Sundowner bar as we wait for my best friend, Eamon, to join us for tonight's concert festivities. Raegan and Lily should be arriving shortly, and I feel like every nerdy kid in those movies waiting for his date to show on prom night.

I look around the dimly lit, mostly empty bar, trying to get my apprehension about tonight under control. Fewer than half of the dining tables are occupied, and only a handful of other people are sitting on green vinyl barstools at the wood bar. A trendy pop song plays loudly from the jukebox in the corner near the restrooms.

I stand, unable to sit, and rub my shoe mindlessly into the faded blue commercial carpet. I've never been jittery for a girl like this before.

I polish off my beer and set the empty pint on the counter. A hand appears from behind the bar, takes the glass, and wipes down the bar top. "Planning dates now, are we? You must really want to get in this girl's pants." It's Chase, my brother. He manages the Sundowner and loves nothing more in life than to give me shit.

"Oh, he for sure wants to get in her pants," Theo interjects. "But she's not legal, and you know Penn and his age rule."

"Fuck you, guys. It's not a date. It's just a group of friends going to a concert." I didn't think through the banter these assholes would dish once they found out I'd invited Raegan and Lily to join us tonight. "She was wearing a New Found Glory T-shirt. How could I not invite her? And don't forget, I invited Lily too. If anything, I'm helping Theo out." I pat Theo on his back.

"Fuck that, man. I'm capable of planning my own female rendezvous." Theo finishes his beer and sets the glass on the counter.

Chase immediately removes Theo's empty and moves down the bar to make another patron a drink, but he stays close by so he can still partake in harassing me.

A clap on my shoulder gets my attention. I turn around to find Eamon and his girlfriend, Maddie. "I'm shocked we're doing this tonight. You don't date. You're a fuck-'em-and-leave-'em, don't-have-any-emotion-or-attachments kind of guy," Eamon states matter-of-factly.

"How long have you been standing there?" He's wasting no time jumping on the give-Penn-shit train.

"Long enough to know that you got it bad for this one. I've never seen you put this much effort into trying to bone someone. I can't wait to see this Raegan chick. She must be a knockout for you to plan all this." He grins before kissing Maddie. After they finally release their lips from each other, she walks behind the bar. Eamon had mentioned she's working tonight, so I bet she's here to start her shift.

"If she's anything like Lily, then it will be worth the effort. That girl can suck a dick like nobody's business," Theo casually informs us.

If any of us is a true playboy, it's Theo, and if he says Lily gives a good blow job, then you know it's top-notch. He's probably set some world record for most received BJs for his age demographic.

"Coming in hot," Chase announces from his perch behind the bar.

I turn around, and from where I'm standing, I have a direct view as Raegan and Lily walk through the door and toward us.

Fuck me.

Raegan is wearing a skimpy shirt, her midriff peeking out the bottom, and the frays of her distressed jean shorts gently rest against her thighs. Her legs are no longer bloody, but bruised and battered. Those steps sure did a number on her. Her brown hair curls down her back, the New York summer humidity adding volume. Her Chucks complete the look, giving it a relaxed flair. She's hot, and I notice a few other guys in the bar are gawking.

Hands off. She's mine.

I'm immediately jealous and protective at the same time. This is a new feeling for me to have toward a girl. I'm shocked at my possessiveness, and a little perplexed, trying to figure out where this is all coming from. I shrug it off because the girls are almost to where I'm standing with the guys.

Lily is in a short dress and sandals. I look over to Theo and see he can't take his eyes off her. She walks over to him, wraps her arms around his neck, and kisses his lips. They're quickly lost in a world of their own.

Raegan is standing behind Lily and Theo. I peek around and wave. "Hey."

Hey? That's your opening line?

I'm acting like an absolute nerd who doesn't know how to talk to a girl.

Raegan gives me a tight-lipped smile and mimics my wave. "Hey."

Do I hug her? Do I fist-bump her?

If she were any other girl, I'd have pulled her in close and kissed her, letting her know what the rest of the evening would entail. But I can't do that in this situation. First of all, she's seventeen, and I'm trying to create an appropriate amount of space because if I smell that fruity hair, I know I'll be a goner. Secondly, I want to claim her as mine, so none of these other assholes can even try to make an attempt, but I'm motionless.

I want to be a gentleman, for once, and get to know her, not just fuck her and leave before sunrise. This is a new feeling for me, and it makes me uneasy because it doesn't feel normal.

I know Raegan is interested in me because Lily told Theo last night, and he's been jabbing me about it all day. Putting all this together, I figure that's why I'm being so awkward about this entire situation.

"You clean up well. No more blood or throw up." I smile at Raegan, then internally cringe. This moment is getting worse by the minute. My usual polished charm is nowhere to be found, and my confidence is dropping exponentially. My dick may even be missing, but I'm hesitant to look down and check.

Raegan lets out a soft laugh. Maybe she senses my discomfort. Thank God Lily pulls away from Theo long enough to save my sorry ass.

"Mmm-kay, and with that, let's do intros. Raegan, this is Theo. Theo, this is my bestie, Raegan."

Theo extends his hand. "Nice to meet you. Lily couldn't stop talking about you last night. And neither could Penn." He lifts his eyes mischievously to mine and lets out a sinister laugh.

Asshole. Why you got to call me out like that?

I glare at him, and it only makes him smile bigger.

Dickhead.

Eamon and Chase laugh. Looks like the Penn-roasting is going to get worse before it gets better. I hope it gets better soon, because these guys are on a roll tonight.

"Thanks, Theo," I overemphasize, wanting to strangle him.

Lily smiles, clearly entertained by my embarrassment.

Raegan shakes Theo's hand. "Nice to meet you too."

Raegan glances over at me. I can't tell if she's nervous or not, but she's carrying a confidence today that wasn't there yesterday. Her eyes wander to the other two jerkoffs whom I choose to hang out with, their jaws slack, holding back laughter, undoubtedly enjoying the show.

"This is Chase." Lily points behind the bar.

Raegan extends her hand and smiles. "Raegan."

"You're even prettier than Penn described last night and *all* day today." Chase takes Raegan's hand and gives it a good shake.

My eyes shoot lasers into Chase, wishing I could detonate him with my stare.

"And last but not least, this is Eamon." Lily turns Raegan's body to face Eamon.

"Hi." Raegan shakes his waiting hand.

"You ready for the crazy that is to be tonight?" Eamon asks Raegan.

She hesitates. "I think so?" Her brain is working, piecing together all the shit these guys are dishing. Her eyes light up and catch mine before her mouth curves into a smile. It's as if she realizes, based on all the things these guys are saying, that I just might like her.

For the first time in my life, I may have caught feelings for someone, and she's off-limits, due to her age and the fact that her brother is Jed

Cline, and there's no way in hell he'd let his little sister hang out with me.

I need to figure this out, quick.

"So, yeah, these are the guys," I say out loud, to no one specifically, annoyed with the antics these guys are throwing around. "We need to head out now to catch our ride."

"Wait! We can't forget Maddie," Lily cuts in, catching Maddie's attention behind the bar, waving her over. "I want to introduce you to Raegan." Lily looks at Raegan. "Maddie was my wing girl last night since you were out of commission. She's Eamon's girlfriend."

"Hey." Maddie offers Raegan her typical warm smile. "Have fun tonight . . . but watch out for this guy." She throws her thumb my way.

Maddie's really gonna give me shit too?

I pinch my lips together.

Eamon leans over the bar and kisses Maddie goodbye while Chase comes out from behind the bar. Theo throws his arm around Lily, in true Danny Zuko style—he's just missing a T-Birds leather jacket.

Raegan stays planted, masking any shyness or fear with a tight-lipped smile.

"After you." I gesture and she flashes me her beautiful smile.

CHAPTER 6

Penn

I stay close, yet keep my distance, as the group heads west, toward the lighthouse. Lily fills the fifteen-minute walk with mindless chatter, nothing of importance, but she gets us all laughing and helps keep my mind from thinking about what Raegan's lips would feel like on mine.

After arriving at the lighthouse, my friend Sam, who is a lifeguard, is waiting for us with a four-person sand buggy that the lifeguards use to get across the beach.

"Hey, man." I reach out and shake Sam's hand. He and I have become friends over the years, as many lifeguards spend their off time on Fire Island.

"We're taking a buggy all the way to Jones Beach?" Raegan asks, excited, her eyes focused on the waves crashing along the beach.

"We're only going to take this to the water tower. There will be a van for us to drive the rest of the way to Jones Beach." I give Raegan a big smile, proud of myself and all the planning and coordination I've done for us to get to the concert.

Sam hands the keys to Eamon while Chase calls shotgun. Theo takes a seat in the back and pulls Lily onto his lap. I take the last seat and extend my hand to Raegan.

Maybe I didn't think this four-seater thing through, but Raegan sitting on my lap—in a group—doesn't break the rules, right?

I quickly convince myself that I'm still in the clear and no rules have been broken.

I capture her hand and delight with pleasure as I pull her close. Her smell intoxicates me, and without thinking, I wrap my arms around her waist, to keep her steady, while the buggy takes off down the sand. My dick convinces me to steal an opportunity and brush my fingers along the exposed flesh peeking out from under her scanty shirt. Raegan's entire body stiffens under my touch.

The wind blows Raegan's hair in my face as Eamon cruises down the beach, expertly avoiding sunbathers and kids playing in the sand.

After a minute, Raegan turns her body so she's sitting sideways on my lap and talks into my ear. "This is so fun!" Her smile radiates.

"I'm glad you're enjoying it. Sam happened to owe me a favor and pulled through on arranging this buggy for us. We'll also take this back later tonight, after the concert."

"Thanks so much for inviting us. I just need to let you know that our curfew is one a.m."

"You have a curfew?" I tilt my head a little closer to Raegan's. I just need one more inhale of her hair, and then I'll stop being creepy.

"Unfortunately, yes." She lowers her head, embarrassed. "Guess most of the girls you hang out with don't have curfews?"

I don't know what comes over me, or why I am continuing to break my rules, but I reach under her chin with one hand and raise her head to look at me. "I don't usually spend time with women who aren't eighteen."

She lets out a soft, breathy laugh, and I use all my restraint not to touch her lips. I remove my hand from her face to try to create space, though it's literally impossible given our seating situation.

"If it matters, I turn eighteen in a little over a month." A devilish smile creeps across her face. She moves one of her hands off the metal side rail and places it on top of my hand, currently wrapped around her waist.

Instinctively, I maneuver so my thumb is rubbing her hand. "When is your birthday?"

"Fourth of July."

Fourth of July.

My mom's birthday. It seems fitting for Raegan to share that day with my mom. Maybe it's a sign or something? Raegan already reminds me so much of her. When Raegan laughed on the ferry yesterday, I turned to look at her and saw my mom. Not in an inappropriate sexual way, but in a simple and natural beauty kind of way. My mom was the most remarkable person I've ever known, down-to-earth and humble. Sincere and fun. Her laugh, just as contagious as Raegan's.

I quickly swallow the pain that fills me whenever I think of my mom. It still happens any time I think about her, even though it's been a long time without her here.

"An Independence Day birthday. Well, we'll need to have a party to celebrate."

"A bit presumptuous to think we'll still be hanging out in a month," she teases and wraps her hand in mine. Her actions most definitely do not match her words, and I should not be this turned on.

Thank God I'm not a pubescent teen who can't control my thoughts, and arousal, or she'd really be feeling how much I'm enjoying her sitting on my lap.

I give Raegan a confident nod, conveying to her that the bet is on and we will still be hanging out in a month. I squeeze her hand three times and enjoy the last minute of the buggy ride with her on my lap and our hands entwined.

Eamon stops the buggy at the water tower, and we all pile into a utility van that Sam also arranged for me. The van is the furthest thing from romantic and is typically used to transport lifeguards and gear from one beach to another.

As with the buggy, Eamon drives, and Chase sits in the passenger seat. Theo and Lily crawl into the back row of the van. Although there is enough space for everyone to each get their own respective seat for this leg of our journey, Lily places herself right next to Theo, so she might as well be on top of him. Raegan and I take the middle row of the van, and I make sure to put an empty middle seat between us, because I need to rein in my actions before one thing leads to another. I buckle my seat belt as Eamon takes the van across the bridge and turns west on Ocean Parkway.

"Raegan?" Lily taps her on the shoulder.

"Yeah?"

"Did you know that these guys all live together in Kismet, in a house that Theo owns?"

"I did not know that." Raegan turns around to face Lily and Theo. "Please, tell me more."

"Theo is a real estate agent and sells houses all over Fire Island, Long Island, and Manhattan. We should connect him with Uncle Rhett." Lily is hustling for Theo, and I internally laugh because Theo probably loves the free publicity she's giving him.

"So, how did you all meet?"

"I'll let Penn tell the story." Theo eyes me, and I know why. We usually come up with elaborate fake stories about ourselves when we meet girls on the island, and I'm certain he's passing the baton to me so I can decide if I want to tell the truth or fib like I always do.

In a split second, I decide I don't want to lie to Raegan. I will lose the idiotic one-fling-a-month bet with Chase, and I don't care. I'll pay him double. Raegan hit me out of nowhere; her presence consumes me, I've never felt this way before, and all I want to do is get closer to her and get to know her more.

"Sure. Where to start . . ." I chuckle.

"Start with Theo," Raegan shouts with enthusiasm, most likely trying to find more out about Theo for Lily.

"Okay. Theo it is." I rub my palms back and forth, thinking about all the shit I could share about Theo, but I decide to just stick with the basics. "Theo is a few years older than I am. Another rich kid who grew up in Manhattan and came to the island every summer. We hit it off when we met five years ago surfing out in Montauk at Ditch Plains. Then he invited me and these two idiots up front to live with him in one of his rental houses. Theo only lives on Fire Island in the summer; the rest of the year, he's at his place in SoHo."

"Hey, dickface! Who you calling idiots?" Chase calls out from the front seat.

Perfect segue.

"Idiot number one up front, my Irish twin, older than me by barely eleven months. We were so close in age our parents put us in the same grade. In the summer, you can always find this guy at the Sundowner, being Mr. General Manager. Chase, tell the girls what you like to do in the off-season."

Chase turns around. "I fish. Usually head down to the Outer Banks and catch tuna."

"I've always wanted to go fishing," Lily shouts from the back seat. "Will you take us sometime?"

"Sure thing. Let's plan it."

I admire my brother, living his life and doing what he loves and is passionate about. Chase always knew he didn't want to work at the ferry company, much to my father's dismay. I don't resent him, but it has undoubtedly put pressure on me to carry on the family business when my dad retires.

"Okay, now Eamon. What's your story?" Raegan asks.

"Eamon grew up out here with Chase and me. We all went to school together on the island from kindergarten through sixth grade, and then we attended the rest of our school years being shuttled out to a high school in Bay Shore. Not to sound cocky or anything, but we were something of a novelty in high school. Everyone wanted to be friends with the kids from Fire Island."

"Fuck yeah, they did!" Eamon calls out from the driver's seat.

"You can find Eamon working part time on the ferries, and he also runs a landscaping and general house maintenance business out here. And you met his girlfriend, Maddie, when we were leaving the Sundowner."

"Yeah, she was bummed that she couldn't make it tonight. She picked up an extra shift because tomorrow is our anniversary, and we're heading off the island for the day, but I'm sure you'll get to hang out with her soon," Eamon chimes in.

I still can't believe he's been held down by the same woman for this long now. I admire his devotion to Maddie. They do long distance most of the year when she's at college, and summer is always their time together.

As storytelling time wraps up, Eamon parks the car. Everyone piles out, and we make our way into the amphitheater. The security guy checks our IDs. Lily passes through without a problem, but he confiscates Raegan's fake ID after she stumbles and can't remember the correct birthday.

Raegan ends up with a big black *X* across the top of her hand, letting everyone know she isn't yet twenty-one and can't drink. The Sharpie brands her and amplifies our age difference even more than before.

"Ugh! I knew that fake ID would never work for me. I don't look like Jasmin from Queens."

"You getting that ID taken away has nothing to do with Jasmin from Queens, and all from you not memorizing the information front and back, like I told you to do." Lily shakes her head at Raegan, as if lying about her fake name and birthday should be second nature.

"I forgot, and then I got scared when I did remember, and by that point, I was already screwed." Raegan frowns.

"Yeah, this venue is super strict on underage drinking. Out on Fire Island we don't have a lot of police activity, and nobody drives, so the Sundowner, and pretty much all the restaurants and bars, look the other way if someone not quite twenty-one comes in to order a drink. As long as you aren't a jerk or shit-faced, we'll serve you." Chase gives Raegan a half hug to cheer her up. "So I guess this means you'll just have to come drink at the Sundowner for the rest of the summer with us."

Why, yes. I suppose it does. Thank you, security guard guy.

I try to leave some space between myself and Raegan as I walk behind her from the security line and to our seats, all in the spirit of this not being a date. She hasn't tried to touch me since she grabbed my hand on the buggy, and I'm grateful yet annoyed at the same time. My head and my dick are at war with each other, and I figure space is the best answer to appease them both.

Lily and Theo, on the other hand, are all over each other, holding hands and making out at every possible moment. I won't be surprised if they sneak off somewhere to *be alone* during the concert.

At the VIP section, Eamon flashes our passes for an escort to our seats.

"Damn, boys. These are great seats." Lily looks around the box area reserved just for us.

Chase goes into bartender mode and pulls beer cans from the cooler. He passes them out to each of us guys, and then one each to Raegan and Lily. "Raegan, if you do drink tonight, make sure to hold the can in the hand that does not have the X." He grins at her, and she sticks her tongue out at him.

Atta girl—don't take his shit.

"Thanks, Chase. I'm good with water for now."

"I'll take a beer." Lily pops open a can, then takes a sip before she starts rummaging through the snack bowl.

I turn to Raegan. "Is this okay?"

"This is awesome. These have to be the best seats in the house. How'd you guys manage to get them?" Raegan looks around, amazed.

Her genuineness is a breath of fresh air compared to the rich New York City girls I usually meet on Fire Island. I know her uncle is loaded, and he's one of the top property owners in New York City alone, but I haven't witnessed Raegan act privileged yet, in any sense.

"Eamon's dad is the head of operations here, and every year he lets us pick a handful of concerts that we want to see, and he gets us a box, leaves a cooler of beer, and plenty of snacks for us. This just happens to be one of the concerts we picked."

"That's so cool. Thank you so much for the invite."

She's still smiling, and I can't take my eyes off her lips. I'm about to reach out and pull her close when the lights go down and the sound of drums and guitar blasts through the speakers, silencing all of us.

In this moment, I realize "no strings attached" won't work with Raegan.

I need strings.

I need to know what makes her heart beat.

I need to be connected to her.

All of a sudden, I need to know everything about this girl.

CHAPTER 7

Raegan

I can't believe I'm at this concert with the hottest guy ever.

I steal another glance at Penn as I jump around to Something Corporate opening up the show. I'm choosing to ignore the pain my legs feel every time they make contact with the ground. My hands are in the air, and I sing along at the top of my lungs. Penn is a sight as he stands next to me at the front of the box, singing and playing the air guitar like he's Jimi Hendrix.

He's carefree and confident, so unlike the guys my age. His black T-shirt fits like a glove, exposing his muscular arms and the web of tattoos crawling up his right arm. I spot an orange-red poppy on the inside of his forearm. It's soft and almost feminine, a drastic difference from the rest of his tattoos.

I want to reach out and touch the tattoo, but Penn's been keeping a solid distance between us since the lighthouse ride. I'm not sure where my courage to grab his hand on the buggy came from, but I was elated when he held it back. I even earned a wink and smile from Lily when she noticed.

Do I get closer to him, or do I stay here?
I don't want to look too eager or desperate ...
Screw it.

The song is loud and upbeat. I dance my way in Penn's direction, brushing my arm against his, making it appear like an accident. My body is immediately engulfed with goose bumps, even though it's boiling out here. From the corner of my eye, Penn freezes for just a moment.

He felt it too.

I've never had a bodily reaction like this to a guy before. It's exciting and I'm craving more.

I glance to the back of the box. Eamon and Chase sit at the table, drinking beers and lightly bopping their heads to the beat. Theo and Lily went to "find the bathroom" a few songs ago, so who knows when they'll return.

The song ends, and as much as I want to brush against Penn again, I need water, or maybe a beer. I look up at Penn. He's running his fingers and palm through his sweaty hair, pulling it away from his face and eyes. I had no idea a sweaty guy could be so enticing. Before I can ask Penn if he wants to grab a drink, a familiar piano melody starts to play, and I pause. It takes only the first few hits of the keys for me to know this is one of my favorite songs by Something Corporate, "Konstantine."

Penn looks down at me, his eyes fill with excitement, and at the same time we say, "I love this song!"

Both our mouths open wide, and I laugh with him.

It's a slower song, not a wedding slow-dance song, but definitely not a jump-around riot song. I want to put my arm around Penn and sway back and forth like I've seen couples do at previous concerts. Though I was eager to "accidentally" brush up against him during the last song, I'm way too timid about making such a bold move now. The confidence I had in the buggy has vanished, instead replaced with apprehension. I wait, hoping Penn will put his arm around me, but his hands remain by his side as the piano intro continues.

"Heeeeyy!"

Oh, thank God, Lily is back.

"He's playing your favorite!" Lily shouts above the extended piano intro, and her voice contains more cheerfulness than I've ever seen her have at a concert. Either she's trying to be my ultimate hype girl, or Theo just gave her an orgasm somewhere in this amphitheater.

She wraps one arm around me, the other around Theo, and as a group, we start to move back and forth in rhythm with each other. Lily leans in front of me and yells at Penn, "Come on! Dance with us!"

Dance. Sway. Stand still. I don't care.

Just put your arm around me.

Penn grins, and with Lily's permission, he wraps his hand tightly around my waist, touching my bare skin, lighting me on fire.

Penn and I sing every word, rocking left to right and on and on, until the very last note.

When the song ends, Lily breaks away from me and wraps both arms around Theo. I lean into Penn's chest, and his fingers linger on my waist for a few extra moments before he pulls his hand away and looks down at me with a soft smile.

Okay, he's back to putting distance between us.

I'm confused. I thought Penn was interested in me, and that's why he invited us here, but his actions have been a little hot and cold all night. I'm no expert about guys, but this is odd.

I need to pull Lily aside and get her take on this situation. She'll know exactly what I need to do.

Maybe I can get her to go to the bathroom with me?

I turn around and find Lily at the back table with the other three guys.

"Do it! Do it! Do it!" they chant in unison, encouraging her to shotgun a beer.

Lily takes the beer from Eamon, wraps her lips around the bottom side of the aluminum, cracks it open, and starts to drink. She finishes the can without spilling a drop.

The things that girl will do for attention.

Penn nudges me with his elbow. I look up, and he gestures with his head for us to join the rest of them.

Eamon hands Penn a sideways can, cut at the bottom. Penn pulls the tab, places the beer can to his mouth, and pounds the beer in a few seconds. He crumples the can and shoots.

"Three points!" he shouts as the can arcs into the garbage can. Chase extends a sideways can toward me. "Your turn."

I shake my head. "I don't drink beer like that."

I've never shotgunned a beer before. I've seen plenty of my friends from school do it at house parties in the city. I know Lily loves to do it because she's actually quite good at it, but I'm not interested in being like them, or ending up with cold amber liquid pouring down my face and shirt because I can't chug it fast enough.

"That's cool, no problem." Penn seems surprised by my refusal but doesn't push it. Instead, he grabs a new beer from the cooler and holds it out to me. His eyes are gentle, like he wants to make sure I feel included, but he doesn't want to pressure me.

"Would you like a regular beer?" he asks. "We also have water and soda, if you'd prefer." His smile is kind, no judgment.

Uncle Rhett would probably appreciate this situation—well, maybe he wouldn't appreciate the fact that Penn's offering me a beer in the first place, but he's not pushing me to drink it. So I give him an extra point, maybe even two.

"I'll take a beer." I wrap my hand around the can Penn is holding, and our fingers touch in the exchange. I watch Penn's face and wonder if he feels the same electric zaps passing between us.

I open the tab and take a sip with my unmarked hand. The bubbles are invigorating and tickle as they go down my throat. I need to pace myself so I don't get too tipsy, because I'm already feeling buzzed being here in Penn's presence. I don't want to end up making a fool of myself or something. Not to mention I don't want to go back to Uncle Rhett's drunk, since he did tell Lily and me only a few hours ago, "No drinking."

The set ends and the lights turn on. The stage workers begin to remove equipment from the first set to prepare for the next one.

"We're going to get some fresh air," Theo announces to the box, as Lily pulls him out of our seating area.

Fresh air? We're in an open theater.

Those two can't keep their hands off each other.

I wish Penn would take me somewhere for some fresh air.

"We're going to meet up with a few friends during intermission," Chase tells Penn and me before he and Eamon walk out of the box too.

We are alone. We are alone.

My hands are sweating as I anticipate what is to come. Lily told me earlier when we were getting ready that intermission would be the perfect time for Penn to kiss me. I wish I had a Tic Tac or some gum to freshen my breath, especially after drinking that beer.

The sound of Penn opening a new beer pulls me out of my thoughts, and I turn to face him. I bring the beer to my lips to take a sip, and Penn mimics me, putting his can to his lips at the same time.

I smile at the cuteness of his copycat before tilting my head back and taking another sip of the refreshingly cold beer. When I stop drinking, so does Penn, his eyes never wavering from me.

He's being cheeky. It's cute and I'm all for it.

"Have you ever seen New Found Glory play live before?" I blab out, trying to fill the silence with words.

"I have. They put on a great show. Have you seen them before?" Penn takes another sip of beer, his eyes still on me.

I've caught him multiple times looking at me throughout the night. I love that with his eyes he is making me feel like the only person in the room, but his body distance suggests I have some contagious disease.

"Yeah, I first saw them at the Warped Tour two years ago on Randall's Island. And the Warped Tour was the concert that opened the door to my love of pop-punk music. That's where I got the T-shirt I was wearing yesterday. I always buy a T-shirt from the bands I see in concert."

"I was at that concert too." Penn laughs and opens his mouth, but then closes it before saying anything more.

"What were you going to say?"

"Nothing. It's not important." He brushes it off, but his mouth twists, and I know he wants to say more, but he doesn't.

"Come on. You can't do that and then not say." I pout, but not seriously.

I'm trying to melt M&M's.

"No. Really. It's nothing." His voice is low and kind as he shrugs.

"Okay." I drop it, not one to whine in order to get what I want. If he wants to share, he will. I'm not going to beg.

"Fine. I'll tell you." He smiles behind his beer can and takes another sip.

I let out a laugh. He caves so quickly and easily. I didn't even have to plead with him.

"I was just thinking that two years ago we were at the same concert. I was twenty-one and very drunk, and you were fifteen and couldn't even drive."

Oh my God. Our age difference bothers him! That's why he's been so standoffish.

But why would he invite me if our age bothers him?

Or maybe my age didn't bother him until I got this big black X across my hand.

Ugh. Play it cool, Raegan.

"I still can't drive. Well, I guess I can, but not legally."

"You don't have your driver's license?" The corners of his mouth turn up in surprise.

"No. I don't really need it living in the city. My uncle has a driver who takes me wherever I need to go." I cringe slightly, thinking about how that probably sounds to Penn. "That didn't come out right. I'm not some rich brat with a driver. I'm fortunate to have someone who helps me get around the city. And when I get to college, I won't have a car, not that it's necessary as I don't really need one."

"Is that who dropped you off at the ferry yesterday?"

My eyes must go wide because Penn continues before I even ask him how he knows that information.

"I saw you and Lily in the parking lot. I watched you hug your driver, and I thought either he was your family, or you were a pretty cool rich girl who hugs the help. I was planning on talking to you after the ferry ride, but then you went and fell down those stairs, so I didn't even have to use my opening line."

I don't know if I should be embarrassed or flattered right now.

"Your opening line—I'm sad I didn't get to hear it. I'm sure it was a good one." I laugh and take a small sip of my beer, not letting my eyes leave Penn's.

"It would have been a good line too. Probably my best ever. Such a shame I couldn't deliver it to you." Penn full on smirks before chuckling to himself.

"Do you have a license?" I'm curious because the only cars allowed on Fire Island are emergency vehicles, and very few permitted cars for people who live on the island year-round.

"I do." He gives me a lopsided grin, almost like he's begging me to ask him more questions.

"Do you have a car on the island?"

"No way. I don't want that much responsibility. But I do have my license for when I go off the island. I either rent a car or borrow one from friends who live in Bay Shore."

"That's cool. Do you get off the island much?"

"It depends. During the summer, I rarely get off. But fall and winter, I usually make a few trips off the island."

"And what about spring?" I ask.

Penn grabs another beer from the cooler and offers it to me. I shake my head. "No thanks."

He nods and opens the can. "In spring, I stick around here. It's my favorite time of year on the island. The flowers bloom and the depressing snow and cold finally starts to turn into warmer days. Have you ever been out here during spring?" He takes a sip from the can.

"No. I'm just a summer vacationer only." I've never even thought to come out here any other time. I'm pretty sure the island shuts down during those seasons, so I'm not sure what there is to do then anyway.

"You'll have to come out and visit next spring." Penn smiles and my heart drops at his statement.

Is he seriously inviting me to visit him here next spring? I don't know how to respond. I was not expecting that. Somehow, all words and facial expressions get stuck inside my body. I freeze up and all I can do is swallow the saliva in my mouth and nod my head up and down.

"I'm such a jerk. I haven't even asked you how you're feeling today." Penn saves me from myself, obviously witnessing my mini freak out, and changes the subject. "Are your legs and head doing better? I should have asked when you first got to the Sundowner earlier, but the guys were riling me up, and I wasn't in my usual state of mind."

He doesn't just save me from myself, but he takes all the heat and puts the spotlight on himself and his awkward moment from earlier tonight. I smile, coming back into the conversation with ease. "Oh. I noticed." I laugh, thinking about how worked up and agitated he looked when Lily and I arrived at the Sundowner.

Penn releases a stifled chuckle, his irritation from the guys still seeming to weigh heavily on him. "Are you feeling better?"

"Yeah, my head is totally good." My knees were hurting earlier, but the endorphins from the concert have made me forget all about it.

Plus, I'm hoping you'll kiss me, and then I won't have any pain anywhere for the rest of my life.

"I'm sure my knees and legs will be hurting tomorrow when I come down from the concert high, but this has been a fun night."

Penn is still looking at me with his irresistible smile. "You are stunning tonight. I mean, not that you weren't stunning yesterday. It's just, you clean up well. Fuck," Penn mutters and shakes his head at himself. "I didn't mean it like that. What I want to tell you is that I think you are beautiful."

I smile. He's flustered, and I'm enjoying watching him struggle. This strong guy who appears so self-confident is nervous, and in a roundabout way, it calms me, because I thought I was the nervous one.

"Thank you. Lily picked out my outfit. I don't usually wear clothes like this. This isn't really me." I fold my arms over my stomach, embarrassed as if I'm being exposed as an impostor.

"If it matters, I actually prefer you in the clothes you were wearing yesterday." Penn leans over and nudges me with his shoulder.

I return his nudge with one of my own, and he stiffens.

What the heck? I do not understand this guy.

"I need to use the head. Do you want to come, or are you okay here?"

"The head?"

"Sorry. Boat talk. The bathroom." He chuckles before giving a smile.

"Oh, gotcha. I'll just stay here." I'm sure the line for the women's room will take thirty minutes, and I don't want to miss the opening song for the next act.

Penn nods before he rummages through the snack bowl and pulls out a bag of Cheetos, throwing it my way.

"I asked Eamon's dad to make sure there were some Cheetos here for you. Sorry there isn't any vodka to wash it down with." He winks at me.

"Ha ha. You're so funny." I roll my eyes at him.

"I'll be back soon." Penn exits the box and heads into the crowd.

CHAPTER 8

Raegan

I sit down and smile to myself. I'm on Penn's radar and he's so out of my league. And beyond his looks, edgy tattoos, and tall frame, I'm finding Penn is also kind and thoughtful. I can't believe how much effort he's put into tonight, from getting here, to the seats, to the freaking Cheetos.

And he told me I'm stunning.

Nobody has ever called me stunning. Sure, Uncle Rhett tells me I'm beautiful all the time, but *stunning*? That was a first.

I'm lost in thought, watching the crew drag amps across the stage and tape down cords when I hear his voice. "I got you something."

I turn around, and Penn is standing by the door, holding the shoulders of a New Found Glory T-shirt.

"I noticed the shirt you had on yesterday got ripped after you fell, so I got you a replacement." His smile is wide and satisfied.

"You saw that?" I didn't even realize the shirt had ripped until this morning when I threw it in the laundry basket.

"Raegan, I can't take my eyes off you." He shakes his head as he affirms what I've felt all night. Neither of us can take our eyes off the other for longer than a few minutes.

I stand up and walk toward Penn, and he holds the T-shirt out to

me. "Thank you. This is really thoughtful."

Do I hug him? Side hug? Full hug? Crap. What do I do?

I wish Lily were here. She'd tell me what to do with just the flick of her head or eyes.

"I thought you could wear it now, since it's more your style and all. I had to get a large because they were sold out of the other sizes."

"That's okay. I'll make it work." It will be long, but maybe I can tie it and make it a little more fitted.

I put the T-shirt on over the halter crop top. Because I'm so short, it fits like a dress, hanging low, almost to my banged-up knees. I gather the material in the front and tie a big knot. I'm not sure if I should try to make it sexier and show more of my stomach, but I decide to just be myself and leave it covering my stomach.

"What do you think?" I extend my arms and curtsy as I give Penn a big smile.

Penn lets out a breath, lifts an eyebrow, and nods, shamelessly checking me out. I indulge in his wandering eyes, having never been the girl getting this much attention, and my self-confidence spills from within.

"It's perfect." Penn steps toward me, and my insides gush at his response.

He's finally coming in for something. Maybe a hug? Or perhaps a kiss?

I mentally let him know I'm ready for either. He's two steps away when Lily enters our area with the rest of the guys.

"Hey! Hey!" Lily calls out. "Next act is up. Wait. What are you wearing?" She points at my new T-shirt.

"Penn bought it for me." I give her a coy smile. Immediately embarrassed from all the attention I'm now receiving.

A chorus of "oohs" pours out of the three other guys. Penn shoots them a look that screams, "Shut the fuck up!"

Lily smiles at me before turning to the guys. "Don't be jerks. I think it's sweet."

"Yeah, it's so sweeeet." Eamon jabs at Penn.

The lights go down, and a guitar riff blasts through the speakers as cheers erupt across the amphitheater, so I guess the hug, or kiss, will have to wait.

Theo, Eamon, and Chase head to the front of the box, their arms fist-pumping the air, excited to hear New Found Glory playing "Hit or Miss."

Lily looks between Penn and me, and I give her a smile and wink, my way of telling her not to worry, that everything is fine.

I assume she's satisfied with my gesture because she walks over next to Theo.

Penn tilts his head toward the front of the box. "Shall we join them?"

"Sure."

He follows me to the rest of the group, and I sing along to all the songs with "the crew," as I am now so affectionately calling them.

The encore ends, and the lights turn back on. I look around and laugh at what a sweaty mess everyone is. These guys are fun, and even though Penn is the one who invited Lily and me tonight, the other three have made me feel welcomed and included, like I'm already one of them. I even shared a fun moment singing into an invisible microphone with Chase and Eamon halfway through the set.

"Okay, guys. We need to leave now so we can make it back in time for Raegan and Lily's curfew." Penn is working to gather the group so we can head back to Fire Island, and I'm uncomfortable for Lily and me being the reason their evening has to be cut short.

"Yeah, don't want you to get in trouble for getting them back late," Theo teases Penn.

"Dude. You're responsible for Lily just as much as I'm responsible for Raegan."

He's responsible for me? I'm giddy at the thought.

Twenty minutes pass before I sit next to Penn again in the banged-up white utility van. Instead of talking, as we did on the way here, Chase DJs from the passenger seat, popping in and out different CDs. Everyone sings along, the volume at full blast. The windows are down, and the warm evening air fills the van, the sweat on my body slowly drying.

Halfway through the drive back to the water tower, Penn lightly brushes his fingers against my thigh in the darkness of the van, and I freeze. The graze interrupts my breathing, and when I finally remember to exhale, it comes out as a heavy sigh. I'm glad the music is playing loud so everyone else doesn't hear the effect Penn's fingers are having on me. He reaches the hem of my shorts and gently rolls a strand of frayed fabric between his thumb and index finger before returning his fingers back down the length of my thigh.

I've never been touched like this before, and my insides flutter. Ever so slowly, I turn my head and look at Penn. The illumination from the light posts on Ocean Parkway allows me to see his eyes. They are an equal mix of curiosity and attentiveness. His fingers linger as he mindlessly draws circles right above my knee and the bruises and abrasions from yesterday's incident.

I don't take my eyes off him as the moment between us passes. A soft smile crosses Penn's face, and I return the same to him. He squeezes my thigh and pulls his hand away. A burning-hot sensation remains on my thigh for the remainder of the drive, and I desperately wish he'd touch me again.

But he doesn't.

The atmosphere within the group shifts once we are out of the van and on the buggy. I pull my hair back into a ponytail to keep it from flying around before we take off. There is no music, no doors, and the warm evening air blows against me as the buggy jostles across the sand.

I'm hit with a wave of exhaustion from all the cardio I did these past few hours, and I think everyone feels the same way. No one talks, and the ride is silent as I watch the moon's reflection off the crashing ocean waves.

Penn doesn't hold my waist on the buggy ride like he did on our way to the concert. This time his arms rest on either side of mine, and his hands hold on to the railing of the front seats, locking me in place between his arms. I face forward on his lap, holding on to the front seat railing too. Even though Penn hasn't touched me, I swear he buries his nose into my ponytail a few times.

He must like the way I smell.

I smile, satisfied, and encourage him to do it again by tilting my head back to his face every so often.

It's getting closer to curfew, but I know Lily and I will make it. Penn has been meticulous about the time, gathering everyone and getting us out of the amphitheater as fast as he could.

Eamon stops the buggy when he gets to Ocean Beach.

"I had fun with you two youngens," Eamon jokes from the front seat.

"Yeah, you two are pretty cool. I approve." Chase holds his hand to the back seat to give me a high five.

I laugh and give him a high five back. "Thanks for letting us crash the concert. I had a great time."

"Let's go," Theo tells Lily as he takes her hand and pulls her away toward the street.

I reluctantly peel myself off Penn's lap, attempting to drag out the moment of connection as long as possible. I immediately miss the warmth of his body once I'm standing on the sand.

Penn gets out of the buggy and puts his hands in his pocket. "Can I walk you to the street?"

"Sure." A little warmth comes back to me because I know I'm only moments away from the part of the night where the date ends, and I'm hoping he will give me a goodnight kiss. Especially after touching my thigh in the van, I'm confident I'll get a kiss. Even if it's just a peck.

I walk up the beach with Penn, and he stops when we reach the first house. Lily and Theo are close, but they are in an embrace and oblivious to our presence.

"I'm so glad you came tonight. I had a great time." Penn's hands stay glued in his pockets.

"Thanks again for inviting us. I had so much fun. I love my new shirt." I tug at the bottom hem, unsettled inside because Penn is still standing there with his hands in his pockets. I'm starting to think I'm not going to get that kiss. So I continue rambling. "Are you sure I can't pay you back for it?"

"It wouldn't be a gift if you did that." He takes one hand out of his pocket.

Here it is. He's gonna pull me in for that kiss.

I lick my lips and hold my breath, waiting. I'm a wreck as I anticipate the kiss.

Penn takes my hand in his. "Have a good night." He gives me a somewhat reserved smile. Long gone is the guy who touched my thigh in the van. He remains where he's standing and squeezes my hand three times, exactly as he did earlier tonight when we were on the buggy heading to the concert. He withdraws his hand from mine. "The island's small, so I'll see you around."

He turns and jogs back to the buggy, not looking back at me once.

CHAPTER 9

Penn

The island's small, so I'll see you around. What was I thinking?
I should have set up a specific time and place to meet up
with Raegan, because it's now been five days since the concert,
and I've seen Raegan only twice, and both times, it has been from afar.

The first time I saw her was after I got off work a few nights ago
in Ocean Beach, and she was with her uncle, having dinner at the
Shipwreck. It looked like they were on an uncle-niece date, and I didn't
want to interrupt, but I eyed her from my spot at the bar with Eamon
and got a few smirks and grins out of her when her uncle wasn't looking.

The second time I saw her was yesterday, when I was working the
ferry in Kismet. She rode her bike up to the ferry as I was pulling away
from the dock. We waved to each other, but because I was in the middle
of maneuvering the ferry, I couldn't get close enough to the edge of the
ferry to tell her I'd be back in two hours. I'd hoped she'd still be there
when I returned, but, unfortunately, she wasn't. I've had to work extra
hours this week, too, so I haven't been able to make it out to any beach
parties in the evening.

Raegan, though, has become a stimulus to my creativity, fueling
my compositions at the piano. In my free time after work, and before I
go to sleep, words fill the pages as I reflect on feelings that are all new

and strange to me.

I should have gone to Raegan's uncle's house at some point over these past few days. I know exactly what house it is, but I've been apprehensive about explaining my intentions to her uncle. At this exact moment, I'm even more hesitant to seek her out at her house because Raegan's brother Jed just boarded my last ferry of the day in Bay Shore.

From the size of Jed's two suitcases, it looks as though he's arriving for the entire summer. Another guy I don't recognize is with Jed, and I can tell he's rich, just from his tailored suit.

Jed is much more refined than me and the local island guys. He's preppy and clean cut. Khakis, loafers, and a polo shirt. I could never imagine wearing such stuffy clothing.

Must be casual Friday.

Jed acknowledges me as soon as he sees me. It's been years since we've hung out, so we don't do much more than exchange a friendly "hello." I pretend as if I really need to focus on getting the ferry across the bay so I don't have to talk to him any more than necessary, because honestly, what would I tell him?

"What's up, man? It's been years. You know what? I'm into your baby sister. She's smart and funny, and we have the same favorite song."

Or: "What's up, man? It's been years. You know what? Your baby sister makes me feel all warm and gooey inside, like a chocolate chip cookie."

Or: "What's up, man. It's been years. You know what? Your baby sister is genuine and beautiful. I've known her for less than a week and have only hung out with her one night, but I can't stop thinking about her."

Fuck. I'm becoming soft as shit.

I'm guessing Raegan hasn't told Jed about the concert, or even me, because he hasn't mentioned anything. More importantly, he's not looking at me as if he wants to kick my ass with some jiu-jitsu move.

I pull the ferry against the dock in Ocean Beach, and, as I was hoping, Raegan is waiting to meet Jed. She's wearing a floral trucker hat, her ponytail hanging out the back. She holds a utility cart handle in one hand, and Lily stands on the other side.

We quickly catch each other's gaze and exchange small smiles.

Just like that, my entire day brightens.

I can't come to terms with how much I have let Raegan take over my mind. I've never felt such a powerful attraction to someone. Thoughts of her consume me entirely.

I deserve a fucking trophy or Medal of Honor for my virtuous acts the night of the concert. I struggled to keep a safe amount of space between us and withstand the physical temptations, and I didn't even kiss her good night. But selfishly I couldn't resist that smile she gave me the two times I wrapped my hand around that tiny little waist of hers, and the few times I caressed her thigh in the van on the way home.

I tried to be good, but never said I was a saint.

By the end of the evening, after I returned her to Ocean Beach ahead of curfew, I realized my respectable actions had nothing to do with the fact that she's seventeen, and had everything to do with the unexplainable connection I felt to her. She's more than just a one-night stand and quick release with some no-name.

I really like her.

I'm completely enamored and absolutely screwed, because "more than" is not what I should be wanting.

I'm trying to appear occupied while I shut down the engines, but I strain to observe Raegan and Jed's encounter.

Raegan jumps into Jed's arms and gives him a big hug. Then she hugs Fancy Suit Guy, and my heart drops, then immediately fills with jealousy. I know I can't be mad or upset by a hug, and he could be a cousin for all I know, but damn, I haven't even given her a proper hug yet.

I remain on the ferry, pretending to clean so I can avoid having to interact with Raegan in front of her brother.

Yes, I'm being a total coward.

They load up the utility cart with Jed and Fancy Suit Guy's bags.

Raegan keeps peeking my way, trying to catch my attention, and I'm now unloading cargo—something I most definitely am not responsible for doing.

I'm breaking into a sweat just to avoid any confrontation.

I'm carrying a cardboard box with a toilet inside for some house remodel out to the dock, and I nearly drop it on my feet when I see Raegan standing in front of me.

"Sorry. I didn't mean to scare you." She gives me a smile that makes my insides pulse. The breeze blows her ponytail, filling my nostrils with her addictive scent, and at this moment I don't care if her brother lays me out on the dock with a punch, because this is heaven.

I glance around, hesitantly looking for Jed, as I place the toilet box on the ground. "Hey." I grin at her, elated to be in her presence again.

"For being such a small island, I've only seen you twice." She sulks.

Oh, so you've missed me as much as I've missed you.

"I know. I'm sorry I haven't been able to connect with you, but I've been working double shifts all week because one of our captains got injured the night we were at the concert. He won't be cleared to work for another week, so I'll be working doubles through next Friday."

I'm exhausted just thinking about how many hours I've clocked this past week. I'm not sure how I'll make it through another week of it, but there is no one else to pick up the slack.

"That sucks. You must be so tired." Raegan pauses, then opens her mouth to say something, but nothing comes out. She rubs her hands together and looks toward the water.

"Are you going to Theo's birthday party next week? I mean, I guess that's a stupid question to ask. I'm sure you'll be there, since he's one of your best friends. I was just wondering, 'cause I'll be there, too, with Lily, since, you know—she and Theo are somewhat an official thing now. And I guess I was hoping to see you." Raegan is nervous and rambling and it's adorable, so I don't respond until she stops fully.

I smile. "Yeah, I'll be there. Actually, I will have that entire day off. Maybe we could—"

"Raegan!"

I'm cut off by the booming voice of Jed calling for his sister.

Maybe we could hang out beforehand is what I want to tell her, but I'm sure as hell not going to say it now that Jed is standing five feet away.

Jed looks surprised to see me talking to Raegan.

I'll take a surprised face over a pissed face.

"You know Wells?" Jed asks her.

"Yeah. I met *Wells* last week." She giggles as she calls me by my last name, and it's all I can do to not reach out and touch her. "You two know each other?" She motions between us.

"Sure. I, along with half of the female Fire Island tourist population, *know* Penn Wells." He says it as a joke, but there is a slight undertone.

"Come on, man. It's not half," I joke back as Raegan's eyes widen.

Okay. Bad joke.

Jed looks between Raegan and me, and before I can say anything, Jed tells her, "Peter needs to get to the house for a phone meeting, so we need to go." He stares at me, assessing the situation.

Raegan looks back to me, her eyes saying, "Sorry." I give her a small, tentative smile because the last thing I want to do is tip Jed off even more on my attraction to his little sister.

She turns and links her arm into Jed's and walks down the dock with him until they meet up with Lily and the guy I now know is Peter, who is now holding the utility cart handle.

They take off in the direction of her uncle's house, and I grab my backpack from the ferry before heading down the dock to start prepping one of the water taxis, since this is where I'll be spending the rest of my day and evening, doing lateral village-to-village rides.

I'm pissed that work is coming between Raegan and me and that I have to wait another week, until Theo's birthday, to finally spend some actual time with her. I miss her laugh and catching her watching me when she thinks I'm not paying attention.

I'm looking forward to seeing how she'll surprise me the next time I get to be with her. She's surprised me twice now. The first time was when she hugged her driver—that showed her kindness. There is no social ladder with her; everyone is equal. The second time she surprised me was when we were at the concert and she didn't shotgun the beer. She knows her limits and didn't give in to peer pressure just because everyone else was doing it. That type of confidence is sexy as hell.

I'm lost in thoughts of Raegan well into the evening, and before I know it, it's late and the passengers have become more drunk and unruly with each trip. I finish dropping off a group in Cherry Grove, and I'm heading back to Ocean Beach with a handful of people on board. I pull up to the dock in Ocean Beach and see Jed waiting for the water taxi. I'm confident he isn't here for a ride.

I stay back and let the deckhand help the passengers off. Finally, when I see no one else needs a ride, I step off the taxi, ready to accept my fate.

"Hey, Jed."

"Wells."

I nod. "What's up?" What's that saying? Kill them with kindness? I need to try that right now.

"When I saw you on the boat earlier today and asked you *what's new*, you conveniently neglected to tell me that you took my sister and her best friend to a concert at Jones Beach the other night."

Oh shit. Yep. He is here to talk about Raegan.

"Yeah, I invited them to join a few of us. It was a group thing." I figure keeping it simple is the way to go.

"You do know my sister is only seventeen." His forehead furrows as he questions me with the authority of a police officer.

Trust me. I'm more than aware. Can I plead the fifth?

"I do know that. She's actually quite mature for her age."

Okay, that second part was not necessary.

Jed cringes. "Even though it's been years since we've hung out, I know you're still a decent guy. But I also know you have a new girl in your bed each week. My sister is not Lily—we both know she'll hook up with anything that moves. I don't want Raegan to be your next flavor of the week."

I don't want her to be that either.

I can't tell Jed how interested I am in his sister because I'm on a fine line already, and it won't take much for this conversation to take a big turn for the worst.

"We're just hanging out. As friends. I've been nothing but respectful." I look him in his eyes and hope he can't read into mine and see that I jerked off to thoughts of his baby sister in the shower last night.

"I appreciate that. The last thing Raegan needs before leaving for college is getting involved in something that ends up messy." His voice is stern, almost father-like, but he emphasizes *messy* by throwing his hands in the air.

"Look, man, I'm not trying to pull her into any mess. Your sister is intelligent and kind, and I'm not trying to add her as a notch on my bedpost."

That's the honest truth.

As much as I'd like to know what Raegan feels like under me, with her lips on mine, Jed's right. She's leaving for college and deserves more than a quick summer hookup. Jed being here on the dock to talk to me shows just how much he cares about his sister and wants the best for her. I want to tell him that I care about her, too, but I'm still trying to process my racing thoughts, so I just let him talk.

"You know Lily has no filter, and she's been spilling everything to Peter and me since we arrived this afternoon, and it sounds like my sister really has a thing for you. I don't want to deal with the aftermath when you break her heart and I have to come kick your ass."

I already know Raegan likes me, but hearing she *really* likes me, well, that strokes my ego in the best of ways.

"I won't hurt your sister. I promise," I tell Jed, and hold my hand to his so we can shake on it.

He grips my hand and shakes hard. "And tell your buddy Theo he better treat Lily right or he'll have to answer to me too."

I nod before Jed takes off down the dock, leaving me with only the sound of waves lapping against the water taxi.

This conversation ended up going smoother than I anticipated. Jed didn't forbid me from seeing his sister; he just said not to hurt her, and that should be easy enough.

CHAPTER 10

Raegan

I am completely obsessed with Penn. It's ludicrous and almost comical just how much I like him after being in his presence for less than twelve hours total.

He worked double shifts all week and had no days off. So I would offer to go to the market anytime someone in the house needed anything, hoping to see him on a ferry or water taxi down at the dock.

I've become an avid bike rider, taking daily, aimless trips to Kismet, hoping I'll happen to run into him. Lily even joins me on Uncle Rhett's dock, lying out, watching every boat that passes in the bay to see if one of them is Penn's.

But nope. Not once did I even see him.

Penn thoroughly consumes my mind. I'm in withdrawal, and I don't even know why. I spent only one evening with him, but I yearn to feel that same elation I felt the night of the concert.

He has to like me.

I think? Right?

The smiles he's given me, how gently he's touched me, there's a connection. But if he's such a player, then why didn't he make a move when he had the chance? I'm starting to think maybe he doesn't actually like me.

At least I'll finally get to see him at Theo's party. Hopefully, I'll get some clarity on his feelings by the end of the night.

Lily is hanging out with Theo this morning and afternoon, and I'm trying to avoid Jed and Peter's invite to join them at the beach, so I get on my bike and head west, to Kismet. Penn did mention when I saw him at the dock last week that he has today off, and I swear he was going to ask if I wanted to hang out before we were interrupted by Jed.

I stop my bike in front of a modest, navy-blue-shingled, two-story house with a fairly large grassy front yard. A narrow wood plank pathway leads to a set of stairs to the raised front porch that wraps around the entirety of the house. An American flag flaps in the breeze, and the only sound filling the air comes from the birds chirping in nearby trees. Two white Adirondack chairs are sitting on the porch, and empty beer bottles litter the handrail. Surfboards in varying sizes and colors lean up against the house, along with a handful of bicycles.

With the exception of the white, purple, and pink impatiens planted near the chicken wire fence, it's clear no females live here. This place is a total bachelor pad and is in pretty good condition, except for some paint chipping off the siding.

Many homes out here have cheeky names given to them by their owners, much like how boats are named. I spot a painted wooden sign hanging on the fence that says, "Boys of Summer." I guess they are paying a little homage to Don Henley. I smile. The house name seems fitting for this motley crew of guys.

I lean my bike against the railing of the plank pathway, walk to the front door, and ring the bell. I hope ten o'clock in the morning isn't too early for Penn or the other guys.

What if he doesn't want to see me?

The thought doesn't cross my mind until I ring the doorbell. I shouldn't have just shown up without an invite.

What was I thinking?

Abort. Abort.

I turn to go down the stairs so I can make a getaway, but it's too late, because I hear the door open.

"Raegan?"

It's Penn.

I pause and turn back to the front door. Standing in the doorway is a shirtless Penn in sweatpants.

Holy crap.

If fully clothed Penn is hot, shirtless Penn is a mind-blowing inferno. His chest muscles are strong and broad, with a light peppering of hair. Blatantly, I gaze down to his defined abs, forcing myself to stop before I go past the waistband of his sweats—I don't want to be *that* obvious. I need a moment to close my mouth because he is absolute perfection.

Penn runs his hand through his morning hair, eyes still half-closed.

I'm speechless.

Apparently, so is Penn.

He blinks a few times. Maybe he's trying to see if I'll disappear?

Should I disappear? What do I do? Where's Lily when I need her?

"I'm sorry I just stopped by. Lily gave me your address. She's busy today with Theo, and you mentioned last week that you weren't working today. So I thought I'd stop by and see if you maybe wanted to hang out? But I realize now you're probably tired and trying to catch up on sleep. It's early in the day, so I can just go, and you can go back to sleep. I shouldn't have stopped by. I'll just see you tonight at Theo's birthday. You're still going to Theo's party, right?"

Shut up, turn around, and go.

"Raegan." Penn takes a step closer to me, reaches down, and places his hand lightly on my shoulder. I immediately stop talking. "I'm glad you stopped by. I actually wanted to hang out with you today, and you saved me a trip to Ocean Beach to come find you."

Knowing Penn planned to seek my company makes my heart flutter, and my confidence gets a little boost as my nerves calm slightly.

"Do you want to come in? I can get cleaned up, and then we can figure out something to do."

Penn opens the door wider for me to enter.

I slip in, and Penn closes the door. I gaze around the surprisingly clean house. No pictures or artwork is on the walls, but at least it isn't dirty. I don't immediately spot any gaping holes in the drywall from a punch or body being thrown into it, and the hardwood floors look like they were just mopped.

"Welcome to Boys of Summer. Nobody else is here right now. But this is the living room and kitchen." Penn points around. An oversized, L-shaped, microfiber couch sits in the living room facing the fireplace where a large, flat-screen TV hangs above the mantel. A dark wood coffee table takes up all the remaining floor space in the room. The kitchen is bright and airy, with an island in the middle and a table with seating for six people. Apples and bananas sit in a bowl on the counter, and I take note that these guys must eat fairly healthy when they aren't guzzling down beers.

"Theo's and Eamon's bedrooms are upstairs." Penn points to the steep set of stairs at the back part of the living room.

I follow Penn down a hallway, and it's all I can do to peel my eyes off his tan and jacked back muscles when he points to a closed door.

"Chase's room." He opens another door and flicks on the light. "Bathroom," he tells me before turning the light off.

He continues down the hallway until reaching an open door. "I wasn't expecting any visitors, so I haven't had a chance to pick up my mess." He gives me an embarrassed smile.

I'm going into a boy's, ahem, I mean, man's room, all by myself. Abril would not be delighted to know this, but Lily sure will be.

I smile as I internally pat myself on the back with my sweaty hand for not being scared and actually showing up to see him.

I walk into his bedroom, and my nostrils are slammed with Penn's smell. Cedarwood and sweet orange, but not fruity in a feminine way. He's all masculine, and there is something about the sweatpants that makes this moment even hotter.

I have to remind myself to stop staring at his naked top half.

I take a quick look around. There's a queen-size bed with a navy-blue comforter tossed to one side. I notice his dirty laundry pile in the corner, containing multiple pairs of cargo shorts and Islander Ferry button-ups. Like the rest of the house, the walls are bare. But what catches my eye is the upright piano and the guitar sitting in the corner. I knew Penn plays piano only because Lily told me after her first night with Theo, but Penn and I have never discussed it.

"You play the piano?" I ask, pretending not to already know.

"I play a little." He looks down at his feet and smiles. It's cute that he's trying to be humble.

"You must play more than a little. You have a piano in your room, and I see handwritten sheet music here." I point to the lined pages with musical notes and words everywhere.

"If you want, I could maybe play for you after I shower. I don't usually play for people, but ..." He pauses and shakes his head as he chews on his bottom lip. "I'd really like to play for you." Penn nods, like he finally talked himself into playing for me. His cloudy grays gleam with a hint of something, but I can't read them exactly. Maybe it's anticipation, or an eagerness to see where this goes.

I squeeze my lips to keep a massive grin from forming. I feel special. *Play it cool, Raegan.*

"I'd love to hear you play. I always wished I was good at playing an instrument. I tried playing the clarinet back in junior high, and I sucked so much the band teacher kicked me out of the class after the first semester." I let out a little laugh, thinking back to how I couldn't even read the music and had to write the letters above each note.

Penn throws his head back and lets out a roar of laughter. "That's hilarious. How on earth can they kick a kid out of band class?"

"I was that bad." I giggle the words out.

"I'm sure you weren't that bad." He gives me a cheeky smile before clapping his hands. "Let me jump in the shower. I'll be quick. You can just hang out in here, if you're okay with that?"

At the mention of *shower*, my eyes betray me, and I glance down at his package. Nothing looks unusually large, and I quickly look back up to Penn's face. He totally saw me eyeing his junk, and he lets out a little chuckle before pressing his lips in a hard line.

Was I looking for a boner? Oh my God, I was. Lily is rubbing off on me.

I clear my throat and manage to squeak out, "Sure. I don't mind waiting."

Penn smiles. "Give me ten minutes."

I throw him two thumbs-up. It's like I can't act normal because I'm in his bedroom. Something about being here is making my brain not work correctly.

Penn walks into the hallway, and a minute later I hear the hum of water rushing through pipes in the wall Penn shares with the bathroom next door.

CHAPTER 11

Raegan

I sit on the edge of Penn's bed and look around. Giving in to my curiosity, I bury my face in his pillow and inhale, memorizing his scent.

I place the pillow down exactly how it was and wait patiently for Penn to return.

I know if Lily were here, she'd tell me this is the time to take my clothes off and wait for him naked in his bed. I laugh at how absurd that is, not sure where her confidence comes from, but there is no way in hell I'll be doing that.

"What's so funny?"

I look over to Penn in the doorway, his wet hair falling into his eyes and dripping on the floor as he holds a towel around his waist with one hand.

I stare foolishly, my eyes on him, as I mentally remind myself to breathe and not lick my lips like I'm a feline and he's some catnip I want to devour.

"I forgot to grab clean clothes." He tiptoes playfully into the room.

Oh my God. He thought I'd be naked in his bed. I was supposed to get naked.

Penn opens a few drawers in his dresser and quickly walks out of

the bedroom. Lily is going to die when she hears about this. She'll tell me something like, "A lost opportunity never returns."

Penn returns a few minutes later, dressed in a pair of cargo shorts and a black T-shirt, his damp hair leaving droplets of water on the neck of his shirt.

"I'm sorry if I made you uncomfortable before. I really did forget my clothes. I wasn't trying to make you feel awkward."

How can he read my mind?

"Oh, that?" I point my thumb behind my head. "Naw. I'm good, not embarrassed or uncomfortable at all."

"Okay. Good." Penn rewards my little lie with a big smile. "So, how was your week?"

"It was nice."

I managed to stay busy, but what I really want to tell Penn is that I spent most of my time since we met thinking about him.

"I went to the beach a lot with Jed and Peter." Penn's face scrunches when I mention Peter.

Ooh. Is he jealous?

My insides are reeling at the thought that this big, strong guy may be jealous of Peter—who's definitely not my type.

"Peter heads back to the city in a few days."

Penn's face settles.

"How was your week? You must be tired from working so much."

"I'm exhausted, but it comes with the territory. I'll be taking over the ferry company in a few years, when my dad retires. Plus, we don't want to upset any tourists by actually making them walk from village to village." He laughs. "So ... I know I owe you a song at the piano, but after that, what do you want to do to pass the time until Theo's party?"

I want to make out with you on this bed.

"Um, I didn't actually have any ideas when I stopped by, but maybe we could go to the beach, ride bikes, or just hang out? I promised Lily I'd get ready with her before the party, so I'll need to head back to Ocean Beach at some point."

"That sounds good. We can figure it out later. I'd love to play for you now." He's fidgeting with his fingers, running his thumb across the palm of his other hand. I can't help but let out a little smile, knowing I might make Playboy Penn a little nervous too.

"Want to sit up here?" Penn motions to the top part of his bed, where a headboard would be, if he had one. "You can take your Chucks off and get comfortable."

Penn pulls the crumpled part of his comforter up in an attempt to make his bed, and puts both pillows against the wall, patting them a few times, creating a little spot for me to sit. It's a sweet gesture.

I remove my shoes before I crawl up higher on his bed and sit crisscross, leaning against one pillow. I make myself at home and take the other pillow, wrapping my arms around it and leaning my head back on the wall.

Penn's smell engulfs me as I snuggle in his bed, and I'm intoxicated by it. I inhale again and something happens to the blood in my veins—I'm not sure if it becomes thicker or thinner, but it's flowing differently within me. It's like I've never truly been alive until this moment.

I'm not sure what to expect. I know we have similar taste in bands, but I have a feeling he's the kind of guy who's well versed in multiple types of music.

I watch Penn's every move as he sits tall on the piano bench. He extends his long fingers above the keys, curving them slightly. I notice his fingers are slim, but they don't look girlish. They have this dexterous and agile appearance, spreading across a large span of the piano.

Penn glides his hands across the piano and presses down on the keys, creating a soft, slow sound as he warms up. His head is tilted down, but his eyes are closed and his body sways and moves to the music. A tranquil look overtakes him. He's both professional and relaxed. This must be his happy place, and I'm thrilled he's sharing this part of himself with me.

He continues to play, occasionally singing. His voice is angelic and doesn't match what I think would come from a six-foot-tall athletic man with tattoos.

I sit in Penn's bed, awestruck.

He plays effortlessly, and it's beautiful. I'm not sure why he doesn't play in front of people, because I would pay to hear this every day.

The music he creates is enchanting. The melodies pull me in. I feel each emotion with every push of the pearly keys. The way he strings a symphony of sound together transports me to a different place and time.

Penn's voice and songs rival those on the radio. He continues on for a while, and I'd be okay if he stayed here all day to play for me.

Penn stops playing and gently places his hands on his lap. I clap in appreciation.

"That was amazing." I'm beaming at how breathtaking and incredible his impromptu performance was.

Penn reaches his hand out to a small, old and faded photo leaning against the music rack. The picture is of a young woman with a small child on her lap sitting at a piano. Penn pulls his hand away almost as quickly as he reached for the photo.

"My mom used to play the piano. I was never interested in learning how to play, though. It wasn't until after she died that I begged my dad to let me take lessons. He found an older lady on the island who played piano and paid her to teach me. I always imagine my mom sitting close by, listening while I play." Penn remains facing the piano and doesn't move to look my way.

The photo must be Penn and his mom. My eyes fill with tears. "I'm so sorry. I didn't know your mom passed."

"It was a long time ago. I don't talk about her very often. It hurts too much. But for some reason, when I'm with you, the hole in my heart that misses her doesn't feel quite as big." He turns his head to me and gives a light smile.

My heart hurts at his revelation, and I pull my legs into my chest, holding the pillow a little tighter as I look at him, wishing he'd look back at me, but he doesn't.

He never talks about his mom, but he's telling me. The fact that he trusts me is touching, and it feels good to be this person for him.

"Thank you for sharing your songs with me. They are so good."

Penn turns his body slightly to face me. "I'm glad you like them. But I should be thanking you, Raegan." He gives me a small smile and his eyes pierce mine. I grin back at him, so handsome sitting there at the piano. "Something's shifted in my music since I met you. It's better, deeper, and comes so much easier than in the past." He pulls his legs out from under the piano and sits facing me on the bed. He moves his hands, and I think he's going to reach out for me.

My breathing hitches with an eagerness I've never felt before. I'm unable to take my eyes off him. Silence fills the room with anticipation and need, and I don't know what to say or do, so I just watch Penn. I take him in without reservation, his tan skin glowing in the morning sun that pours in through his bedroom window.

Penn rubs his palms together. "Have you ever heard of a heart song?"

"A heart song? No. What's that? Is it like a love song?" I'm shaky as I say *love*. I know this—what we have—these few moments in person isn't love. It's lust, for sure. But it's different. It feels special. And I can only hope Penn is feeling it too.

"Not necessarily. It's more of a song that speaks your feelings without you having to find the right words. Have you ever had thoughts so overpowering and consuming, be it elated, or discouraged, or even upset, but you didn't know how to put them into words?"

Um, yeah. This moment would qualify. I have no idea how to describe how I'm feeling.

"Well, that's a heart song. My parents came up with the idea and always had heart songs for each other."

My heart bursts. His parents' love story sounds exceptional. "That's really sweet." I curl my lips into a smile.

"I have one ... a heart song ... for you." Penn doesn't take his eyes off me as he speaks, but he doesn't move any closer.

He has a heart song for me?

Is this what he does to all the girls? Play them the piano and tell them sweet things?

My heart drops at the thought that I'm just another girl for Penn, another summer fling. Jed wasted no time telling me to steer clear of Penn, that he's nothing but a player, and it only fueled my desire to know him more. I didn't come here looking for something serious. That's the point of this summer, I remind myself. Get some experience and go to college. So why do I care so much if this is his "thing"?

"Sure. Is this the same song you play for all the girls?" I sound insecure and like a total brat, and for the life of me I can't figure out why I care so much.

"What?" A look of confusion crosses Penn's face. "No." I sense hurt in his voice. He waits a moment before his hand reaches for my leg. His fingers graze my calf, and once our eyes meet, he pulls away with a sigh.

I immediately feel the emptiness from the removal of his hand, and a burning sensation lingers.

Glancing beyond my shoulder and out the window, Penn slowly

speaks, "I don't bring girls to my room, let alone play songs for them. These are all firsts for me." His eyes shift to mine, a curious wonder within them. "You're a storm, Raegan. A hurricane. I want to rush into the center of it, completely unprepared. You make me want to do all these things I don't normally do. I want to play a song for you."

"Oh." I'm embarrassed by my rude attitude and don't know what else to say. His words hit me right in the heart. I've been obsessing over him since the day I met him, and I suddenly know why. I want more than just experience in the bedroom. I want to know Penn. I want to feel a connection. I like him. Like, a lot.

I've never been someone's hurricane. I'm not sure I've ever even been someone's rain shower, but if I'm his hurricane, then he's my tidal wave, my storm surge, crashing into me and breaching my defenses.

"So don't you worry, Rae. This is my first heart song to you, and to anyone. Ever."

The way my shortened name rolls off his tongue melts my insides. It captivates me. And I can't stop looking at him.

I always correct people when they shorten my name to Rae. My parents named me Raegan because that's what they wanted people to call me. But for some reason, when Penn said *Rae*, it felt right. And I don't correct him.

He places his hands on the piano, and I listen to the elegant sound that vibrates around us. I don't immediately recognize the song until the melody starts, because it is usually played on a guitar, but he's transformed it into a beautiful piano piece.

It's Eve 6's "Here's to The Night." Penn sings the chorus loud.

This was not what I was expecting.

Penn finishes the song, and we both sit in silence.

My head is spinning as I attempt to solve this musical puzzle and figure out what he just tried to tell me through the heart song.

The song is complicated.

It's hopeful, yet pessimistic.

I'm confused.

Is he telling me this won't work? Is he saying let's just capture the moment? How do I respond?

A simple thank-you doesn't seem sufficient.

"That was ... beautiful. Nobody has ever played a song for me like that before." I take note of his strong body and look at him, trying to reach his eyes.

As if he can feel my gaze, Penn turns his head away from the piano, looking at me. He doesn't break his stare as he slowly moves his legs to the side of the piano bench. He hesitates slightly before leaning over onto the mattress, strands of hair falling over his dark eyes as he infiltrates my space.

My heart beats uncontrollably, and that feeling is the only way I know I'm still alive, because this feels like a dream, like I'm floating.

I move his pillow off my lap, setting it on the mattress, and Penn reaches for my arm. Heat rushes between my legs at his touch. I reposition myself so my thighs are resting on my calves, my shins pushing into the plush mattress. Penn gently draws me near, and my shins sink farther into the comforter with every inch closer he pulls me.

Penn reaches out and brushes his thumb over my bottom lip. I inhale slowly as the pad of his finger swipes once more across my lip, and I delicately nip at his finger. Penn's face lights up in response, and he bites down on his bottom lip, shaking his head at me like I'm in trouble. His eyes grow even darker, black pupils taking over the stormy grays. I know he's about to kiss me, and I'm begging him with my eyes to do so.

Penn leans in closer, then stops, dropping his finger from my lip, and I instantly feel the void between us.

"Why'd you stop?" *Please don't stop.*

Penn exhales. "God, if you only knew how much I want to kiss you." He pauses, looking as though he wants to say more, but he doesn't.

"You can kiss me."

My boldness in saying things to Penn is new to me, but it feels normal, not at all as if I'm as inexperienced as I truly am.

Penn reaches out for me again but stops inches from my face, then withdraws his hand. "Please don't say that. If I kiss you, then things will get complicated." His voice strains, and the words tremble out of his mouth.

Complicated? Complicated is okay ... look at Noah and Allie in The Notebook. *Lots of complications, but it worked.*

I want to ask Penn what he means by *complicated*, because his words don't match the way his eyes devour me, or the feel of his thumb as it swiped my lip only moments ago. But as quickly as my newfound boldness came, it's gone, and I'm embarrassed and unsure of what to do next.

Do I awkwardly hang out with him for the rest of the day and just ignore this? Or should I just head back to Ocean Beach and avoid it?

There's no way I can spend the rest of the day with him and pay no attention to the fact that we are both attracted to each other and just almost kissed.

I push off my shins and stand, my feet firmly on the ground. "Maybe I should go?" I offer, even though it's the last thing I want to do.

"I don't want you to leave, but ..." Penn clutches on to his shaking leg, and his head drops, unable to look me in my eyes. He doesn't finish his thought.

I'm positive that I misread this entire situation.

My time here at his house has been incredible, but also nothing short of confusing. He plays me his songs, talks about his mom, but then pushes me away. Right now, my pride is hurt.

"Would it be better if I left?" My voice cracks, but I clear my throat and remain strong, even though I have no reason to ask him the same question again because I'm pretty sure I know what his answer will be. I'm already slipping my feet into my Chucks and bending over to tie them before Penn responds, "Probably." He continues to look down at the ground, his hands doing nothing to keep his leg shaking at bay.

Gone is the confident guy who took Lily and me to the concert. "I'm sorry." He looks up at me, and his dark pupils have been restored to normal size, giving way to the softest gray eyes I've ever seen. His lips are tightly closed, and he gives me a small half smile.

He's beautiful but broken, and I'm feeling humiliated. I need to get out of here. I walk toward his bedroom door to see myself out.

"I'll still see you tonight?" he asks, his voice hopeful. I turn around from my spot in the doorway, meeting his gaze as he sits still at the piano.

"Yeah." I nod before walking down the hallway and out the door. The wind is blowing hard and I look up at the sky to see dark, puffy thunderstorm clouds coming in from the west. Crap. I didn't realize there was going to be a storm today. I need to get back to Ocean Beach before it hits. I jump on my bike and ride back to Uncle Rhett's as fast as I can in an attempt to beat the rain.

CHAPTER 12

Penn

Theo's beach party is raging, and there are a lot of people I've met and known over the years, but there's also a handful of people I don't recognize. The full moon is out, and it's cooler than usual for a mid-June night thanks to the quick thunder and lightning storm that passed through earlier today. It was right after Raegan left my house, drenching the beach and leaving in its wake some cooler weather. So I'm keeping warm in my hoodie, thrilled that for the first time in two weeks I'm out at a party and I'm not in my Islander Ferry uniform.

If Raegan wasn't coming tonight, I'd have just stayed home, bought Theo a twelve-pack, and called it good. But I can't get Raegan off my mind. She's set up camp in my head, and it's not a bare-bones, one-night campground, but a massive "I'm going to get comfortable and have all the amenities" campground.

She's here for an extended stay and I'm welcoming it.

Eamon ran power from the house of our friend, who lives right on the beach, and set up a few speakers to play music. Much to my dismay, the music has been an ongoing sequence of rap and hip-hop songs. Sisqó's "Thong Song" is blasting, and the grinding on the beach is intense. I've already declined a few offers to dance from women I've

messed around with in the past, quickly realizing they no longer hold the same appeal.

I'm searching for the only person I want to dance with tonight, and I can't find her anywhere. I'm restless, thinking she may not actually show. After my little stunt earlier today in my bedroom, who knows if she's even still interested in seeing me?

After Raegan left my house this afternoon, I sat around and kicked myself, thinking about how close I came to kissing her. I've never had self-restraint like this before. The medal I get for my abstinence better be fucking gold, cause my balls are blue and are cursing me nonstop.

I replay in my head, for the hundredth time, our entire morning at Boys of Summer. It killed me to see her in my bed, wearing a Sugarcult T-shirt, smiling as I played the piano. All I wanted to do was pull her in close, kiss her, and tell her how she's changed my life in the short time I've known her.

And then I gave her a heart song.

Like an idiot.

Seeing Raegan's face light up after I sang the Eve 6 song reminded me that I promised Jed I wouldn't hurt her—and if I kissed her, I would be breaking that promise. Now I think I may have hurt her either way because I can't erase the sad look on her face when she left my place earlier.

I spent an extended portion of the afternoon thinking about the fact that I let Raegan get up and leave. I didn't ask her to stay; I didn't try to stop her. I just watched her walk out the door without explaining my feelings. I don't even know if she will want to talk to me tonight.

I've never been good at feelings anyway. My mom meant everything to me, and after she died, when I was a hormone-raging thirteen-year-old, I shut down and pushed everyone away. I loved my mom more than anything. I wouldn't talk to my dad or even Chase about those deep dark feelings that took hold of me on the inside, the days I could barely get out of bed, look at a piano, or even eat. I've kept it all locked in and bottled up. Eventually, the pain faded, but the memories of my mom stay ever-present in my mind. If she were here today, I imagine her hitting me upside the head with one of her rolled-up gossip magazines for the way I've been acting with Raegan. "You're being too hot and cold," she'd say. "Don't mess it up."

It may be too late for that now, Mom.

Over the years, I've become an emotional shell, swearing off ever caring about someone as much as I did my mom. This is why I've never been in an actual relationship before. It hasn't been worth the risk of possibly losing someone I care about again. But somehow, a certain seventeen-year-old is making me break all my rules. In a short amount of time, she has thawed my heart to the possibility of letting someone in. The thought petrifies me. But I want to see where it goes because I'm intrigued by everything she represents—happiness, laughter, and a calming sense of peace in her presence.

I know I need to fix our almost kiss and her leaving my house earlier today. I've thought through all the options and how they could play out. I've narrowed it down to two scenarios.

Option one: I apologize with words. Dig deep into my heart and tell her how I feel. Take the risk and make myself vulnerable, unlike anything I've ever done before. Maybe she accepts it, or maybe she slaps me and tells me I'm an asshole. It's risky because I need to make sure I say the right words, and I have no idea where to even start. But it seems like something a mature guy would do to ask for forgiveness.

Option two: I apologize with a kiss. The moment she walks onto the sand, I'll grab her by the hand and pull her close, wrap my other hand around her waist, and give her a fairy-tale dip of a kiss in front of everyone. Girls like that romantic shit. She'll for sure forgive me.

This one seems like a sure win, but is a beach party, in front of all these people, really the place she wants our first kiss to be?

Is it where I want our first kiss to be? I've undeniably grown a vagina.

The two options bounce back and forth in my head as I stand near the keg with Chase and Eamon. Beer in hand, palms sweating, I've never been this restless waiting for someone to arrive at a party.

Theo has been making his rounds, hitting up everyone here tonight to say "thanks." He's currently standing with a crowd of his New York City buddies who came to the island this weekend to celebrate him. Most of those guys aren't too bad, but Chase, Eamon, and I don't tend to mix well with these polo-shirt wearing, slicked-back hair sporting, "I work a fancy job and make more money than you" Manhattanites, so we keep ourselves distanced.

I swallow my beer and hear catcalls and whistles. Before I lower my beer from my mouth, I know Lily and Raegan have arrived. Sure enough, I glance over, and as cliché as it sounds, my breath is taken away. Raegan is wearing a dark-purple top, with a jacket and jeans. Her brown hair is half pulled back and falls with perfect waves. She walks next to Lily, who is dancing her way onto the beach, her belly button ring on full display in a short shirt and jeans.

Raegan is smiling and laughing, a stark comparison to the sad girl who walked out of my house earlier today.

I want that smile to mean she isn't mad or upset at me, that maybe I still have a chance to figure out how to make this work. I need to know what this feeling between us is, and why I want to be a different person around her.

Raegan scans the crowd, giving a few shallow waves to other people on the beach. She finally looks over to the keg, and when we make eye contact, her smile fades. I push through the feelings of disappointment and widen my smile before I hold up my red cup and point to it—

universal code for asking if she'd like a beer. She shakes her head and mouths, "No."

Well. Shit. She's smiling at everyone but me. I should have run over there and done option two first.

Raegan looks away, giving her attention back to Lily. I know she said no, but I need to bring her something. I need an excuse, any excuse, to be near her, to talk to her. I grab a bottle of water and a can of soda from the cooler next to the keg, deciding I'll bring her a peace offering, then go in with the forgiveness kiss.

Yes, you still have game. You can do this.

As I walk back toward her, some guy I don't know pulls her into a hug.

Oh, hell no. She's not his to touch.

She's not mine, either, but I don't like seeing his filthy hands on her.

He moves his hands down her back, drops them lower, and gropes her ass.

What the fu—

Raegan tries to pull back, but the guy has a tight hold on her. Raegan's face clearly says she's uncomfortable, and she puts her hands on his chest, trying to get away from him. Lily throws her hands in the air, screaming something I can't hear over the music. Lily pushes the guy, and he doesn't even budge. He lets out a dickface laugh, and I instantly fill with rage.

I drop the water and soda in the sand and sprint toward Raegan. "What the fuck, man? Get your hands off my girlfriend!"

The guy immediately lets go of Raegan and puts his hands in the air like a guilty perpetrator. He takes a small step away from Raegan. "Whoa, whoa, whoa, man. No harm, no foul. Didn't realize this fine piece of ass was taken."

I spot a barbwire tattoo around his biceps and know this guy is definitely a douche. He probably wears his sunglasses inside of places too.

"Taken or not, she was obviously uncomfortable and didn't want your hands on her. Show her some respect. You can't just go around touching her, or any girl, for that matter."

Theo, Eamon, and Chase rush over next to me, ready to have my back if needed. An equal number of Manhattan-looking guys approach. Friends of the asshole, they appear to be weekenders—definitely not rich enough to own a rental out here.

I point my finger back toward town. "Get the fuck out of here!"

"Or what?" The dickface shrugs, and that's all it takes for me to lose my composure. I punch the guy square in the jaw. All hell breaks loose. Fists are flying. It all happens so fast.

I get in three more good punches before I get sucker punched by one of the other city guys. He's drunk, so his aim is crap, but he hits me pretty hard. My eye and cheekbone instantly throb.

Rather than defend myself and beat the shit out of his ass, which is what I would typically do, I reach for Raegan and draw her to my side. "I got you," I say, and pull her away from the mayhem. We start to walk away, but I'm shoved from behind, the momentum catching me off guard.

I'm still holding on to Raegan's hand, and the push causes her to fly down into the sand.

I turn around and throw a punch into a different guy's face, and he immediately goes down into the sand, resting his palm on his cheek, blood dripping out of his nose and onto his arm. It looks like a bloody massacre, but I'm sure I only broke his nose—the blood should stop ... eventually.

Raegan places her hand in my outstretched one, and I help her up.

She brushes the sand off her jeans and then savagely kicks the guy in the ribs while he's still down. "Jerk!"

Hell yeah. Raegan may be short and petite, but she is certainly capable of taking care of business. As if she needed one more reason for me to be attracted to her.

CHAPTER 13

Penn

"**C**ome on. Let's get out of here." I squeeze Raegan's hand and we sprint toward Boys of Summer.

It only takes a few minutes for us to reach the house, my adrenaline pumping and my face throbbing. I'm still holding Raegan's hand, and we haven't spoken a word to each other.

So much for my romantic apology.

Raegan follows me inside and heads to the kitchen, grabbing a bag of frozen vegetables from the freezer.

She gently places the cold veggies on my eye, and I wince at the contact. "This should get the swelling down." Concern floods her eyes. The hit wasn't so bad as to require an ice pack, but I'll gladly take any attention Raegan wants to give me. I reach up and take hold of the bag.

"I'm so sorry you got hit defending my honor as your *girlfriend*." She looks up at me and shakes her head as she half rolls her eyes. I'm pretty sure she's finding it all humorous, but I can't tell for sure if she's impressed or not.

"Sorry. The whole girlfriend thing just kind of came out." It really did. I know she isn't mine, not even close. But there was no way I was going to let that guy get away with putting his hands on her.

"Are you hurt?" I brush my knuckles across her cheek, knowing I'm

treading in dangerous territory, yet again. A charged sensation between her face and my fingers shoots up my arm and to my heart, beating fast with desire. Desire unlike any I've ever had.

Just kiss her and get it over with.

She flinches at my touch. I know I'm giving her whiplash with all my back and forth, but I don't remove my hand.

"I'm okay. Luckily, it was just sand and not concrete."

"I wanted to talk with you about earlier. I—"

I'm cut off from giving Raegan my romantic apology speech when Chase, Eamon, Maddie, Lily, and Theo walk into the house, followed closely behind by Jed and Peter.

Last I heard, Jed wasn't coming to the party tonight, so I'm surprised to see him waltz into the house with the rest of my friends. His macho-big-brother attitude puts a damper on this whole thing I'm trying to get going with Raegan. Especially because last I saw Jed, I told him that Raegan and I were just friends. I don't think "just friends" touch each other's faces the way I'm touching hers right now.

I pull my hand away from Raegan, and her eyes go empty, sad almost, and it kills me even more inside to disconnect from her. But I know Jed sees the moment Raegan and I just shared because he's eyeing me from across the room.

Raegan turns to the front door and acknowledges her brother before surprising me by not stepping away from my side.

I do a complete once-over of Jed, and his T-shirt is covered in blood and ripped, but it doesn't look like any blood is his because his face is intact. Chase and Eamon are carrying the keg, fists pumping the air.

Looks like the party is moving here, and my alone time with Raegan will have to wait. I welcome the interruption because it will give me some time to get my head on straight and figure out how I'm supposed to play this out.

The group reenacts the fight, telling Raegan and me the play-by-play of how Jed and Peter happened to be walking by right as the fight broke out. Jed jumped in to have my back and ended up taking care of the original asshole who started the whole thing by putting his hands on Raegan.

"Don't forget Theo! He took out those other guys who were trying to get Jed! It was so sexy," Lily interjects.

"Sexy, huh? You like that?" Theo grabs Lily's hips and starts kissing her.

I'm jealous of Theo and Lily. My usual urge to puke at such a public display of affection is missing, along with my balls, because all I can think about is what I would give to be grabbing Raegan's hips and pulling her in for a kiss right now.

"That's my little sister's best friend. Get your tongue out of her! And, Lily, is that your outfit, or did you forget half your clothes?" Jed rolls his eyes.

"Get a room!" I yell in an attempt not to look soft, though I'm still holding the frozen veggies over my eye.

Raegan laughs and looks at me from the corner of her eyes.

Lily breaks away from Theo and sticks her tongue out at everyone. "Your room?" she asks Theo and raises her eyebrows suggestively.

Theo walks over to the stereo system and pushes play. "In Too Deep" by Sum 41 blasts out of the speakers. Theo turns the volume up, walks back to Lily, takes her hand, and leads her up the stairs. Yet another moment I wish belonged to Raegan and me, but I already had Raegan in my bedroom once today, and I absolutely blew it. I send a wish out to the universe that I get a second chance, but it's not feeling promising.

"Be careful," Jed says in a stern-big-brother kind of way to Lily as she walks by.

"I appreciate how much you care about me, but I'm a big girl." She struts up the stairs behind Theo.

"Poker, anyone?" Eamon asks, looking at the half-bloody group of us in the living room. Before anyone responds, he's already clearing off the kitchen table and setting up the chips and cards.

Without a word, Chase fills up a plastic cup from the keg, walks over to the table, and takes a seat.

"Deal me in!" Peter excitingly says as he unbuttons his sports coat and parks himself in a seat at the table.

Who wears a sports coat to a beach party anyway?

Jed approaches closer to where Raegan and I stand. "Hey, man. Can we talk?"

I look between Raegan and her brother. "Sure." I'm not expecting this conversation to go in my favor.

"Seriously? You're gonna talk about me when I'm standing right here?" Raegan chimes in with a hint of sarcasm in her voice.

"I just need to chat with Penn for a moment. And we're not going to talk about you in front of you. We're going to chat over here." Jed points to the opposite corner of the room.

Raegan rolls her eyes. "You're such an ass."

Jed walks to the other side of the room, and I toss the semi-thawed veggies on the counter and follow him. I have not forgotten our discussion last week, and I'm sure I'm about to get version 2.0.

In the five seconds it takes to move across the room, I prepare my response to Jed. "Yes, I'm still just friends with your sister. No, I don't want to be. Yes, I've been respectful. No, I haven't kissed her yet." Ha. None of that will work. I'm going to have to wing it like I've been doing this entire time.

Raegan walks over to Maddie and starts to talk with her, though she's looking my way, so I give her a small smile.

"I may have overstepped a little last week on the dock, trying to dictate who Raegan can and can't be with." Jed's standing close to me, arms folded across his chest, and he speaks loudly, so I can hear him over the music, but his tone and delivery is friendly.

I'm reading his face, trying to figure out his angle, because I was not expecting this. But his face gives nothing away. We just look like two friends in the corner of the room hanging out.

I tilt my head. "A little?"

"Okay, maybe I overstepped a lot. I get protective of Raegan. You don't have a little sister, so you don't know the stress of it. Her heart is pure, and she's innocent in more than one way. I just want to make sure she doesn't get hurt. I know you're a decent guy—sure, you like to sleep around, who doesn't?"

I chuckle because I'm pretty sure Jed sleeps around just as much as I do, or as much as I used to, anyway.

"I spent a lot of time with Raegan this past week, and I hear how she talks about you and how her face lights up at the mention of your name. But today I spent it with a sad Raegan because apparently you wouldn't kiss her when she was at your house earlier."

I let out a big laugh and nod. I'm trying to process what he's saying, and what it means, but I'm surprised by his lighthearted demeanor.

"Are you here to thank me for keeping my hands to myself?" I glance over to Raegan and find her still watching us, looking only half-invested in her conversation with Maddie. I flash her a grin, and she blushes.

"Yes. And also, to let you know that if you want to date Raegan, I'd be okay with it."

I release my hold on Raegan's eyes and look at Jed, confusion swirling in my head.

What? Date her? This conversation is not going the way I envisioned.

I thought for sure I'd need to grovel at his feet just for him to be okay with me taking his sister to the beach or lunch some afternoon. But here he is, and I haven't had to kneel at all. "Wow. I feel like there's a catch. What's the catch?"

"No catch. Raegan and I talked a lot this afternoon, and as much as I hate it, I need to be all right with her growing up." Jed looks over to his sister and winks at her. I glance and she's smiling from ear to ear, almost as if she knows exactly what Jed is telling me right now.

Jed takes his dad role seriously. It's a bit overprotective, but I guess if I had a little sister, I'd want to make sure she doesn't end up with some douchebag too.

I don't take my eyes off Raegan as I chuckle and tell Jed, "You guys are strangely close."

Jed laughs and puts his hand on my shoulder, dragging my attention away from Raegan to him. "Just keep it casual," he says, his voice firm. "We both know this won't go beyond the summer because she leaves for college in two months. But if you're going to be with her, keep it monogamous." He removes his hand and takes a step back, reading me while he waits for a response.

Casual and monogamous? Jed's words swirl in my head. I definitely know how to keep things casual, but I've never been a long-term, steady and exclusive guy.

"Yeah. Casual and monogamous. You know. Casual ... hang out at the beach, take her out on dates, bring her flowers, say goodbye before she leaves for college, and monogamous ... you only do this with her for the entire summer, no other broads." He shrugs, looking at me like it shouldn't be a problem.

I'd love to have Raegan for the entire summer, and I've got no problem with what Jed's laying down. I want to be the casual and monogamous guy for her, but I still have my eighteen-year-old rule in the back of my mind.

"So ... this is your blessing?" I'm flooded with unexpected feelings. I know Raegan talks about me with Lily because Theo mentions things, but knowing Raegan talks about me with her protective older brother, and he's okay with me and her being together, makes my insides twist.

I've never had twists for a girl.

Yet another first with Raegan.

"Yeah, I guess it is." Jed nods before quickly looking over to Raegan.

I move my eyes to her. Maddie is no longer with her, and she's sitting by herself on the couch, hands clasped in her lap, waiting. I can't contain the massive grin I'm giving her. Raegan's eyes twinkle through the dim light of the house, and her mouth curves into a smile.

All I hear is the thump of the bass from the song playing through the stereo. I know the song, but at this moment can't remember any of the lyrics or the name of it.

All I see and feel is Raegan.

"Wrap your shit up and make sure you are clean." Jed pulls me out of my trance and points at my dick.

I shake my head up and down. Laughing at how absurd this conversation is. "Yeah, man, no worries there. I'm safe and clean."

"Treat her right, let her go easy, and don't make me regret this." He extends his hand for a shake.

I clasp his hand and squeeze. "I'll try my hardest."

And I honestly mean it. I'm going to give *this*—me and Raegan—all I've got, and since it's only for the summer, I don't want to waste another moment. I want to throw her over my shoulder and take her out of this crowded and loud house and have it just be the two of us. My mind is consumed with thoughts of finally getting to know her, kiss her, and touch her.

"Deal me in the next hand," Jed calls out to the guys as he pulls his bloody shirt off and walks away from me and toward the table.

I look back at Raegan, still sitting on the couch, her knees now turned into each other, her left leg shaking. She watches her brother take a seat at the kitchen table before looking back at me, and when her eyes meet mine, she smiles. I can see her tongue pushing against her bottom lip. It's unintended, I'm certain, because her leg is still shaking in what I hope is anticipation and need. I tilt my head toward the front door, letting her know I want to get out of here.

I don't miss one movement as she presses her palms against the couch cushion and pushes her body up. She straightens her jacket and tucks a piece of hair behind her ear before she walks toward me. My heart is racing—it may beat out of my chest. I can't believe how overjoyed I'm feeling, knowing I get to be with her.

I step into her space, leaning into her ear. "Would you like to go for a walk?" I pull away and watch her beach glass green eyes sparkle.

She bites down on her lip. She has no absolutely clue how sexy she is. "I'd love to." Her eyes are suggestive of wanting to finish our conversation from earlier, before everyone else barged into the house. I'm ready to redeem myself for this afternoon.

I reach down and lock my fingers in hers, both of us ignoring the whistles and hoots from Eamon and Chase at the kitchen table, and I walk Raegan out the door.

As I cross the threshold, my eighteen-year-old rule flies out the window.

She's close enough.

I don't think about any consequences. I'm taking Jed's permission and running with it.

CHAPTER 14

Raegan

Once the front door closes, Penn looks at me peculiarly. It's like he's seeing me for the first time ever. "Come on. Let's walk."

I oblige, instantly forgetting how disappointed I was earlier today when he didn't kiss me in his bedroom. We walk hand in hand toward the bay and I want to skip around like Snow White while she's in the forest with all her animal friends—I'm elated. My hand is so much smaller, but it seems to fit perfectly in his and I don't ever want to forget this feeling, the beginning of whatever this is blooming between us.

I know Penn wants to talk about what happened at his house this morning because we had a moment in the kitchen right before everyone walked in.

My mind is racing, and an anxious pit forms inside me as I think about it.

I'm not sure exactly what Jed said when he pulled Penn aside back at the house, but Penn's face is lit up, and he couldn't stop smiling even if he wanted to. Also, we're holding hands right now, and Jed allowed me to leave the house with Penn, so I'm guessing it was good.

As much as I want to talk about it, I decide to wait for Penn to bring it back up because I don't want to ruin this moment.

Instead, I walk at Penn's side for a few minutes in silence, stealing glances at his silhouetted face in the moonlight. Each time I do, he doesn't look down at me, but smiles, like he knows I'm looking at him.

When we reach the strip of sand on the bay side of the island, Penn bends over to remove his Sperrys, and I do the same, taking off my Converse and socks.

"Come on." He softly tugs at my arm, drawing me closer to him. He wraps his arm around my shoulders and leads me a few more feet until my toes touch the bay water and small ripples form at our feet. Even though the air is cold, the water is warm.

I look up and give Penn a timid smile. The warmth from his touch goes beyond my arm and through my entire body.

I'm safe and protected and wanted.

I gaze up at the sky, which has cleared from the earlier thunderstorm clouds, before looking over at Penn. His mind appears preoccupied as he looks up at the starry sky. He shifts his eyes down to me and smiles before turning his body to face me. He slowly and deliberately glides both hands down the arms of my jacket. He might as well be dragging his fingers over my skin like I'm a fragile piece of glass, he's that delicate and focused. His eyes flicker against the moonlit water until his fingers reach mine once again and interlock.

"So, about earlier today, when we were in my bedroom. I really want—"

Penn pauses, and my heart drops as he unclasps his hands from mine, reaches for his pocket, and pulls a vibrating pager out.

"Shit." His face tightens. "I'm sorry. I need to go to the dock. Work emergency. I swear if it's not one thing, it's another." Penn's forehead creases, and he gives me a small smile before he walks over to our shoes and reaches down for his and hands me mine.

"Oh, okay." Damn. Our night is getting cut short. This is so frustrating. At this rate, with all the interruptions, we'll never be able to discuss the *almost kiss*. I'm not an anxious person, but all day my stomach has been in knots, and I've barely been able to eat because I'm so riddled with nerves. Earlier the nerves were from Penn not kissing me in his bedroom, and now they are from me overanalyzing what each and every touch and look from Penn means. I retrieve my socks and Converse from Penn's hands, planning to walk barefoot until my feet dry, and offer him a small smile. I'm trying to hide my disappointment. I don't want to come off as too eager or childish—too young. I also don't want to be a burden or get in the way. He has a job to do, and I can't expect him to tote me around with him all night.

"I can just head back to the house and wait for Lily to be done with Theo," I offer, looking everywhere but toward Penn.

Penn stops walking and shakes his head. "Don't go back. Come with me." He smiles and extends his hand for me to take.

He wants me to go with him?

I press my lips together, attempting to hold back the delight swirling within. I'm not sure why I want to hide my emotions, but I'm trying to figure all of this out as I go. I know from Lily there are unspoken rules that must be followed so as to not appear too desperate.

I'd love nothing more than to spend the rest of this beautiful night with Penn, and it is still early.

"I mean, only if you want, but it'd be fun to spend some more time getting to know each other." He gives me a childish shrug. For a guy who always seems so sure of himself, he looks worried. It's hard to get a good reading on Penn sometimes. But I'm happy to hear he's not ready for the night to end either.

That's all I need to know. Forget looking desperate, I'm in.

I reach for his hand. It's warm and instantly comforting. His palms are rough and callused from working on the ferries. I've held a few guy's hands at school, but they never felt this *experienced*. They were soft and juvenile. Penn's hands are strong and make me feel safe. "Okay. Sure. What are we doing?"

"I'll get more information when we get to the dock." Penn leads me off the small, sandy beach, and within a minute we arrive at the Kismet dock.

The Sundowner takes up one entire side of the dock, and the outdoor patio is crowded with patrons, drinking and eating, all bundled up for this unusually cold evening. The other side of the dock is lined with one-stop shops—beach chair and boogie board rentals, wine and beer store, and souvenir hut, all closed for the evening.

Tucked in the back corner next to an ice-cream parlor is a door that leads to a small office. Penn uses a key to open it and goes inside.

I sit on a bench outside and brush the sand off my feet. I don't want to walk any farther on the dock without shoes. I'll never forget that one time the entire soles of my feet were covered in splinters after I went barefoot on the dock. Abril sat for hours with tweezers, pulling splinters out, one by one. Lily sat by my side and held my Popsicle as I clutched the arms of the chair as each sliver slid out of my feet. Thinking of Lily, I smile. I don't want my time with Penn to end, but I'm looking forward to getting home later and dissecting this entire evening with her.

Penn is in the office, and I watch him through the window in the door. He's talking to someone on the phone. Nodding occasionally. He looks out the window, running his hand through his hair, and smiles at me with his perfect grin. It's good that I'm sitting, because my legs go weak when he smiles.

Penn's work ethic is commendable. Besides Jed and his friends, I don't know any other guys his age, but I'm pretty sure most guys in their twenties don't work as hard as Penn does. He seems to constantly be on call. Picking up shifts to cover for people, taking on tasks that are below the job of a captain, but he does them because they need to get done. I've yet to ever see him complain. He takes pride in the family business, helping his dad however he can.

There is a clear difference between our lives. I come from a life of privilege, having never been without, living a life most could only dream of, thanks to Uncle Rhett. I'm promised anything I could ever want for my future, and yet I'm missing the drive and desire for what's next. Penn seems to have it all figured out. His life is simple, and he's content, but he's had to work hard for everything. Nothing fell in his lap, including his job at Islander Ferry. Even though his dad owns the company, Penn told me his dad still made him pay his dues to get to where he is today.

I admire the life he's created for himself. So self-assured.

Penn looks at me again and holds one finger up, letting me know he's almost done on the phone. I smile and nod, wondering where we'll be headed once this phone call ends.

Penn hangs up and walks outside. He locks the office door and dangles a set of keys with a bright yellow foam floating key ring hanging off it. He runs his other hand through his hair, pulling the falling strands out of his eyes. I love his tousled hair. It's always a mess, but it gives him a mysterious appearance. If the ferry business doesn't work, he could be a magazine or even an underwear model.

Oh God. That'd be hot ...

Penn's sulking face turns my dirty-thought smile into a questioning one. "Good thing I only had two beers tonight, and it was a while ago, because one of the captains has food poisoning and I need to run a water taxi for the rest of the night."

He blows out a lungful of air, looking frustrated, shifting his eyes across the dock.

I'm disappointed too. It's like the universe is doing everything in its power to keep us from finally talking about earlier today. I guess when the time is right, we'll eventually connect.

I reach for my socks. "I didn't realize you worked the water taxis too."

"Yup. I do it all. And, unfortunately, when it's a family business, you have to drop everything to help when needed. Do you want to come with me? Saturday nights are always great for people watching."

He really is a busy guy, and I definitely want to go with him. I'm not ready to leave his side, and I'll take any time I can get with him. I don't care if we're sitting in silence on the beach, or talking over a noisy water taxi, I just want to be with him, near him. I'm excited, imagining where those keys are about to take us. Sure, we won't be alone, but at least we get time together.

"Sounds fun. I love people watching."

"Great. Jump on." Penn crouches down in front of me, his back toward me.

"What are you doing?" I smile. He looks like he's pretending to be a gorilla or monkey. He just needs to make some "ooh-ooh ahh-ahh" noises.

Penn pats his shoulder. "Jump on my back. I'm giving you a piggyback ride. You don't have your socks and shoes on, and this dock needs to be sanded. I don't want you getting any splinters."

I hop on Penn's back, wrapping my arms around his neck, feeling every muscle pressing against my chest and stomach. Penn's hands wrap around my thighs, and I swear he rubs me one extra time with his thumb. I freeze at the rush from his touch.

Penn stands up, now that I'm secure on his back, and I feel how broad and strong his shoulders are. It's like he was built to carry me.

I rest my face in the crook of his neck. His aftershave saturates my nose. It's intense, and I want—need—more, because it just became my favorite scent. I'm immediately hooked. I never knew you could be addicted to a person's smell.

Penn runs down the dock, pretending twice to dump me in the water. I let out a scream, and he laughs as my body floods with happiness each time. I know he won't throw me in, but I hold a little tighter to his body, and it's the most satisfying feeling in the world.

Penn stops at a water taxi tied up at the end of the pier and carries me on board. He places me down on one of the bench seats that lines either side of the boat, and rummages around until he finds a towel for me to finish getting the last bits of sand off my feet.

Penn heads to the enclosed portion of the taxi and starts the engine. I quickly get my shoes on and join him inside. There is nowhere for me to sit next to him while he's at the wheel, so I take a seat on the bench across from him, facing his side, knowing I'll have the best view of him all night.

I think back to the first day I saw him on the ferry, and at that time I never could have imagined I'd be here with him.

CHAPTER 15

Raegan

"First stop, Ocean Beach, to pick up our deckhand, Jon."
Penn pulls the taxi away from the dock and takes off.
The water taxi goes much faster than the large ferries. I'm
grateful we're sheltered in the enclosure; otherwise, my hair would be a
knotty mess and I'd be freezing because it's chilly tonight.

Penn expertly maneuvers the taxi through the water. Shifting the
throttle to increase and decrease the speed as needed, one hand on the
wheel, observing everything on the water. On stretches where we are
going straight, he glances at me and flashes a cocky smile, like he knows
just how good he looks standing behind the helm.

We pick Jon up in Ocean Beach. Penn explains to me before we
get him that Jon is what they call a salty sailor. I'm not sure what that
means until we pull up to the dock and I see him—late fifties, untamed,
red handlebar mustache, all-around scruffy, with an anchor tattoo on
one forearm and a mermaid on the other. His voice is deep and raspy—I
assume he's a smoker.

Penn takes the water taxi laterally down the island, heading east. He
stops at the dock in each Fire Island village. If there are people waiting
who want to go farther east, they jump on board. I'm not worried about
seeing Uncle Rhett or Finn out here tonight because they are hosting

a dinner party at their place in Ocean Beach. But it's possible I'll see some of their friends, and if I do, I'll deal with it when it happens.

Once we reach Watch Hill, at the very east end of Fire Island, Penn turns the taxi around and heads west, following the same pattern of stopping and picking passengers up to go west, until we reach Kismet. And then we repeat the east-west pattern for the rest of the night.

Jon manages the passengers, taking their cash when they get onboard and reminding them to get off when we get to their location. Jon makes some jabs at Penn, but he is nothing but pleasant to me.

Penn did not lie. The people watching tonight is phenomenal. There are so many drunk people, saying and doing absurd things. One guy almost goes overboard because he's jumping around, trying to impress the girls he's with. Another guy from the same group ends up throwing up off the back of the taxi, and somehow some older drunk woman ends up in just her bra and shorts, her shirt nowhere to be found on the taxi. It must be floating in the Great South Bay somewhere.

According to Penn, this is a mild night. I can only imagine what a more eventful night looks like. It's nonstop, organized chaos.

Penn seemingly knows half the people who come on board. Guys pop their heads in to say hi or crack a quick joke with Penn, and a ridiculous number of women come over to say hi to him, by name, too—too many for me to even count on my two hands.

I hate that he has this playboy reputation because he's been anything but that with me. I'm a little insecure watching these beautiful women eye him and practically drool at his feet. I don't entirely understand why Penn wants to spend time with me when he could have any of them.

I try not to dwell on this too much, and in between the pickups and the drop-offs, the interruptions from guys he knows, and women he's probably slept with, Penn and I talk, mostly short spurts of information passing between us.

The conversations are effortless.

I find out that Penn was voted in his senior yearbook superlative as "Biggest Flirt." I laugh and tell him Lily got the same one at our school. He tells me about his love for sailing, and how he hopes to one day sail across the Atlantic from the Caribbean to the Canary Islands. He's been too busy this summer to spend much time on the water for leisure sailing, but he said once things slow down at work, he'll take me out for a sail. He even told me that if he wasn't taking over the ferry business, he would pursue his love of music further. From what he played for me earlier today in his bedroom, I'm sure he'd be rich and famous. He's got the talent—and the looks.

I tell Penn about my dad leaving, and how Uncle Rhett took us in. After he tells me about his love for sailing, I tell him about my love for gymnastics.

I've loved gymnastics since my first class when I was five years old. Abril signed me up so I could meet other kids from the Upper East Side, and she could get an hour break.

"But my mother ended up pulling me from all my gymnastics classes after a few years, just as I was starting to show potential for being a gymnastic athlete. Telling me that no businessman would take me seriously in a leotard. So I was put in golf lessons four days a week because 'that's where business deals occur,' and then I was expected to play on competitive teams throughout middle school and prep school." I'm exhausted just thinking about those days. I'm glad that golf is finally over. I still don't know how I managed to practice and compete so often and still ace all my classes. Honestly, I don't ever want to pick up a club again in my life.

"Whoa. Your mom sounds ... extreme." Penn looks like he has other words he'd prefer to use to describe my mother, but he settles on that.

"You have no idea. I don't think I even want to be a lawyer." It's childish admitting this out loud. "But it's my mother's expectation, so I have to do it. There's no bargaining or discussions with her. What she says goes."

I'm used to it. I know she does it out of love because she wants only what's best for me, but the closer I get to leaving for Berkeley, the more I know I don't want to do law. Problem is I don't know what I want to do instead. Being a lawyer has been ingrained in me for so long, it's the only future I see, even if it doesn't inspire or fulfill me.

"You should do what makes *you* happy and not anyone else." He looks at me, somewhat sad. I don't want him to feel bad for me. I've got a great life. Sometimes I have to do things to appease my mother, but it could be worse. I should count myself lucky she's still alive, unlike Penn's mom.

"Yeah, maybe one day." I leave it at that, afraid to let my mind wander to thoughts of what I would really do if I had a choice. I don't want to get my hopes up. The need to please my mother outweighs my desire to figure out my own dreams.

The rest of the evening passes too fast. I enjoy the time we spend sharing with each other, and the subject of the almost kiss doesn't get mentioned by either of us. Penn focuses on the water while he navigates the taxi in the bay, but he steals glances my way throughout the night. I gift him a small smile each time our eyes connect, speaking silent words to each other. It's as if he wants to confirm to me that I'm the only one he sees tonight.

It's undeniable that he's the only one I see tonight.

I look at the clock as a group of passengers offload in Fire Island Pines, and I know, based on the time, that I'll need to get off when we stop in Ocean Beach.

Disappointment creeps in again, knowing that we still won't get to discuss the almost kiss. I should be okay with it by now, and I know there's always tomorrow, but after spending all evening talking about everything but the kiss, I'm craving closure on the subject.

Jon unties the lines from the dock, and Penn pulls the water taxi away.

I rub my palms across the top of my thighs, feeling the denim, attempting to release whatever the pit in my stomach is doing.

"You're thinking about something."

I look up to Penn watching me. "Yeah, I was just thinking I'll need to get off in Ocean Beach." I can't wait until I'm at college and don't have to think about curfew. I'll be able to stay out however late I want, or even overnight somewhere, and not worry about needing to get back home.

I am counting the days until I reach that level of freedom, but I'm afraid it may come too late for Penn and me to have that together.

"I was just thinking the same thing." His grin gets even bigger. Almost as if he's proud of himself for reading my mind. "You won't make curfew if you don't get off then, and I don't want you being late." Penn laughs. "I'm sorry this night didn't end up being very fun."

"What are you talking about? I thoroughly enjoyed the people watching."

And every minute I got to look at you.

And each story you told me.

"It did end up being a pretty good night for that. But you'll have to come again because some nights are *even more* wild."

Twenty minutes later, Penn pulls up to the Ocean Beach dock, and to my surprise, I do not see anyone on the dock waiting for a ride. All night each docking has been back-to-back offloading, then onloading passengers, so I'm hopeful we'll get a few extra minutes together before Penn needs to head off for the next stop.

As the passengers are getting off the taxi, Penn takes my hand.

"Come on. I've got five minutes, and I'm walking you as close to your uncle's as I can."

I smile internally, not wanting him to see how elated I am that he's going to walk me.

Penn stops at the side of the taxi and continues to hold my hand until I'm safely on the dock.

"Don't you have to keep working?"

"Yeah, but there's no one here right now, and Jon will be fine until I get back." Penn looks back at Jon, and they exchange a thumbs-up. He then jumps off the taxi and joins me on the dock, taking my hand once again.

"Thanks for tonight. I had fun."

"Me too." Penn smiles down at me before releasing my hand and wrapping his arm around my shoulder. I wrap my arm around his waist and rest my head against the side of his torso. I'm again overwhelmed by his smell and the feel of his strong muscles. He really is a giant next to me.

I walk down Bay Walk with Penn, breathing in every moment of tonight, committing each minute to memory. When we are two blocks away from Uncle Rhett's, Penn stops under a light post and takes my hands, locking his fingers between mine, pulling me a step closer.

Penn's eyes burn with something I've never seen in any guy. Passion? Desire? I'm not sure, but they are soft and kind as they watch my every move. Our chests rise and fall in rhythm as my heart beats erratically. Gone are the carefree conversations from tonight on the water.

This feels momentous and meaningful.

We are so close we could kiss. All he needs to do is bend down, and I just need to go on my tippy-toes. But I don't because the loud, gnawing voice in the back of my head tells me I'm reading too far into this, trying to make this moment be more than just friends saying good night.

Penn releases one hand from mine and reaches for a piece of hair falling in front of my eyes. He slowly runs his fingers through the strand before tucking it behind my ear. His thumb touches my cheek as his fingers wrap around my ear and hold my head. I don't realize I'm holding my breath until I let out a loud sigh. The feel of his hand on my face shoots shivers throughout my body.

"Raegan, I really like you. But the fact that you're seventeen is causing some internal conflict." Penn pauses and takes a gulp of air, but he keeps his hand on my head, rubbing his thumb across my cheek.

His words circle through my head, and I can't believe this is happening. Penn likes me.

"I like you too. And I'll be eighteen in three weeks." I press my lips together as I look up at his. I want so badly to kiss him, but I'm too fearful to make the first move.

"Trust me. I'm counting down the days until your birthday."

Penn unclasps his other hand from mine and wraps his hand securely around my waist, pulling me in even closer, and my breathing hitches. I move my arms and drape them around his shoulders. Our height difference is amplified standing with each other like this because I'm not able to fully lock my hands around his neck.

I try to swallow, but my mouth is suddenly so dry. My legs shake as I look into Penn's eyes, wide and glowing. Thank God he's holding me because I can barely stand.

Penn lightly licks his lower lip as he leans down, and his eyes close when his smooth lips gently touch mine. The kiss is soft, and Penn hums against my mouth, squeezing my hip with the palm of his hand. All the tension I've been holding thinking about the almost kiss from this morning releases from my body, and I relax into his embrace, weightless.

Penn slowly pulls away from my mouth and rests his forehead on mine. His fingers rap on my waist, almost as if he's playing the piano keys. My fingers tingle as I draw my hands down his chest, stopping just above his heart, feeling his rapid heartbeat in pace with mine. A sense of relief washes over me to know this moment is intensely charged for him too.

Our eyes connect. I'm hungry for more as Penn grins and brushes my bottom lip with his thumb. "I want to keep seeing you, and I want to be the *only one* seeing you when you turn eighteen. But we can't do more than kiss until then."

My heart doesn't slow down. If anything, it beats even faster.

He wants to see me? I'm not even sure what that means, but I don't care.

My hands are sweaty with eagerness, and there isn't anything that could wipe this smile off my face.

He pulls me into a close embrace, his arms tightening around my shoulders. I move my arms around his torso and squeeze, giving him a hug. "I can wait," I speak into his chest as I breathe him in.

"I'm glad." He places a tender kiss on the top of my head. "Good night, Raegan. I'd love to see you tomorrow. The guys and I will be hanging out. You and Lily should stop by. We'll be on the beach in Kismet."

I bounce lightly on my feet as my insides vibrate. "Sounds good. We'll come find you." I look up at him one last time as we release from our embrace. "Good night, Penn."

I walk toward Uncle Rhett's, and when I'm two houses away, I look back once more. Penn is still standing there.

He raises a hand to wave goodbye and shouts, "Heart song: Good Charlotte, 'Seasons,'" before he turns and runs back toward the dock.

CHAPTER 16

Raegan

I wake in the morning to thoughts of Penn and that kiss we shared under the stars. I lift my fingers and touch my lips, still unsure if it really happened, but the flutters in my heart remind me it was every bit real.

I can clearly remember how his eyes were focused so intently on mine, how his hands held me close but not too tight, and how he tucked my hair behind my ear, like every good rom-com movie.

"He's your perfect summer fling," Lily told me right before we finally fell asleep last night. "He's experienced and can teach you what you need to know for when we get to college. You can get your nerves out with him. And damn, he's hot. I bet he's all dominant in the bedroom. You're gonna have so much fun with him."

I fidget with my fingers, thinking about it. "I'm not sure we're even going to get that far this summer. He doesn't want to do more than kiss until I'm eighteen."

"Oh, he's a dude. All he wants to do is have sex with you. He just doesn't want to go to jail, so he's gonna keep it in his pants till your birthday."

The thought of messing around with Penn fuels me, as if I just drank a triple espresso and I'm bouncing from foot to foot, unable to

settle. But at the same time, I'm also scared of messing around with Penn because I have no experience and don't know the first thing about pleasing a guy.

I just need to take things day by day. I've been on the island for only two weeks; I still have a lot of summer left. And today Lily and I will go to Kismet in our bikinis and hang out with Penn and the guys. Maybe we'll go to the beach and play some volleyball. Or maybe we'll go to the Sundowner, and the guys will sneak us a few beers, or maybe we'll all get on our bikes and ride around. For being such a small island, the options aren't endless, but I'll gladly do anything just to spend more time with Penn.

Uncle Rhett must be up making breakfast because I smell bacon wafting from the kitchen downstairs. I look over at Lily. She's still knocked out cold—that girl can sleep through anything. I consider waking her but decide she probably still needs her beauty rest, so I throw my hair into a messy bun and head down on my own.

I see her before I hear her. Hair pulled back into her signature tight bun, power suit pressed and starched to perfection. Her no-bullshit aura engulfs the kitchen. With her, there is no casual mode. She lives in constant work mode.

I stall for a moment, hiding behind the wall, trying to determine whether I'm ready for her to dampen the high I'm still riding from my kiss with Penn. I'm not in the mood to face her today. I can sneak back upstairs and pretend to sleep the day away, or deal with her head-on.

"Raegan. Is that you over there?"

Well, damn. No need to decide anymore. She sees me.

Her authoritative voice carries through the entire house. I'm surprised I didn't hear her from the bedroom earlier.

I hesitantly step into the kitchen. "Mom. Hi. What are you doing here?" I look around the kitchen, everywhere I can, to avoid making eye contact with her. Her presence makes me uneasy. She changes the entire dynamics of a room full of people.

I glance at the clock. It's not even ten yet. I spot Jed sitting at the granite countertop bar, stuffing half a pancake into his mouth. I give him questioning eyes, and from behind our mother, he shrugs. He unfailingly gets along with her better than me. Something I've always been secretly envious of.

"Well, finally, you decide to wake and join the rest of the world. I was about to send Jed up there to get you." She shuffles a stack of papers on the kitchen counter before placing them into her black leather briefcase.

"Where's Lily? You need to eat. You're getting too thin. Come get a plate." My mother pats the counter next to her, beckoning me closer.

Too thin, too fat, hair too long, hair too short. I can never get it right with her.

I cringe and lift my chin in an attempt to look confident. "Lily's still sleeping." If she's smart, she'll stay in the bedroom the rest of the day to avoid the Spanish Inquisition that's coming. I pull a plate from the walnut custom cabinet next to my mother and add two pieces of bacon and a single pancake from the stove, dousing them with maple syrup.

"Go wake her up after you eat. We're leaving in three hours, and you still need to pack."

"Um. What do I need to pack for?" I cut a piece of pancake and place it in my mouth as I look at Jed. I'm yet again given a shrug, but his mischievous smile tells me he knows more.

"I'm taking you girls to Saint Lucia for your high school graduation present. We'll be there for two weeks, staying at the best five-star resort they have. Jed is going to join us too."

"Oh. Wow." I've always wanted to go to Saint Lucia, and I'm

incredibly grateful that my mother planned something for me, but the timing sucks. I don't want to leave this island to go to another island.

I want to stay here and hang out with Penn. A lot can happen in two weeks. Penn could meet someone else and forget all about me by the time I return.

"*Oh. Wow?* That's it? How about, 'Oh. Wow! Thank you, Mom!' A little more excitement and gratitude would be appreciated. Do you know what I had to do to rearrange my schedule to make this work? And I came all the way out here to the island to surprise you and pick you up ..."

And there it is. Classic Elenore Cline, always finding a way to make every situation about her. Wanting each and every person to know what she's done for them lately. She continues talking, but I've tuned her out, my posture getting more rigid the longer she goes on.

I pull back my shoulders and inhale deeply before taking a big bite of bacon, chewing to delay my response. "Thanks, Mom. Saint Lucia sounds like it will be a lot of fun. I'll go wake up Lily and tell her the good news; then I'll pack." I plaster on a smile as I walk to the sink.

"Great. I have a few calls to make, but a private water taxi will pick us up here at the house and take us back to Bay Shore, and we'll take a Town Car from there to JFK to catch our flight. First class, of course."

Of course. I wouldn't expect her to fly with the peasants in coach.

I hold back my eye roll and toss my half-eaten bacon and pancakes into the disposal before I rinse my plate and place it in the dishwasher.

When I turn back around, my mother is no longer in the room. I wipe my wet hands on the tea towel hanging off the oven and glare at Jed.

"What?" He throws his arms up innocently, his mouth full of bacon.

"Are you actually looking forward to this? How am I going to survive two weeks with her? I've never spent that much consecutive time with her before."

Jed strides over and pulls me into a hug. "It'll be fine. You know Mom. She'll end up working a lot, and you won't have to be with her the entire time."

I bump my head against Jed's chest and let out an aggravated sigh. He rubs my shoulders, a kind attempt to release some of my annoyance.

Jed knows all about my struggles with my mother, and I'm sure he assumes that's what my crappy attitude is about. But Jed doesn't know about last night with Penn, and I can't tell Jed just yet that I don't want to be away from Penn.

"Ugh. I better go wake up Lily," I grumble, and Jed nudges me out of the kitchen.

"See you soon, sis."

I walk up the stairs and into my and Lily's bedroom.

All I want to do today is ride a bike to Kismet and go to the beach with Lily, Penn, and the other guys. I don't want to pack for a two-week trip. I know I sound like a pouty child, but last night I finally kissed Penn, and now I won't get to see him for two weeks.

I cautiously wake up Lily, as she isn't much of a morning person. I recap what my mother told me about the trip.

Lily, of course, is far more excited about Saint Lucia than me.

"This is perfect. I've been trying to figure out how to end this thing with Theo. He's so sweet, and my God, he has taught me some mind-blowing stuff in the bedroom that I can take to California, but I don't want to give my entire summer away to just one guy."

"Yeah, that sounds horrible." I roll my eyes. "How utterly tragic to only get one guy."

"Oh, shut up! You just got one little taste from Penn last night. Wait until you get more and realize everything you've been missing."

She dramatically places the palms of her hands over her heart.

I swear, Lily's already lived three full lives with all the sexual knowledge she carries.

I walk into the hallway, finding both my and Lily's suitcases in the closet, and I drag them back into our bedroom. "We better start packing. I don't want to be late and upset my mother because we are not on schedule. Plus, I want to make sure I have time to go to Penn's place to see him and let him know I'll be leaving."

I drag my feet into our walk-in closet, still thinking about how much can change in two weeks.

"Great idea. I can break things off with Theo then too." Lily leaps out of bed, saunters into the closet with me, and starts throwing outfits and swimsuits into her suitcase.

About an hour later, Lily and I park our bikes in front of Boys of Summer. I take a few yoga breaths, in and out through the nose with my mouth closed, to calm myself.

It's only two weeks. Don't stress.

I follow Lily up the front porch stairs, and she knocks. My leg bounces up and down as someone inside approaches the door.

It's Chase, and he's standing there, grinning. "Hey, ladies. I heard you may be stopping by today. Theo's upstairs. You know the way." He steps to the side, lets Lily in, and then looks at me. "And I'm supposed to tell you that Penn and Eamon both got asked last minute to work a ferry this morning, but they should be back around lunchtime. Penn wants us to all grab food at the Sundowner and then go to the beach. So you are welcome to hang out here or come back later this afternoon."

Lily pauses from inside the house and glances back at me. She knows exactly where my head goes—the thought that I wouldn't get to see Penn before I leave for Saint Lucia never even crossed my mind. I chew the inside of my cheek. I'll be gone by the time Penn is off work, and I won't get to say goodbye.

"You should go down to the dock and see if you can catch him. Maybe he'll be doing a drop-off or pickup?" Lily suggests.

I have about an hour before Lily and I need to ride back to Ocean Beach so we can catch the private taxi to Bay Shore with my mother and Jed. Lily's idea is perfect. My best chance to see Penn is down at the dock.

I need to get there. Now.

I look at Lily. "You're amazing. I'll be at the dock. Meet me there when you're done." I don't know how she can be so casual about hooking up and breaking up with Theo. Penn and I shared one kiss, and my world is about to end because I'm leaving for two weeks.

I run down the stairs and hop on my bike, riding it all of two minutes until I'm at the dock. I stop by the small office he took me to last night, and it's locked up. I cocoon my eye against the window on the door, looking in, just in case someone is hiding out in there. I sigh. "Damn." I can't even ask one of his coworkers where he is.

I walk over to where the ferry and water taxis dock.

Nothing.

I sit on a bench next to the long water taxi line, filled with waiting passengers.

Fifteen minutes later, after zero boat sightings, Lily appears.

"Okay. All broken up and all good." She clasps her hands together in victory.

I shake my head and laugh, her ridiculousness pulling me from my anxiousness of wanting to find Penn. "It was that easy?"

"Yup. He was on the same page. No hard feelings, and we'll still be friends, so it won't be weird for you and Penn." She lifts both hands loosely, palms up in a "Who cares?" gesture, then shrugs before sitting down next to me.

What a strange breakup, but if it works for them, then great.

I smile, happy for my best friend.

I'm not sure what Penn will say when I tell him I'm leaving. Will he even care?

Oh my God. What if he doesn't care?

That thought hadn't crossed my mind until right now.

"Lily." I grab her hand. "What if he doesn't care that I'll be gone for two weeks?" I look at my best friend for answers.

"Are you kidding me? He'll care. Trust me. He's going to be disappointed. But this will be good for your relationship."

I don't think a kiss qualifies as a relationship. But I don't tell her that. I let her continue with her Lily-isms.

"It's like I always say, absence makes the heart grow fonder, and patience is a virtue." She tugs my hand until I look at her.

Um, pretty sure I've never heard Lily say those clichés before, and I laugh as she successfully pulls me out of my head.

I turn back to the bay as a water taxi pulls up next to the dock. I jump off the bench, looking to see if Penn is on board, muttering *please* repeatedly under my breath. He's not on board, but I see Jon, and I hold on to a little bit of hope that he knows where Penn is.

"Hey, Raegan. Nice to see you again. Where are you heading?" He extends his hand, wanting to help me on board the water taxi, and cut all the waiting passengers.

I wave my hands in front of me. "Oh, I'm not going anywhere. I'm looking for Penn. You don't happen to know where he is?"

Please know where he is. I need to see him.

"Yeah, he's on the ferry in Bay Shore and should be arriving here in about ..." Jon pauses and looks at his gold Casio calculator watch before looking back at me. "Twenty minutes."

Twenty minutes? That will cut it close for us to get back to Uncle

Rhett's in time, but I don't care. My thoughts scatter, too hopeful to think straight, but I can be quick—at least I'll get to see him.

"Thank you, Jon!"

I drag Lily with me farther down the pier to where the ferries dock, and we wait for Penn to arrive.

Fifteen minutes later, I spot a ferry coming from across the bay. This has to be Penn.

The ferry approaches, and on the top deck is Penn in full captain glory, complete with his uniform and Wayfarers. But today he's wearing a backward hat, and his unruly hair curls out underneath.

My heart skips a few beats as flutters overtake my chest and stomach. He gets hotter every time I see him.

I can't contain my grin, and I'm elated that I get to see him before I leave. Eamon waves to me from the side as he ties the ferry up to the dock.

He reaches down to his walkie-talkie, clicks the side button, and tilts his chin as he talks into it. "Captain, there's someone on the dock to see you." He winks at me and I beam.

"Hey," Penn shouts down from the side of the top deck and waves. "I can't get off right now because we have a few more drop-offs east of here, but I should be back in an hour. Do you want to grab lunch and head over to the beach later?"

I can't believe I'm going to have to yell my goodbye over the rumble of the ferry engine and chatter of passengers.

"I'd love to but can't." I have to yell loud for him to hear me. "My mother surprised Lily and me with a trip to Saint Lucia. We leave in less than an hour. And we'll be gone for two weeks."

"Two weeks? What am I going to do without you for two weeks?" His words sound casual, but his eyes tell a different story. Then he laughs, perhaps at how needy he sounds. A lighthearted feeling passes through me at the thought that just maybe he'll miss me as much as I'm going to miss him.

"I don't know. It will be hard, but you'll survive." I lightheartedly exaggerate, then giggle, because I should be taking my own advice.

"Hang on." Penn holds up his tattooed arm before disappearing, only to show up on the dock a minute later. He takes my hand and rubs my palm with his thumb.

"We're boarding new passengers and then taking off, so I only have a few minutes."

I bend my head forward and rest it on his chest, grateful for the comfort he brings.

"You're sad. Why are you sad?" He reaches under my chin and lifts my face to his. His eyebrows raise, and his lips are pursed.

The fact that Penn picks up on my sadness puts a lump in my throat. He's observant.

I tilt my head from side to side and sigh. "I wanted to spend my summer here on the island."

With you ...

Penn reaches for my hips, so sure of himself. "It's Saint Lucia! Go have fun. Well, not the kind of fun Lily likes." He playfully eyes Lily as she remains seated on the bench.

"Raegan will be just fine." Lily smirks. "We're going with her mom and brother. How much fun do you think we'll truly have?" She rolls her eyes.

"Jed's going too?" Penn sounds surprised.

"Yeah, we just found out about it earlier this morning," I say.

"Well, I'm glad I got to see you." He pulls me in closer. I run my hands up his chest and clutch my fingers at his shoulders.

Penn leans into my ear. "I'll still be here, waiting, for when you get back." He leans away to look at me, and his hands engulf my face before his lips connect with mine. His kiss is needy and wanting. I arch my back as I lift my heels off the ground, attempting to push my body closer to his. I run my fingers through the hair falling out of his hat at the nape of his neck. Penn moans, then smiles into the kiss. I take note that he likes that.

I taste faint hints of salt water from his morning on the ferry, and he mustn't have shaved this morning because his face is more scruffy than last night and prickles against my skin.

I like that.

A lot.

Penn squeezes my hips, and my insides tingle. If I'm this stirred by a simple kiss, I can't wait to find out what I'll feel when it's more.

"Yeah, Raegan. Get it." Lily punches the *t*.

I smile into Penn's lips, and he reluctantly pulls away, laughing. I look over to Lily, who's doing a little jig on the dock.

Penn bends forward, resting his forehead on mine. "When you get back, it'll only be a week until your birthday." He locks his eyes with mine and gives me a playful smile.

My chest tightens, and the countdown to eighteen is fully on.

"Yo, Penn!" Eamon calls from the ferry and points to his wrist.

"I've got to go. Can't let the ferry get off schedule." He presses one last quick kiss to my lips and runs back to the ferry.

Penn takes his post at the helm, so sure of himself and absolutely in control.

I touch my lips, the feel of him still very present.

"It's thrilling, isn't it? The butterflies and twisting feeling in your stomach. When it's your person, it feels right."

Words of wisdom like I've never heard before from Lily. I didn't know she was even capable of having butterfly feelings. I always thought it was just lust and desire with her.

I'm sure learning about butterflies. Each moment with Penn becomes the new best feeling in the world. I want to hold tight to all the flutters. Penn and I are nothing more than a few hangouts and two incredible kisses, but it feels like so much more. My feelings for him came fast and unexpected. He said he'll still be here waiting for me to get back. *But will he really?* He's a guy, an extremely attractive guy. I know he has women throwing themselves at him left and right. It's not that I don't believe him—I'm just worried about what these two weeks apart will do.

CHAPTER 17

Penn

"Chug, chug, chug!" Chants echo throughout the packed Sundowner as Theo and I polish off another pint. Bass is thumping from the DJ booth set up in the back corner. It's slumber party night, and I'm chilling with my fourth or fifth beer—I can't remember exactly. Summer is in full swing.

I got off work at a reasonable time tonight, so I came here right after to meet up with Theo for a few drinks, and it's turned into dinner. Chase is behind the bar, mixing cocktails and pouring beers. Maddie has the night off, so she and Eamon are hanging out by themselves back at Boys of Summer. Chase keeps the alcohol flowing to our table as we finish our burgers.

"Dude, you're the only one in here with your shirt on, and it's a *button-up*. At least throw a white T-shirt on or something." Theo chastises my clothing choice for the evening because I'm still in my uniform and not wearing my "PJs"—aka, boxers—but I'm surrounded by plenty of dudes who are, Theo included.

"Take a look around." Theo motions around the Sundowner. "There are so many chicks who want to hook up tonight, and they are wearing so little clothing. How are we going to choose who we get to bang later?" Theo gazes around the bar and restaurant, assessing and evaluating his options.

My answer is easy. I'm not choosing any because none of them are Raegan. They aren't even tempting—prancing around in their lingerie, asses on full display, tits pushed up to their chins as they get low on the makeshift dance floor next to the DJ booth. You'd think we're at a strip club, and not what's supposed to be a family-friendly business during daylight hours.

There's only one girl on my mind, and she's been two-thousand miles away for seven days now. Her trip is halfway over, and I selfishly wish she was back here, now. Seven days to go until I get to see her again.

I shrug and toss a ketchup-dipped fry in my mouth, choosing not to validate Theo's question.

Even without a response, Theo can read my reaction. "*No shit.* You're still holding out for Raegan? Dude. I commend you. This is the least action you've gotten since before you were seventeen. Your dick must hurt from not gettin' any." He snorts.

I'm saved from responding to Theo by Chase, wearing a pair of gym shorts and no shirt, holding three pints.

"This round's on me." Chase sets the beers on the table and pulls up an empty chair.

"You off yet?" I ask, hoping to change the conversation to anything but hooking up with one of these chicks in here.

"Nope. One of the bartenders never showed, so I'm covering for him all night. Just taking a quick break to eat." He takes a swig from his beer, then wipes the foam off his upper lip.

One of the cocktail waitresses, surprisingly dressed in a practical silk pajama set that covers all her assets, stops by and places a basket of chicken wings with a side of ranch in front of Chase.

"Thanks, Monica." He looks up and smiles at her, watching her every move.

"No prob, *boss.*" She winks and runs her brightly painted fingertips across Chase's shoulder blades as she walks back to the kitchen.

"Damn. She's smokin' hot. Are you fucking your employee?" Theo asks, with zero judgment. He's had to let two admins go in the past year alone because he's become *romantically* involved with them—meaning he slept with them. I'm not sure how he's never been sued.

"Not yet, but soon." Chase puckers his lips and nods. "She's only an employee for a few more days; then she's taking a full-time waitress job at Shipwreck, and I can finally tap that." He rubs his palms together, salivating over thoughts of his wings—or thoughts of Monica. I can't tell.

Theo reaches out a fist to bump Chase's, and they both laugh.

So much for trying to get away from the topic of sex ...

"You've been eye-fucking that group of girls over there for the past hour." Chase looks from Theo over to a table of barely dressed college girls. "Which one are you taking home for the night?"

"Haven't decided yet," says Theo. "I guess whichever one Penn doesn't want." He looks at me and smirks, challenging me to admit that I'm not taking any girl home tonight, that I'm waiting for Raegan. He's being a real prick.

The old me would have jumped at the chance to have first pick. I'd saunter over to their table, knowing exactly which one I'd snag before night's end. I'd give her one of my lines, and be back at her rental within the hour, getting at it like bunnies. But those days are in the past. I can't explain it and don't understand it at all. I'm completely consumed by a girl who barely makes it to my shoulder but makes my heart so fucking full.

She called me two days ago from Saint Lucia, and I was so damn thrilled to hear her voice. I tried to stay positive when she told me she was leaving for two weeks. I didn't want her to know how upset I was that she'd be gone that long, but I don't think her mom has ever given her this kind of attention or time. So I wanted to make sure she went and didn't have any worries about my dedication to whatever we have between us.

I've never given Raegan the phone number to Boys of Summer because none of us answer it, let alone check the message machine. So she looked up Islander Ferry's main number on the Internet in Saint Lucia and called. It just so happened I was in the administrative office, waiting for a ferry to load before heading out, and the operator put her through to me.

I was elated when I heard her voice. I've never been a phone guy, lacking the desire to spend time talking and getting to know someone that way, but I could spend all day talking to her on the phone. She has no idea of the effect she has on me. I know the guys see it, and I undeniably feel it, but Raegan—she doesn't know the power she has come to hold over me in the short amount of time I've known her.

I'm not going to lie. I was afraid that she'd meet a guy down in Saint Lucia and he'd steal her away from me. A sense of relief washed over me when I realized how much effort she went through to call me. I'm hoping it's a sign that she wants me just as much as I want her.

We weren't able to talk today because she was leaving early to go on a zip line excursion and then spend the evening on a catamaran with Lily and Jed, but we made plans to talk tomorrow. I'm ready to finish this last beer, then head home and get some sleep, because doesn't time move faster when you're sleeping or some shit like that?

"Earth to Penn." Theo waves his hand in front of my face, snapping me out of my daydream.

"They're all yours for the taking," I respond, as Raegan's green eyes and beautiful smile fill my mind.

"Such a shame." He shakes his head at me and beckons to a tall blonde over at the barely dressed college girl table.

She looks between her two friends, a brunette and a redhead, and they all giggle before they stand and stroll over to us.

"Hey, ladies." Theo pats his leg, and Blondie sits down, immediately whispering something into Theo's ear.

Redhead and Brunette are eyeing Chase and me, waiting for us to decide who gets whom. They're going to be standing there awhile because Chase's cocktail waitress is glaring at him across the room from under her notepad and pen, ignoring the table whose order she's in the middle of taking. He's not about to mess up finally getting his chance with her when she's no longer under his employment.

And me, well, the old Penn would have taken Redhead, hands down without question—I've found her type to always be a little extra spicy between the sheets. But there's no way in hell I'm about to give either of them the time of day. My heart's been stolen and locked up, and it is eagerly waiting for the return of its five-foot-nothing owner.

"Ladies. I apologize about my friends here." Theo gives Chase and me the evil eye for not being the good wingmen he expects us to be. "But there's certainly enough of me to share with all of you, if you're interested." His devilish stare turns suggestive as he smirks at each of the girls.

Blondie, Brunette, and Redhead look at each other with curious faces, reading one another without saying a word before they all nod in unison.

"Are you shitting me . . . ?" I mutter under my breath. He's taking all three of these half-naked girls back to Boys of Summer, which means his room, which is directly above mine, will be thumping and moaning all night.

Theo moves to stand, taking Blondie with him, and extends his hands to Brunette and Redhead. He winks back at Chase and me before escorting them out of the Sundowner.

I've decided to ride the rest of the evening out here. I don't want to be at the house any sooner than necessary. Hearing Theo bang these three isn't on my list of life "must dos." I'm sure Eamon and Maddie will leave the house and come here once Theo arrives. It'll be fifteen minutes, tops.

Sure enough, ten minutes later, Eamon and Maddie arrive. We have a few drinks before last call. I'm buzzed but not drunk, and we offer to stay after closing time to help Chase with the final cleanup. While Maddie vacuums, Eamon and I gather wet rags and wash down the tables and chairs. Chase, plus the bartenders and servers, cash out the registers and split up their tips.

Once the bar and restaurant are clean, the four of us walk the three minutes to Boys of Summer.

Lucky for us, the ménage à trois—plus Theo—seems to have ended. They are all probably passed out from too much alcohol and sex, as there's no noise coming from upstairs.

I fill a large glass with water and pound it before refilling and taking it down the hall to my room. I change out of my work clothes, finish the second glass of water, and let my head hit the pillow.

—

"Okay. So orange is your favorite color, you secretly love country music, bell peppers are your favorite vegetable—but only the red, especially not the green—and you don't drink soda. How about favorite chip flavor? Are you a BBQ or sour-cream-and-onion lover?" I throw another question at Raegan, eager to add more information about her likes and dislikes to the ongoing list in my head. This has become our daily game when she calls me from Saint Lucia.

"Neither. You already know this. Cheetos all the way." Raegan giggles into the phone.

"Ah, yes. How could I forget about the Cheetos?" I laugh, remembering our first encounter on the ferry. I lean back in my chair inside the dingy Islander Ferry administration office in Bay Shore as I wait for the last ferry of the day to board.

I've never considered myself a destiny type of guy, never had feelings run that deep to even let the thought of fate consume any part of my mind. Life was always just *life*. Live my days as they come, enjoy them as best as I can, but never focus on why things happen. That's too fucking philosophical for me. But ever since that first day on the ferry, I find myself wondering how and why Raegan appeared in my life.

Why does she share the same birthday as my mom?

Why does her laugh bring me back to my childhood and make everything feel safe and comfortable?

Why does she make me want to be a better person in all aspects of my life?

Why is she the last thing I think of before I go to sleep, and the first thing I think of when I wake up?

I'm terrified about how much I like her. It's a *I want to sit on the phone and just listen to her breathe* kind of like. If the guys knew just how deep this went, they would call me *whipped*, but I call it *enamored*.

I'm completely and utterly captivated by her.

We've been on the phone for a good fifteen minutes now. I have only a few more minutes before I need to depart on the ferry. I open my mouth to ask just one last question—Nintendo or Sega? I'm a guy—I need to know this.

Before I can ask, Raegan whispers into my ear, "Only one more sleep." I hear her inhale deeply, and my heart grows at the sound of her anticipation.

"Trust me when I tell you that I've been counting." I smirk into the phone.

I'm like a kid waiting for Christmas morning. My eagerness for her return is borderline codependent, but it is refreshing and fun. I just have to get through tonight, and I'll get to see her tomorrow. I took a morning shift, so I'll be free when she arrives in the evening. But I don't want her to know. I want to surprise her.

"So what are you doing tonight to celebrate your last night there?"

"Well, my mother's working—surprise, surprise. Lily is off with that guy she met on the first day, and Jed's been MIA for the last few days. So I'm going to an early dinner at the Italian restaurant here at the resort; then I have an appointment for a massage in an outdoor cabana right by the ocean. I'll end the night on my favorite hammock—remember that one I told you about the other day?—where I'll relax and read until I can't keep my eyes open any longer."

"That sounds like a great way to end your vacation." I want to add, "I wish I was the one taking you to dinner. As well as the one to give you a massage so I can run my fingers up and down your naked body, then snuggle with you in the hammock, and kiss you good night."

But I don't. She's been in Saint Lucia longer than I've been with her in person. All those words need to wait until she's back and I can say them to her face. Plus, I need to reel in my thoughts because I'm working my way to a full-blown hard-on in the Islander Ferry administration office as I think about rubbing my hands all over her.

"What are you doing tonight?" Raegan's voice stops my mind from going too far down the dirty train.

"I'm meeting the guys at the Sundowner for a late dinner; then I'm gonna head home and crash." I worked a lot these past two weeks, picking up extra shifts, not because I had to, but because I wanted to. Without Raegan around, I found myself bored, and the party scene just hasn't been cutting it for me.

"Is it PJ night at the Sundowner again?" Raegan lets out the same laugh, *my mom's laugh*, like she did when I told her about slumber party night at the Sundowner when Theo went home with the three chicks.

"Ha. No theme tonight. Just grabbing some food and a few beers." I don't want her to be concerned about me going out. I want her to trust me, but I don't want to admit my deep feelings for her quite yet because honestly, I don't even know how to do that. Based off my prior track record, I don't inspire a lot of trust from the opposite sex, but I'm a work in progress. I haven't been with any other woman since I met Raegan—hell, I've not even looked at or given any female the time of day since I met her.

Raegan says something into the phone right as Jon busts through the door. "What the fuck, man? Everyone's boarded and we're late. Tell your little girlfriend that you gotta get off the phone and get your ass on the boat."

I look over at the clock. *Shit.* We were supposed to leave four minutes ago, and I haven't even done my prelaunch check at the helm. I've never been late for a departure like this before. Thank God this is the last ferry of the day, so there won't be a snowball effect of delays for the rest of the evening's schedule.

"Rae, I'm so sorry. I don't know what you just said, but I'm running late and have to go." I hang up the phone as soon as I hear her say, "Okay. Bye."

I rush out of the office, make my way onto the ferry, and safely complete my prelaunch checklist. Once we pull away from the dock and are somewhere in the middle of the Great South Bay, I finally breathe. We are about ten minutes off schedule, but luckily the passengers don't seem too upset if they even notice we are delayed.

At least I was able to end the call with Raegan quickly and didn't have to make up a little white lie as to why I won't be on the dock tomorrow when she arrives. I can't wait to surprise her. I just need to get through this ride, then dinner, and sleep before I get to wrap Raegan in my arms and kiss her lips again.

CHAPTER 18

Raegan

As beautiful as Saint Lucia was, I've been counting down the hours and minutes until I get to see Penn. After flying, driving, and now ferrying, I'm unable to hold back my eagerness. We arrived at JFK two hours ago, and my mother stayed back in the city, repacking before she flies off tomorrow for an estate visit—now that her obligation to try to be an actual parent is over.

Something came up at work for Jed, and he needs to stay in the city for a few days, so it's just me and Lily on the ferry back to Fire Island.

I was hoping Penn would be the captain on this ferry, but it's some guy I've never met before. Penn had to get off the phone so fast last night I didn't get to ask him if he'd be working today.

I loved my phone time with Penn when I was in Saint Lucia. It wasn't until the fifth day that I finally called him from the phone in my hotel room. I know the international phone charges are outrageous, and I don't ever abuse my mother's, or Uncle Rhett's, wealth, but I needed to hear Penn's voice and keep in touch somehow. If my mother saw the charges on the room bill when we checked out, she didn't mention it.

Even though he told me he'd still be there waiting, I kept thinking that maybe he would meet someone else, or one of those women who knew him from the water taxi would try to hook up with him. The thoughts haunted me, and Lily finally said, "Just call him." Such a simple solution, but somehow the thought never crossed my mind.

Our calls were fifteen to twenty minutes long when we spoke. Our conversations were lighthearted. It was comforting to hear his voice and have a few laughs together.

I feel the exact same about Penn now as I did before going to Saint Lucia, and, if anything, the feelings may even be more intense because I basically had two weeks to myself on a beach with nothing to do but read trashy romance books the resort sold at the gift shop, and think about Penn while Lily was off running around with some mystery guy she met on the first day. She did split her time, though, half with me and half with the new guy.

I didn't mind, really. I had a lot of time to myself to think about life, college, and what career I would pursue if it were up to me and not my mother.

That is still to be determined. I'll spend more time thinking it through after I get to Berkeley and start taking classes, but for now, it's still a political science major for me.

Luckily, my mother had to take care of one work emergency after another in her hotel suite, so I barely saw her, and when we were together, we managed to have a decent time. She didn't ask a hundred million questions every day, and the time we spent, when she wasn't working, was pleasant. Maybe there is still a little bit of hope for us to have a Rory-Lorelai Gilmore relationship.

Jed flew to Saint Lucia with us, but he did his own thing most of the time. With the exception of a thrilling zip line adventure through the trees and a sunset catamaran sail, he took his own excursions and kept evenings to himself. I wish we would have gotten more time together, especially since Lily was off skinny-dipping and riding ATVs with her boy toy, but I understand he needs space to relax too.

The ferry pulls up to the Ocean Beach dock as the last slice of sun sets behind the horizon, casting the sky in an orange-red hue, the color identical to Penn's poppy tattoo on his arm.

"Look who it is." Lily taps my arm and points.

No way. Penn's here, on the dock. With flowers. Butterflies flutter in my stomach as our eyes connect, and he waves with a huge smile.

I sit up straight and alert until the ferry comes to a complete stop and is tied to the dock. I jump out of my seat and wait, as patiently as I can, in the line to get off the ferry. Once my feet hit the wooden dock, I run toward Penn. Our bodies crash as I jump into his arms, my legs wrap around his torso, and I bury my face in his neck. Penn holds me with ease and tightens our embrace.

This reunion feels like it's been a year in the making, and not two weeks. I didn't realize it was possible to miss someone so much. All his familiar smells infiltrate my body and mind.

"I missed you so much," he whispers into my ear before setting me on the dock.

"How'd you know I'd be here?" I press my lips together to keep from smiling too big.

Penn runs his fingers up my arm and tugs on the hem of my shirt before pulling away. "You forget that I've got eyes all over the island, and especially the ferries." His smirk makes my legs melt, and all I can do is smile.

"Think Lily could take your suitcase back to your uncle's house for you? I want to take you somewhere." His tongue darts out, and he quickly licks his bottom lip.

I can feel my face flush with heat. "Take me anywhere."

Preferably your bed.

Lily happily adds my bag to the utility cart and heads off to Uncle Rhett's. She's been quieter than usual, but I'm sure she's just sulking because her "superhot sex god" was left in Saint Lucia. I don't feel guilty about leaving with Penn. I'm finally getting my time with him, and I know she understands.

Penn takes my hand and leads me down the dock to the bike rack. We stop in front of a bike that's been modified to be an ultimate beach cruiser. It has thick wheels for easy riding on the sand.

"Where are we going?" I question, very aware of my fast heartbeat.

"It's a surprise." A slow smile builds on Penn's face. "Hop on. This is my chariot." He gestures to the back of the bike. The bike has a soft cushion on the rack behind the seat and welded foot pegs on the lower part of the frame for the passenger's feet to rest on.

I throw my purse into the milk crate attached to the handlebars, which already holds a backpack and blanket.

Penn has something planned, and I can't wait to find out.

I sling my leg over the back seat, wrap my arms around Penn's stomach, and rest my face on his back. I inhale a mouthful of Penn's scent as he takes off, riding west.

I'm finally back with him, and we are going to be alone, at least until my curfew. I'm having heart palpitations thinking about what may happen now that we are on the same island ... together.

Penn rides us through Atlantique to Fair Harbor and all the way to Kismet. The wind blows my hair, and the evening weather is finally cooling down a bit, though it's not cold enough for a sweatshirt. Occasionally, Penn takes one of his hands off the handlebar and reaches back to touch and squeeze my thigh. I tighten my grip around his chest. I can't seem to get close enough to him to fill the craving I've missed these past two weeks.

Penn continues past Kismet down the half-dirt, half-sand street that is Burma Road, and stops the bike in front of the Fire Island lighthouse visitor center. Many years ago, it used to be the Keepers

Quarters. I look up and smile, seeing the black-and-white-striped brick tower rising into the evening sky. This is one of my favorite places on the island, and I haven't come once this summer.

Penn rests the bike up against the brick wall, grabs the blanket and backpack from the milk crate, and hands me my purse. I take it and put the strap across my shoulder before accepting Penn's waiting hand. I intertwine my fingers with his rough hand, finally with each other again.

"Your travel outfit is an Ataris tee with a skirt, huh?" Penn tugs on the bottom hem of my shirt with his free hand as we walk up the wooden steps to the entrance.

I look up at him, and a rush of exhilaration passes through my chest into my stomach. "Yeah, it's an 'In This Diary' song kind of day." I give Penn a heart song and grin.

Penn smiles. "I love it."

Penn pulls a set of keys out of his backpack. He unlocks and opens the door.

"You have a key to the lighthouse?" I'm surprised.

Penn looks at me over his shoulder. "I've got friends all over this island."

Of course he does. I've been slowly learning this. He knows almost everyone out here.

"I've been coming here for years, and yet I've never been inside the lighthouse." I look around the dark and empty room, thinking of all the stories this place must hold after more than one hundred fifty years of use.

"Well, let's head up. One hundred and eighty-two iron steps to the top. After you." Penn gestures as he pulls a flashlight from his backpack and turns it on, illuminating the steep steps in front of me.

I climb the spiral staircase with Penn close behind. His hand occasionally grazes my back and hips as we make our way up. I'm swinging my butt with extra emphasis to try to steal more of his attention because my body devours each and every touch.

We reach the last step and Penn hands me the flashlight so he can unlock the small wooden door that opens to the outside observation deck. I follow him outside and stand, speechless, transfixed by the wonder in front of me.

I can see three-hundred-sixty degrees for miles and miles. The sky is so clear. I can even make out the Manhattan skyline.

I look up and see the rotating beam sending a flash of light toward the ocean in a steady cadence.

"We're lucky. There's no wind tonight. Sometimes I'm up here and the wind is gusting at thirty knots." Penn shares as he lays the blanket down on the ground and sits with his back against the tower, his knees bent and feet planted on the deck.

He pats for me to sit down between his legs.

I happily oblige. Settling my back against his chest, erasing all distance between us. I rest my head on him, close my eyes, and draw in the scent of Penn. We're snug. If Penn's legs were straight, they'd almost hang off the edge of the metal railing.

Penn points up at the sky. "You see that bright star there?"

I open my eyes and look, trying to follow the line of his finger. "Yeah. Maybe? Actually, I have no clue where you are pointing. I see a lot of stars." I laugh.

"It's the brightest one in that bunch right over there. You'll find it." He's patient, and then I finally spot it.

"I see it!" I squeal.

Penn chuckles. "That's Vega. One of the stars that makes up the constellation Lyra."

Penn talks with passion for at least five minutes, telling me a strange mythological story of a musician named Orpheus and his lyre, and how he lost the love of his life twice. It is an odd story to share in this moment, but he provides elaborate details about not just the stars that make up Lyra, but other constellations nearby too.

"Stars bring you joy." I enjoy hearing his enthusiasm. It's one more thing that makes him more appealing, as if I need another reason.

"Stars remind me of my mom. She is the one who taught me how to use stars to navigate the waters at night. She used to wake my dad, me, and Chase up in the middle of the night whenever there was a meteor shower. It didn't matter what time it was—we'd be on the beach, watching. She'd even call me and Chase in sick to school the following day so we could all sleep in and recover." His voice sounds distant as he talks about his mom, and I turn slightly so my shoulder leans on his chest and I can look at him.

Penn's lips close tightly together at the thought of his mom. He clears his throat. "You do something to me that helps me talk about my mom. I don't usually talk about her this much." He aimlessly draws his fingers up and down the back of my shirt as he talks, and a warmth infuses my chest at his gentle touch.

"I like hearing about your mom." I truly do. His face and entire demeanor changes whenever he talks about her. He's lighter. Almost joyful.

Penn wears a shield of armor in the form of muscles and tattoos. He tries to look tough and unapproachable, but I'm quickly finding the opposite. He has a sentimental side, and I want to continue piercing his shield to know what else lies beneath.

CHAPTER 19

Raegan

Penn wraps both arms around me tightly and nuzzles his face into my neck. "Seriously, I missed you like you wouldn't believe." The warmth in my chest extends into a pleasant sensation throughout my entire body.

"I missed you too. Saint Lucia was incredible, but I wish you could have been there with me. This, right here, is exactly where I want to be. The view from up here is amazing."

I take a deep breath and inhale the faint ocean's spray. The breeze prickles my skin with goose bumps as I admire the water illuminated by the moon.

"I thought you'd like this." Penn wraps my hair in his hand, pulling it to the side, as he places a small kiss on my neck.

"I'm sure you bring all the ladies up here." I say the words before I think them through. "I didn't mean that to be a jab. It's just, I thought, maybe this is your *thing*. You know, you bring them up here, look at the stars, and make it romantic." I'm not sure why I'm still talking. The words are just coming and I can't backtrack.

I freeze, embarrassed, but Penn turns my face toward him.

His eyes narrow, focusing on me. "You're the first girl I've ever brought up here." He presses his lips to keep from smiling.

"M-me? I figured this was just your MO," I stammer.

"I only come up here once a year these days." He stops talking and pulls his hand away from my face. His eyes break away from mine, and he stares toward the water.

I mentally scold myself for going on about this being a place he brings "all the ladies." I'm curious why he comes up here only once a year, since he has a set of keys and all, but I can't bring myself to ask now. I'm humiliated from my previous words. I look down and stare at my knees. We sit in silence for a few moments, then Penn begins to run his fingers up and down my back. I settle into his touch, waiting for him to talk.

"I come here each year on the anniversary of my mom's death." Penn doesn't take his focus off the water.

I reach for his hand and hold it tight against my chest. "Oh, Penn. I'm so sorry."

"This year will be ten years." He sniffs a small breath and continues. "She died of ovarian cancer. It happened so fast. One day, she told me she was sick, and less than three months later, she was dead. This is where I came the day she died. My dad had to carry me down the stairs over his shoulder to get me home.

"For a long time after it happened, I was angry. I hated my dad. I was furious my mom was taken from us. I became an asshole. This lighthouse was the only place where I felt like I had a connection to my mom. I would come up here and look at the stars."

Penn doesn't so much as look at me. The moonlight reflecting off his eyes makes them appear glazed over, almost as if he's holding back tears. I don't care what anyone else says, Penn has a soft side to him, and I love that he continues to share with me and show me more of who he is.

My eyes fill with tears for Penn and the loss he's struggled with since his mom died. "Thank you for bringing me here," I whisper.

Penn squeezes my hand three times.

I squeeze back three times and watch a smile break across his somber face.

Penn looks down at me. There is an exhilarating charge between us. There is also a heavy tension in the air from everything Penn just unloaded.

Penn moves his head toward mine, his stare burning the side of my face.

I hesitantly lean in and press my lips to his.

I can't breathe. I'm frozen. My senses magnify. The waves crash louder, and droplets of saltwater mist across my arms. My eyes are closed, but I still see the lighthouse beam shine in the darkness as I taste Penn's lips on mine.

Penn's hands move to my hips, and he flips me, pulling me onto him so I'm straddling his lap. His fingers gradually find my bare skin under my shirt. He pushes his tongue against my lips, asking for permission, which I willingly grant. Of the few prep school kisses I've had, no kiss has ever felt like this.

Penn's hold on my hips gives me the confidence to lightly bite and tug his lower lip. He responds with a deep moan, and the swell in his pants grows against my thigh.

Holy crap. Did I do that?

I slowly move my hands to Penn's chest and cautiously explore and touch every solid inch of him. I comb my fingers through his hair at the base of his neck. Twirling his hair in my fingers, I gently tug, and he responds with a groan.

Penn pushes and pulls his hands back and forth on my hips, encouraging me to grind up against him. My thin cotton underwear leaves little protection between my throbbing core and his board shorts.

Penn moves one hand to my lower back while his other finds my breast under my shirt. He pinches and tugs at my nipple through my bra. The irresistible feeling is explosive, and I crave more.

I reach down and unfasten Penn's shorts before tugging them down.

Penn kisses and nips at my neck, both hands now palming and squeezing my breasts under my shirt.

There's an ache between my thighs. I'm ready to explode. I set free the hardness in his boxers.

Penn pulls back from my neck, his eyes dark and unwavering. "Fuck. Rae. You're gonna be the death of me," he says breathlessly.

"Nobody calls me Rae," I mumble.

Penn shakes his head slowly, side to side, biting his lower lip. "May I call you Rae?" he whispers back in my ear, nipping at my lobe. His warm breath tickles my ear, and the skin on my body tightens.

"Yes," I whimper.

I peek down, and I'm shocked to see a massive penis in my hand. I've never touched one before. Sure, I've made out with a couple of guys at parties, but I never let it get close to passing second base. Jed was always a fear factor, but I was also scared and nervous. *What if I don't do it right? What if he laughs at me? What if ... what if ... what if ... ?* I've always been full of those.

My heart beats out of my chest as I try to remember everything Lily has detailed to me during our late-night sleepovers. She is my resident expert in everything from hand jobs to blow jobs to sex positions. I never pay much attention to her explanations and details, mostly because I've been too timid to even look at a penis in real life, let alone hold one in my hand.

I quickly try to recall all the bits and pieces of Lily's description of how to give a hand job. *It's all about your pressure, the stroke, the pattern, and how you move your hand. Don't forget to listen to the guy's breathing, and when you hear him make noises or grunts, it means he likes it, so keep doing that ... but don't do too much of the same thing. That gets boring. You want to change things up, and don't forget about his balls. Give those some love too ...*

I suck in a giant breath and move my hand to the tip right as Lily's voice comes back into my head. *Okay, also guys leak a little when they get hard. It's called precum. Use that shit to lube up the penis if you're gonna whack him off ...* I feel the bead of wetness, and I use my thumb to rub it around the head. Penn lets out another moan, closes his eyes, and lays his head against the lighthouse tower.

I push my shoulders back, satisfied with myself, and overlook any flaws I may have with this hand job because Penn just made a long and low moan that sounded a lot like pleasure—and I'm responsible for it. I wrap as much of my hand as I can around his throbbing hardness and start to move up and down his length.

I set a rhythm as I stroke and listen to his breathing, all the while watching his face.

Penn's fingers brush up and down my arms a few times before settling on my hips again. His hands move from there to my thighs. One of his hands finds its way under my skirt and gently trails between my legs.

Penn shoves my underwear to the side and slides a finger inside me. I tingle and burn as pleasure floods my body. Moving his finger in and out, he keeps pace with my strokes. Or maybe I keep pace with him. I have no clue, but the hair on my arms prickles.

The pressure inside builds as Penn slides another finger in, and I'm suddenly a volcano about to erupt.

Penn's free hand clutches around my ass, and he slowly moves me, up and down, in rhythm with his strokes.

I release my grip on Penn's erection, unable to multitask with the never-before felt pleasure coursing through my body. I place both hands on Penn's shoulders and use the leverage to lift my knees off the ground, allowing my hips to go higher. Penn quickly finds a place inside me I never knew existed.

"Please. Penn. Don't. Stop." I pant out each word, the euphoria building deeper within.

"Come on my fingers, Rae."

With those words, I let it all go and ignite. A noise I've never made before escapes from my mouth as I ride the wave of ecstasy that's coursing throughout my entire body.

My breathing is heavy when the last of my elation passes. My knees fall to the ground, and I sit back on Penn's thighs. He bites down on his lip and gives me a smug smile. He looks like a kid who just got an A+ on his spelling test.

That was hot, and now I want to make him feel just as good as he made me feel.

I look down and see Penn is still hard. I hear Lily in my head: *If all else fails, put your mouth on it and suck it like a lollipop …* I lower my head and take as much of his fullness in my mouth as I can.

A faint taste of soap, mixed with Penn's everyday scent, fills my throat and nostrils as I try to remember to breathe through my nose.

Penn responds with a growl of pleasure as his hands gather my hair, which has fallen around my face, and he pulls it back with one hand into a thick ponytail. He places his other hand behind my head and softly pulses my head back and forth on his length, setting the rhythm.

His erection is so much warmer and smoother than I imagined. I'm trying to figure out what to do next, not wanting to appear inexperienced. I start licking, sucking, and bobbing my head up and down with his presses, ensuring I take appropriate amounts of time on the head and the shaft, just like Lily explained.

I move my hands and cup his balls through his boxers. Penn's breathing becomes deeper and more rhythmic. The doubt and apprehension I had earlier about pleasuring him vanishes, and a sense of power overcomes me, knowing I'm making him aroused.

"I'm about to go." Penn pulls his hand back from my head and lightly taps my shoulder to notify me, but all it does is encourage me to go at it harder. A few more heavy breaths from Penn, and he releases in my mouth. It keeps coming, much more than I expected. A million things run through my mind, but the one thing that stands out most clearly is Lily, yet again: *Don't spit. Swallow that shit. Guys are super enthusiastic when you swallow.* I gulp the salty, warm liquid down my throat, surprised my gag reflex doesn't kick in. When I'm certain Penn has emptied the last of himself, I pull my mouth back, avoiding eye contact. I press my lips together, and my hands tremble slightly as I cup them in front of my mouth. Nerves take over my body, and I'm suddenly unsure if I did it right.

I sit back on Penn's thighs, looking everywhere but at him. He bounces his legs, forcing me to awkwardly meet his eyes. He reaches to my thighs and calmly runs his fingers up and down. My gaze drops to his lips, and I giggle.

"What's so funny?" Penn inquires as he tucks himself back into his boxers and shorts.

"I can't believe I just did that." I touch my throat.

"That was the most remarkable blow job I've ever received. Nothing funny about it," he says matter-of-factly.

"You're just being nice." I smirk. I'm hesitant, trying to decide whether I should tell him more, but he's been so open and honest with me, I want to do the same for him. "That was my first one." I look everywhere but Penn's eyes.

"Your first what?" He reaches out to my cheek and turns my face so

I'm looking at him.

My face burns. I know I'm turning crimson red. I'm mortified.

"That was my first blow job, and the first time I've orgasmed like that." I pause.

Screw it.

"Um. That was the first time I've ever touched a ..." I pause and point to his crotch, embarrassed to say the word. "A penis," I quickly declare, covering my face with my hands.

"That blow job was fucking fantastic! And I'm honored to have given you that orgasm with just my fingers." Penn pulls my face into his and kisses me until my muscles relax.

"Is that what I taste like?" he asks as he pulls away.

"Mm-hmm. Do you like it?" I teasingly give him my best sultry and seductive eyes, not sure who I am at this moment.

"My God, Rae. You are an innocent little vixen. Never sucked a cock and yet you swallow it all down like a champ, every last drop. I'm so turned on. You have no idea." He sits up straight and pulls me into him, holding me tight. I feel him breathe me in deeply.

I'm intoxicated by his words, knowing I have the same impact on him that he has on me.

When he finally releases me, I pull my cell phone out of my purse and see it is past midnight.

Crap.

I sigh and stand up. "I need to head back. Curfew and all." Great reminder for Penn that I'm still not eighteen.

Penn stands. He folds the blanket, tucking it under his arm, and we walk back inside the lighthouse. He grabs the backpack, and we begin our descent down the stairs.

A sated feeling overwhelms my ability to think clearly. That was the most enthralling experience of my life, though I can't help but notice how quiet Penn is. He doesn't try to touch my back or brush against me, like he was on the way up the tower.

Maybe I did something wrong? Was I supposed to make it last longer?

I had no clue what I was doing up there.

Maybe he didn't like it? But he said he did.

I'm so confused.

Penn locks up the lighthouse and we walk to his bike.

"So. Rae . . ."

Here it comes. It's going to end here.

"Rae?" Penn touches my arm and pulls me out of my thoughts.

"Oh, um. Sorry. What'd you say?"

"I want you to know that I feel extremely guilty for what happened up there." He points to the top of the lighthouse.

Why on earth is he guilty? I wanted that just as much as he did.

"What? Why?"

"I shouldn't have let it go that far, but I wasn't thinking straight, obviously." He scrubs a hand down his face and reaches back to his shoulder.

"I don't feel like you took advantage of me, if that's what you're worried about."

Penn reaches out and touches my arm. "I'm glad you don't feel that way because that is the absolute last thing I want you to feel. But we really do need to keep it to kissing only, until your birthday. We only have a week. No more tempting me." His eyes grow wide. "You were like a sorceress up there." He laughs and runs his fingers down my arm.

"Me? Tempting you? You tempt me!" I laugh and slap his hand away.

"We need to wait. It's just a week. We can do it."

"Okay. No more magic." I point my index-finger wand at him, pretending to cast a spell on him. "Boop!" I tap my wand to his nose.

My humor is rewarded with a handsome smile. "You are such a dork. Come on. Let's get you home."

Penn bikes us from Kismet to Ocean Beach, pointing out more stars and constellations along the way. I hold on tight to him as I commit every star to memory.

We arrive at Uncle Rhett's right at curfew, and Penn wraps me in his arms and holds me tight, picking me up off the ground.

"No more leaving for two-week surprise trips this summer. I missed you too much." He places me back on the ground. "The guys and I are going to the beach tomorrow. Do you and Lily want to meet us there?"

I've yet to spend any time with Penn on the beach, and I can't wait to see him in his swim trunks and no shirt, looking like the Greek god he is.

"That sounds fun. Count me in. I'm sure Lily will want to come too."

"I can't wait." Penn wraps his arms tightly around me and bends down to press his lips tenderly against mine.

I'm not sure how I'm going to make it a week with only kissing him. After getting a taste of what *more* is, I'm hooked.

CHAPTER 20

Raegan

There's a knock at the door, and I place a bookmark inside the page I'm reading. "Come in."

The door cracks open, and Jed pops his head in. "Happy birthday!"

"Thanks." I set the book on the side table next to my bed, welcoming the interruption.

"Have you been sitting here, all alone, on your birthday, reading? That's sad!"

Lily has been gone since early this morning, working on her surprise for my birthday tonight. I have no clue where she is or when she'll be back.

Lily doesn't know how to celebrate my birthday without noise. She loves big and grand.

For my sixteenth birthday, she sent me on a scavenger hunt around the island, and I ended up in front of a giant cake, from which a contortionist popped out and put on a performance with fire and glass. It was dangerous and brought in quite a crowd of people.

Last year, for my seventeenth, she organized an amateur sand sculpture contest on the beach. I was the judge, and there were prizes for the winners. It was an entire-day activity. First place went to a group

of college guys who created an underwater aquarium with sea turtles, sharks, and coral. It was fun, but a bit overwhelming with all the people.

I'd have been just fine with a store-bought cake and doing something low key, like going to the movies or getting our nails done. But I appreciate all the effort Lily puts into making my birthdays special.

"Some of us enjoy quiet time alone. We can't all be extroverts." I stick my tongue out at him.

"Well, Lily should be back soon." Oh, great, Jed is in on tonight's surprise too.

"So you know what she's planning for tonight?"

I'm a little surprised Jed's involved. He's been going back and forth to Manhattan a few nights a week since we got back from Saint Lucia, something about a work crisis. It's unusual for him, but I guess as his job responsibility increases, his presence at the office is needed more.

"I sure do." He smirks and leans up against the doorjamb with crossed arms. I'm curious because all she's told me is that Penn and his friends have been invited too.

Unfortunately, last night Penn told me the Islander Ferry had to add a few extra water taxis to the shift tonight, for the holiday rush, and he now has to work and won't be able to come to my surprise. He was apologetic and promised he'll make it up to me tomorrow, or later in the week, when the rush settles. I get it. Work has to come first, but it's disappointing.

Penn and I have spent every minute that he wasn't working this past week either at his house, the beach, or the Sundowner.

We make out when we're alone, though he has been very adamant and clear that we can only kiss, and that the night at the lighthouse was a moment of weakness on his part.

On nights when I've had a few Smirnoff Ices and my confidence is high, I sometimes try to make him break the rule, but his restraint is honorable. In fact, the "we can only kiss" rule has built up some pressure within me, and my expectations of what is to come next has only amplified. Lily, too, can't believe Penn has remained unwavering this long.

Surprisingly, Uncle Rhett has been very lenient with curfew, and when I fearfully walked into his house, way past curfew after I accidentally fell asleep on Penn's couch while we watched a movie, I didn't get grounded or even scolded. Uncle Rhett must realize that our time under his watch is limited, and he's giving Lily and me space to grow up. It's freeing, and I allow myself to imagine what even more freedom will look like when I get to Berkeley.

"So, what are you doing until we leave tonight?"

"Well, I'm not sure when Lily will be back, and Penn is working all day and night. So I guess just reading? Unless you want to hang out?"

"Oh, I see. I'm number three on your list now?" He laughs, walks over to my bed, and pulls me into his arms for a hug. "I remember when I was your number one." He tousles my hair with his hand, and I swat him away.

Jed and I have always been close, even with the six-year age gap, but for some reason, this summer we've both been more distant from each other. I haven't opened up to him much about my relationship. He tolerates me hanging out with Penn, but I get the feeling he doesn't want details.

"So how's work? Did you get that emergency all sorted out?"

"Oh, yeah. It's all sorted. But I'll probably need to keep going back and forth to Manhattan every few days for the rest of the summer."

"That sucks. You must be pretty important these days." I give him a smirk, wanting to tease him a bit and inflate his ego.

"Naw. I'll never be that important. I just do my job."

That's one thing I love about Jed. He's always humble, even though

I'm sure he'll be running that firm in ten years.

"Helllooo. Are you kids up there?"

Jed and I look at each other and smile.

"Abril's here!" I throw the covers off and run to the stairwell.

This is the first summer Abril has not spent on the island with us. Over the past few years, as I've gotten older and less in need of a babysitter, Abril took on new responsibilities from Uncle Rhett. She is now his personal assistant, overseeing and managing all his appointments and travel schedules. So she is around the townhouse in the city often, and I still get to spend time with her.

This summer, however, Uncle Rhett gifted Abril with the entire summer off, fully paid, as a thank-you for her devotion and service to the family for the past eighteen years. She just got back from a visit to see her parents.

I run down the stairs and jump into Abril's sturdy arms.

"Happy birthday, my sweet girl."

"Thank you. How was Puerto Rico?"

"It was wonderful. I'm so glad I was able to go. The weather was perfect." She places me down on the bottom stair, and I'm still not close to being at eye level with her.

"Maybe one day you can take me there and I can meet your parents."

"I would love that. I still can't believe you'll be moving away soon, and I won't get to see you all the time." Abril's eyes begin to water, and I stare at my hands and frown. This woman raised me, and I spent almost every day with her for the past eighteen years. I will miss her.

"I'll still be around—no need to cry," Jed says from behind me on the stairs.

Laughter fills the foyer, and Abril pulls me in for another warm hug.

"Ugh, that passenger ferry was too full for my liking." The distinct voice of my mother carries as she walks out of the kitchen and into the foyer.

Lucky me.

Not only did I get to spend two weeks with her in Saint Lucia, but she is here again for my birthday. She's making an earnest effort to get involved with my life before I leave for college, apparently.

"Hey, Mom." Abril releases me from her embrace as my mother pulls me into her arms. I internally sigh and take a shallow breath so she won't hear it.

"Honey." My mother pushes me away at arm's length and looks at me. "Happy birthday. You look ... different," she deadpans, and I wait for the criticisms to come.

I reluctantly speak. "I do? Well, maybe it's because I'm now eighteen." I lift my chin in an attempt to look confident.

And maybe because I've been messing around with Penn.

She'd be livid if I told her that, so I hold back my grin, not wanting to give my mother any more ammunition.

"I can't believe you came into my life eighteen years ago. You are incredible. You know that, right?"

Amusing words from my mother. I'm irritated, but force a fake laugh. "Of course, I do. I mean, Jed wasn't much to compete against, with all his adolescent bad decisions," I taunt, wanting to pull him into this conversation to take the spotlight off me.

"Hey! I heard that!" Jed yells as he strides over, pulls our mother into an embrace and kisses her cheek.

"Jedediah, can you believe your little sister is eighteen today?" My mother beams like she's so proud to say she raised us, though she's done nothing more than pass us off to Abril all these years.

"Seems like only yesterday she came barreling into our lives, and I've been pushed to the side every day since." Jed laughs and pulls me by my shoulder into an embrace. "You know I love you, right?"

"Don't be mad that you aren't the favorite child, Jed," I mock.

"Favorite child? Who are we talking about? You, Raebird? Sweetheart, we've barely seen you this summer. You cannot qualify as the favorite if you're never around." Uncle Rhett and Finn enter the foyer, laughing.

It's true. I have not been around the house much. I'm either out in the sun or with Penn somewhere.

Wanting to soak up every minute possible with Penn consumes me. I feel guilty for not taking time to be with Uncle Rhett and Finn much this summer.

"Where have you been spending your time, Raegan?" my mother questions, acting concerned, though I know she truly doesn't give a damn.

"Oh, just out and about." I give Jed my laser beam eyes, using them as a warning not to say a peep about Penn. I don't want my mother to know about him. I cross my fingers, hoping Uncle Rhett and Finn don't say anything either. They don't know how much time I've been spending with him, but I'm sure they know a little something.

CHAPTER 21

Raegan

Everyone walks into the living room, and Abril brings out a plate of chocolate chip cookies she brought with her from my favorite bakery in Manhattan. We eat the cookies while sitting on the couch, catching up. I manage to avoid too much one-on-one attention from my mother, as most of the afternoon is spent with everyone discussing their jobs. Since I don't have one, I have practically nothing to contribute.

I'm lost in a distant and empty stare, thinking about Penn and the fact that he won't be able to make it tonight, when Lily strolls into the house, carrying a large cardboard box. I look at the clock above the fireplace. It's three o'clock. Jed jumps up from the couch and takes the box from Lily's hands, and she whispers something into his ear before he walks upstairs with the box.

She shoots a glance at me and points her finger. "Raegan! Close your eyes. You can't see inside this box."

I remain in my spot on the couch and close my eyes. "How long do I have to keep them closed?"

It's silent for a few moments until I hear Jed come back down the stairs.

"Okay, you can open them now," Lily singsongs.

It's not like I could see inside the box, so I'm not sure why I needed to close my eyes, but that's Lily—making everything an experience.

"Uncle Rhett, what time is dinner?" Lily walks toward the couch.

Uncle Rhett is catering a small, family-only birthday dinner for me; then he'll have friends over to watch fireworks and celebrate the Fourth of July. This has been his routine for the past eighteen years, and I'm relieved to have an excuse to leave afterward.

"We'll start early tonight, at five, since I know you kids have better things to do than hang out with us boring old farts."

"Perfect. Raegan, Jed, and I need to be somewhere by eight." Lily smiles big.

What is she planning?

"Sounds like you kids will have a fun time celebrating Raegan tonight. And, as I understand, we are not to expect you home until late tomorrow?"

I remain still and only move my eyes between Uncle Rhett and Lily as I process what he said. We're doing something overnight, and I want to know what it is.

"That's right." Lily beams an even bigger smile and looks at Jed with strange eyes, almost like she's willing him not to spill any of the beans. I cup my palms under my chin and rest my elbows on the table, waiting for more information.

I'm excited about an overnight party, but when I remember Penn won't be there, my excitement dies.

"Jedediah will be with you the entire time, I assume," my mother chimes in, again trying to pretend like she's actually involved and cares.

"Sure will. I'll be with them the entire time." Jed smiles at me, then winks at Lily. Seriously, what has Lily planned, and just how involved is Jed? This is elaborate.

"So ... Raegan, I need you to leave the house for a little bit. Maybe go to the beach or something, come back in an hour, and then we can get ready for tonight." Lily stands up and pushes me out the front door.

I smile and give Lily a silly salute, which I can tell she loves by her huge smile. "Yes, ma'am." I walk out the front door and head over to the Ocean Beach dock to see if I can find Penn on one of the ferries or water taxis. If he's there, maybe I'll be able to go for a quick ride to the next dock, just to get some time with him, and then walk back to the house to get ready.

I get to the dock just as a ferry pulls up, loaded with people. Eamon is on board, tying the lines to the pier. I recognize another captain, whom I met in passing earlier in the summer. Sadly, though, I don't see any sign of Penn. He must be on a different boat.

Eamon waves. He then yells over, "Penn isn't here."

I give Eamon a small wave before weaving my hand through my hair, attempting to hide my disappointment. "Thanks for letting me know."

"Oh! By the way, happy birthday!" Eamon smiles.

I tilt my head to the side and furrow my eyebrows. "Thanks. How'd you know?"

"How do I know? It's all Penn can talk about. 'Raegan turns eighteen on the Fourth of July. I can't wait for Raegan to turn eighteen. Only three more days till Raegan is eighteen,'" Eamon says in a high-pitched voice that sounds nothing like Penn, and more like a gossipy thirteen-year-old girl.

I laugh. "No way. He didn't say all that."

"Swear on my life." Eamon opens the ferry gate to let passengers off. "He's bummed he can't celebrate tonight. Things have been crazy on the boats with the holiday and everything. You should know, though, that the only place he wants to be tonight is with you."

I shuffle my feet and kick at the ground. "Yeah. I get it," I say. But

I don't believe my own words because without Penn, tonight won't feel complete.

"I'm sorry I can't make it tonight either. We'll make it up to you and have you over at Boys of Summer sometime soon to celebrate."

Oh, bummer. Eamon can't make it either. Maybe it will end up just being me, Lily, and Jed? It wouldn't be terrible to just be us three tonight, but I do have fun whenever I'm with Penn's friends too.

"Sounds good. Thanks, Eamon. If you see Penn, can you tell him I said hi?"

"Of course. Have fun tonight. I hear Lily has put together quite an event." He laughs and gives me a wide grin.

"Yeah, I can only imagine what she has planned." I shake my head.

I wander from the dock down to the beach, knowing I have about thirty minutes until Lily has ordered me to be back at the house to get ready. I hope Lily isn't going to pick my outfit tonight. I just want to wear a T-shirt, throw some curls in my hair, and call it good.

On my walk back to the house, I realize I haven't packed for any sort of overnight trip. I'm starting to stress, wondering what I need to pack, because I just found out I won't be sleeping at home tonight.

When I return to the house, Lily is missing, yet again, so I grab my toothbrush, hairbrush, and extra clothes since I can't ask her what I'll need. At least Lily not being here allows me to get ready in peace. I know my outfit choice will drive her nuts, and I imagine she'll tell me something along the lines of, "It's nice to spend time on your hair and makeup and wear something a little sexier than a T-shirt every once in a while." I chuckle to myself and head downstairs for dinner.

I'm surprised to see Lily sitting at the table with Uncle Rhett, Finn, my mother, Abril, and Jed. I didn't hear her come in the house because she's being extra stealthy and sneaky today.

Dinner passes like any other catered event Uncle Rhett hosts. The food and service are top-notch, and Abril baked her famous two-tiered almond lavender cake with eighteen candles for me to blow out. I barely take a bite of the fancy cake before Lily drags me out the front door. Jed is following close behind with our overnight bags. Apparently, Lily previously packed me a bag, so she combined the additional stuff I packed earlier with what she already packed for me. How she forgot my toothbrush while packing for me, I don't know, but I'm glad I remembered to grab it.

The adults tell us to have fun and remind us to be responsible at the same time.

I was looking forward to maybe finally being a little irresponsible tonight, but I'll have to settle for full responsibility because Penn won't be there. My heart twinges at the thought, but I know I'll end up having a good time because Lily is in charge, and she won't settle for a mediocre celebration.

Lily, Jed, and I make our way to the Ocean Beach dock. The sun will set in about thirty minutes, and twilight bounces across the cloudless sky in a mixture of golds, pinks, and purples.

A water taxi is at the dock, and hopelessly I cross my fingers that Penn's on board. But as we get closer, I see it's Chase and Theo, each holding the end of a banner that reads "HAPPY BIRTHDAY!"

I let out a laugh and swat Lily's arm. She stands tall and gives me a glowing grin.

"Oh, girl, just you wait. This is only the beginning." She runs her hands through her long hair before flipping it back over her shoulder.

I smile at Chase and Theo, who have become my friends over the past month, and silently swallow the sadness of it not being Penn.

Collectively, the group cheers, "Happy birthday, Raegan!" as Theo lights the end of a sparkler, waving it in the air.

Things with Lily and Theo are normal. Lily has already moved on from Theo and her Saint Lucia fling with some new guy she met who will be on the island for another week. She'll see him a few more times and then move on to the next one.

I'm impressed at how easily Lily moves on from guys. My thoughts race, and I'm overwhelmed every time I think about how I'm going to move on from Penn at the end of summer.

"Aww, guys. Thanks so much." I'm still looking, hoping Penn is hiding, but he's not here.

"Jump on board. Let's get this party started!" Theo says.

I make my way onto the small, private water taxi, with Lily and Jed behind me.

"Where are we going?" I turn to Lily.

"That's for us to know and you to find out," Lily yelps with zeal.

Chase gives the captain a nod, and the boat comes to life, then flies west.

We reach the dock in Kismet, and everyone piles off the water taxi. We walk the short distance to Boys of Summer, which is covered in glowing lights that rival Clark Griswold's. They are strung across every inch of the roof. There is communal happiness between everyone as we laugh and stare up. I can't wait to see what they will look like once the sun has set completely and it's pitch-black out.

As I walk into the house, I see streamers hanging from the ceiling, banners, more balloons, and a Pillsbury Funfetti cake with my favorite rainbow chip frosting on the kitchen counter.

I give Lily a side hug, and she wraps her arm around my shoulders and squeals, proud of her work. I think about how lucky I am to have this group of new friends who put all this effort into celebrating me tonight.

I shift my attention to the living room, and there stands Penn in the center with a massive grin on his freshly shaven face, his hair slightly damp, but combed. He's not in his Islander Ferry uniform, but instead wears a stone color, short-sleeve button-up and a pair of navy blue cargo shorts. His hands are in his pockets, and he tilts his head to the side, rocking back and forth on his heels.

I raise my fingers to my parted lips, a strong awareness of my heartbeat pounding throughout my body before I run to him and jump into his arms.

I bury my mouth in Penn's neck. He smells delicious and is as handsome as ever.

"You're here," I say, my words muffled, hypersensitive to his solid embrace as he holds me.

"Happy birthday, Rae. Did you really think I could miss your big day?" His breath tickles my ear.

I pull my head out of his neck, looking into his rainy gray eyes. I give him the biggest smile. My heart is perfectly whole now that Penn is here for my birthday.

He sets me on the ground but holds tight to my hand. Next to Penn is his piano. It's been moved from his room and is covered in twinkle lights, candles, and flowers.

"You guys, this is awesome." I look over to Lily, standing there with perfect posture, shoulders back, neck exposed, admiring her work. "Is this what you've been up to all day?"

A slow grin appears. "Mayyyybe," she says, and giggles. "Let's drop all our stuff here and head to the beach before there are no spots left to watch fireworks." She quickly turns and begins to gather the group.

With our hands full of beach blankets, snacks, and a cooler of drinks, we walk down the path to the beach. Sandwiched between Penn and Chase, I ask, "How'd you guys get time off? Isn't this the busiest weekend of the summer?"

"It wasn't easy, but we knew we couldn't miss your birthday." Chase smiles at me. "Being manager at the Sundowner has some perks. I was able to get my assistant manager to cover for me. Plus, I'm pretty sure we'll end up there later tonight, anyway."

"Aww. It means a lot that you would do all that just to be here for me." I nudge him with my shoulder.

Penn gives me a wink and smiles. "I had to trade, beg, and barter with every employee at Islander Ferry to get tonight off. Finally, one of the guys took pity on me after I explained to him that tonight was your birthday. I just got off when Chase and Theo went to meet you guys at the dock in Ocean Beach."

I don't have words to explain to Penn how ecstatic I am that he's here, so I just squeeze his hand three times. Our own little silent communication.

When we reach the sand, it's already crowded with people claiming their spots for the fireworks. I admire the sky because it has turned a deeper shade of orange and pink.

"Look over here," Lily says. I take my eyes off the sky. Eamon and Maddie are standing in the middle of a circle of driftwood, blocking off a section of beach.

"What's this? How early did you guys have to come to claim this spot?"

"We built this driftwood VIP section yesterday," Lily says. "And we've all been taking shifts throughout last night and today to keep it claimed as ours."

"Is that where you've been running off to?"

Lily laughs. "I guess you could say that, between decorating the house, baking you the mother f-ing cake of all cakes, and planning yet more surprises for later, I've been busy."

"Eamon, I just saw you at the dock."

"That was my last ride of the day, and I was trying to throw you off the surprise trail." He laughs as he wraps his arm around Maddie's shoulder.

"You guys are seriously the best." My eyes fill with tears. This group has become a second family to me, and I don't ever want things to change.

CHAPTER 22

Penn

I lay out a blanket and sit in the sand, but not before pulling Raegan down next to me and wrapping my arm around her. She's glowing tonight in her Simple Plan T-shirt. The last bit of light from the horizon sparkles off her eyes. I'm ready to skip the fireworks and after-party and fast-forward to the part of the night I've been patiently waiting for, when I get to have Raegan all to myself.

It's hard to believe that I've known Raegan for only five weeks because I don't remember life before her. Raegan takes away the pain of losing my mom, inspires me to write music—and just knowing that I'll get to see her gets my ass out of bed in the mornings. My heart beats differently in her presence. I have become this mature version of myself. It scares the shit out of me, having feelings and being a nice guy, but it's been slowly growing, and I may even like who she is helping me become.

I'd be lying if I said it's been easy to keep my dick in my pants for this long. I've had to rub it out in the shower more than I'd like to admit.

All in the name of being a gentleman.

I'm not entirely sure what Raegan is expecting tonight, and I don't care if we don't have sex. I've never felt this way about anyone before,

and it is about more than just sex for me. I want to be with her, in whatever capacity I can have her.

I sit with Raegan by my side as we wait for the sky to turn dark so we can watch the fireworks. Jokes and one-liners fly back and forth between us guys while we kick back with a few beers.

I've only had two beers, wanting to ensure my focus remains sharp the entire night. Raegan has not had any beer, and she seems exceedingly antsy. Wanting to calm her down, I give her shoulder a squeeze and whisper into her ear, "You are absolutely breathtaking tonight. Eighteen looks good on you."

She turns her head to me and smirks. "Eighteen will look good on you later." She immediately presses her lips together, almost unsure if she actually just said that.

"I can't wait for eighteen to be on me later." I brush my nose against Raegan's ear, then travel my gaze over her, taking in every inch before I steal a soft kiss. She tastes sweet, like always, and her fruity hair infiltrates my senses. My chest expands and I feel breathless, just from this simple kiss.

Raegan moves her hand dangerously close to my dick. I playfully swat it away, not only because we are out in public with her brother sitting two people away, but also because I don't want her to start something we can't finish right now.

I pull back and Raegan frowns. "Patience, Rae. We have all night."

"Uggghhh. Fiiinnne." She rolls her eyes and dramatizes a frustrated sigh.

She's adorable when she tries to be funny.

"Let's take a picture." I pull a disposable camera from my backpack and ask Lily to take one of us. Standing up, Lily takes a few pictures of Raegan and me, and the flash blinds us because it's so dark out. I hope the pictures develop right. We'll probably all end up with red-eye.

Lily then moves along and takes photos of the rest of the group on the beach.

The sky lights up red and blue, and my focus shifts up as my hand remains securely on Raegan's thigh. A loud boom shortly follows as the fireworks trickle down to the horizon, with bright blues and greens filling my eyes.

I turn and take in Raegan watching the sky.

She radiates beauty, and her eyes light up whenever a firework goes off. She finally takes a beer from Lily, after much insistence. Lily whispers loudly, "Drink this. It will chill you the fuck out. You are so wound up you'll never be able to orgasm later when Penn finally gets you to himself."

I stifle my chuckle, and Raegan tenses, knowing I heard Lily. I squeeze Raegan's thigh, as I grin with confidence, knowing I will deliver a mind-blowing, heart-stopping orgasm to her later.

"Lily!" Raegan half shouts. "Keep it down. I don't need Jed knowing what's going on later."

"Girl, you think he doesn't know? He's already had the *talk* with Penn. You know he takes the fatherly role very seriously. It's kinda sexy."

"Ew! Lil, that's my brother, and since you are practically my sister, he's practically your brother. You can't say things like that." Raegan shakes her head.

Lily shrugs and places the beer can on Raegan's lips. "Sip," she demands, and Raegan takes a swig of the beer.

My thoughts go back to just a couple of days ago, when Jed pulled me aside to remind me of our talk from earlier in the summer. "Don't fucking break my sister's heart." He senses the closeness Raegan and I have with one another. I don't know if he's aware that we haven't slept together yet, but I told him that I care about Raegan and only want the best for her.

Jed's words have sat in the forefront of my mind as I've been attempting to navigate for the first time ever what it means to sleep with someone I genuinely care about. Plus, I've never slept with a virgin before, so I have to remind myself to take it slow and be gentle.

Nothing tonight will be aggressive.

Every touch will be with adoration and longing, and I will worship her until she knows just how astounding she is.

Raegan jumps a little when some illegal fireworks start to go off only fifty yards away on the beach. I move my arm around her shoulder and squeeze tight, letting her know I've got her and will keep her safe. Raegan looks over at me as the fireworks finish, and she presses her lips together into a smile, a look of expectation bursting from her eyes.

I blow out a long breath and smile as I stare back at her. It's too dark to see, but I know her eyes are as green as a jade gem tonight.

After the fireworks end, Lily stands up. "Okay, guys. Back to the house!"

My chest seems to expand, knowing we are heading back to the house and I'm one step closer to having Raegan alone.

I rub my hands together before helping Raegan up. I gather our blanket and help pick up the empty beer cans. As the group begins to walk ahead to Boys of Summer, I reach out for Raegan's arm and pull her back to me, wanting to savor just a couple of extra moments with her on the beach.

She lets her body fall into mine, and I wrap her in an embrace, dropping the blanket to the ground and bending over to rest my head on top of hers.

"You don't know how happy I am that you are here. I was so sad when I found out you had to work tonight." I move my head off her, and she looks up at me. "I can't wait to see what else is planned for tonight." She pulls her lower lip with her teeth, letting me know her thoughts are anywhere but here. I'm intoxicated, and not from the beer, but from her. I'm wholly overwhelmed by her.

"I'm glad I was able to find someone to cover for me at work because the night is just getting started. We have a few more activities to appease Lily and her birthday plan; then you will be mine the rest of the night." I wrap my arms around Raegan's waist as she reaches up, almost able to link her fingers around the back of my neck. I lean down, pressing my lips to hers. Her lips part slightly, and I take the opportunity to slip my tongue into her mouth. She tastes like beer and smells like her coconut lotion. I reach one hand up and caress down her cheek and neck to the top of her shirt, where I rub a curled index finger against the hem.

Thoughts of removing this shirt from her body later tonight fill my mind. I've spent many afternoons at the beach with her in a bikini, so I know what perfection lies underneath, but to finally be able to explore and touch and kiss her olive skin awakens my curiosity and my dick. Since I met Raegan, I've fantasized about her in my bed so many times that my muscles tense thinking about finally giving in entirely to our spark.

I don't take for granted what a lucky asshole I am, and I keep that thought in my mind as I pull away from the kiss. Raegan sighs when we separate, and I pick up the blanket I dropped and clasp our hands together.

Raegan and I walk up the street and see Boys of Summer glowing in Christmas lights. A loud bass thumps inside as we stand at the bottom of the stairs, looking at the lit-up roof. Raegan's smile is ear to ear. "How many lights are on the house?"

I quickly multiply the number of boxes and how many lights were in each box. "Close to twenty thousand, I think."

"What? No way!" She laughs.

"Yes way!" I give it back to her with an equal amount of enthusiasm.

"Lily and I took a trip off the island a few days ago to buy the lights. I'm surprised we found them with Christmas being six months away."

"You helped with this?" She rubs her forehead and shakes her head in disbelief. "When did you do that? You've either been working or with me."

I hum and sway along to the music blasting inside. "You almost caught us, but Jed covered."

Raegan reaches up and pulls my head down to give me a quick kiss on my cheek. A second later, the front door opens, and a rap song blares from inside. Lily and Maddie dance their way onto the front porch, each holding a bottle of Smirnoff Ice.

"Get your ass up here, Raegan!" Lily shouts over the music.

Raegan shakes her head, laughing, as she does a double-take between me and her best friend.

Lily runs down the stairs and takes Raegan's hand. "Come on. Let's go inside. We have more surprises."

Raegan gives in to Lily's exuberant spirit and follows her up the stairs. I bounce lightly in place as thickness forms in my throat, thinking about how much I care for this girl.

I'm making my way into the house behind them when the music stops. Jed walks out of the kitchen, holding the birthday cake Lily made.

The cake is engulfed in sparklers, all eighteen of them flaring a massive cloud of smoke. We sing "Happy Birthday" at the top of our lungs, off-key, and when we have one line left of the song, the fire alarm goes off.

Beep, beep, beep.

Chase runs over to the alarm, trying to turn it off.

Raegan keeps trying to blow the sparklers out, but her wind does nothing, seeing as they are professional-grade sparklers. Flames are flying at Jed, the embers landing on the hardwood floor. The rest of us stomp them out as we see them burn. Smoke billows up to the ceiling, and Jed's veins stand out on his neck while his hands clench the cake plate. He darts his gaze around the room before running to the kitchen with the *beep, beep, beep* still coming from the fire alarm.

Jed throws the entire cake in the sink and turns on the faucet. The water extinguishes the sparklers—but also soaks the cake, destroying it into a mound of wet flour and frosting.

I look over to Raegan for her reaction. Her eyes are wide and bright, and she's laughing.

"Nooooooo!" Lily cries out and runs over to the sink, grabbing two globs of cake in her bare hands, shaking them up in the air. "Jed! You know how hard I worked on that cake."

"Lil, it was about to catch the entire house on fire. I didn't have a choice." Jed looks defeated and apologetic, though he only did what was needed so the house didn't burn down. He steps closer to Lily, and her nostrils flare before she bares her teeth.

"It's okay, Lily." Raegan jumps in to console her friend and protect her brother. "We don't need cake. We can drink these Smirnoff Ices instead." Raegan chuckles and pulls back a swig of it.

I can tell Raegan doesn't want to drink tonight, but it instantly appeases Lily, and she wipes her hands clean, quickly forgetting about the wet fire cake.

Lily gathers everyone around the kitchen table, and we play one of our favorite card games, Oh Hell. Raegan sits to my left and steals touches on my leg. I repeatedly tap my foot on the floor each time her fingers graze me, attempting for it to be a distraction, but it doesn't work. I don't dare ask her to stop, but I wish time would speed up because my impatience to be with just her tonight grows. The beer on the beach and the one Smirnoff Ice must have gone straight to Raegan's head. She's giggling and most definitely a little buzzed. The game finally ends, and Maddie comes out of nowhere, annihilating us all, taking the overall win for the game—a gift certificate to the Sundowner, courtesy of Chase.

After Maddie's win, Lily announces it's time for the next activity, shooing everyone into the living room, and I know I'm up.

I rub the back of my neck, avoiding eye contact with all my friends. I never publicly play my songs for people. Sure, the guys hear me playing in my room all the time, and I've played for Raegan, but that's different. This feels like a concert, and I need to perform at my best. The idea of sitting at the piano with everyone watching and listening to each word I sing is unsettling. But this is something I asked Lily to add to tonight's activities.

I want Raegan to know what she means to me. How special she is. I want to play for her.

I wipe my sweaty hands on my shorts and shake them in the air before I take my place at the piano and give Raegan the first of her birthday presents.

I clear my throat, close my eyes, and push the ivory keys, a melody of vibrations consuming the room. I wrote this song for Raegan after the first day we met on the ferry, when she tumbled down the stairs and I took her to the doctor.

I've always been very private about my music, using it as an outlet for my anger and sadness, never once writing a love song. This is another thing Raegan has done to me. She's opened my eyes to see I have a part of myself that can be overpowered by true feelings for someone else, and not just lust.

A month ago, I was coming unglued about these feelings. But I'm sitting here tonight, knowing Raegan is eighteen and we are only an hour or so away from what I hope to be the most incredible night of her life, and mine. A sense of calm and peace covers me, unlike anything

I've ever felt before.

I continue to play the song and sing the words wrapped up inside my heart. I glance at the guys. They look dumbfounded. They cannot believe that I, Penn Wells, am this infatuated man, bleeding my heart on the piano for a girl. I look to the other side of the piano where Raegan and Lily are holding hands. Raegan's eyes are filling with tears and pierce mine, reaching the uncharted depths of my soul where no one else has ever been.

Raegan must know that with this song I'm all but saying, "I really, *really* like you, and I may even love you, as unbelievable as this is." I maintain eye contact with her as I keep playing, singing the words directly to her. I want her to know what she means to me, and I don't care what the rest of the room thinks.

I end the song, and Raegan remains still, watching me. Lily is the first to clap, breaking the spell cast between Raegan and me. Everyone else begins clapping too. I feel wide awake and energized now that the song is over, and I do an idiotic half bow from my seat on the piano bench.

Raegan slowly slides down next to me. "Can you play some more?" Her eyes are big, and I hope they are filled with the same desire and need I have for her.

Admittedly, what I want to do is throw her over my shoulder and take her to the next part of the evening. But everyone begins chanting, "Encore, encore, encore," so I have no choice but to jump back into another song. This time I play a more upbeat mainstream song so everyone can sing along and dance.

Ten songs, a warm beer, and an hour later, I decide it is time for this party to end. I keep messing up lyrics and keys because I'm unable to think about anything else but Raegan. I can't wait any longer. I grab my beer and hold it in the air.

"To Raegan! Happy eighteenth birthday! We may not have a cake, but this is one fucking fantastic night." My eyes lock with hers across the room, where she's dancing on the coffee table with Lily and Maddie, and she tilts her Smirnoff Ice my way and smiles.

There is an eclectic cheer from our small group of friends as everyone lifts their drinks and shouts, "Happy birthday!"

I walk over to Raegan and lean down into her ear. "You ready for the next part of the night?"

"I've been ready since before the fireworks." Her voice is raspy, and I watch her chest rise and fall with each breath she takes.

Lily pops into our space. "Here's your bag."

Raegan hugs her best friend and smiles. "Thanks, Lily. Tonight has been perfect."

"Everything but that waterlogged cake," Lily jokes.

"I said I was sorry!" Jed yells from the kitchen table, where a new round of Oh Hell is starting.

"Yeah, yeah, yeah," Lily lips back to him.

"So. Why don't you two head off? We'll clean up here and see you tomorrow." Lily squeezes Raegan's arm and shimmies.

I take Raegan's bag in one hand, and with the other, I take her hand. My foot jitters against the hardwood floor as I glance at the door, ready to make our exit.

"Catch you guys later." I wave to the group and lead Raegan out the front door.

"Wells!" Jed calls before I close the door. I pause and look back into the kitchen. He points to his eyes and mouths, "I'm watching," then directs his fingers at me. I give him a nod and shut the front door.

Trust me, Jed. I don't want to fuck this up.

And finally, I'm alone with Raegan.

Alone. So alone.

Just her and me. Hand in hand. And I'm scared shitless.

This is really happening.

I've never spent an entire night with a female. It's always just been about the sex, but tonight I'm going to fall asleep with Raegan next to me and wake up together in the morning.

Like a true couple.

Raegan has been worth my endless days of work and no sleep to plan and execute tonight, just to see that smile on her face.

I want this to be different from any other time I've had. I want to erase every woman I've been with before because she is so much more.

"So, where are you taking me?" She grins and runs her tongue across her lip.

I wet my lips. "You'll see."

She shakes her head and giggles as I lead her to my bicycle. She jumps on the back, and I ride off to Cedar Street, hooking a left, and a few minutes later we reach the boardwalk streets of Saltaire.

Leaning up and into my ear, Raegan says, "Saltaire has always been my favorite village on the island. I think it's the fact that the streets are all boardwalk, and there is a small brick church with a bell tower. Lily and I used to ride our bikes there when we were younger. We always said we'd get married in that church. Not to each other, obviously." Raegan laughs.

I ride one more street down, turn left, and stop the bike in front of the red brick church with a white arch door. "This church?" I turn around to look at her.

She beams under the moonlight. "Yes! That's the one."

"You know, when Chase and I were kids, we'd play capture the flag or cops and robbers every day with summer kids, and this church was always a base or a jail. And now that we're older, Chase and I sometimes end up here when we're walking home after a night out at the Sundowner or Shipwreck. We sneak into the bell tower and sit, usually talk about our mom, or sometimes we don't talk at all. Just enjoy the silence of the night. It's become a quiet place for us." I smile at Raegan before turning back to the handlebars.

"I like that we share this place together." She squeezes her arms around my stomach. "I wonder if we ever played together when we were kids and just didn't know it. You spent time with Jed. We had to have run into each other a time or two." Raegan places her head on my back.

"I've wondered that a few times myself. But we stopped playing those games by the time we were eleven, and you would have only been five, and I can't imagine your uncle or Abril letting you run around the island at that age."

I feel her cheek rise higher on my back. "Yeah, you're right."

I'd love to go up in the bell tower and create a few new memories with Raegan, but I'm ready to get to our next stop.

As if Raegan can read my mind, she breaks the silence. "So, aren't you taking me somewhere?"

I laugh, loving her little bout of boldness. "Sure am." I run my hand up her arm before I lift my feet off the ground and pedal a few more streets down till we reach our destination for the evening.

CHAPTER 23

Raegan

Penn stops the bike in front of a quaint cottage with cedar shingles and white shutters on the front windows that's perched among the reeds. The cottage is tiny, and there can't be more than one bedroom inside, which I guess is all we need.

Leaning the bike against the side of the cottage, Penn takes my hand, along with my bag, and leads me to the front door. After scooping me into his arms, Penn carries me inside like we're a married couple.

My insides jolt at the thought, and I quickly push it away. This is not going to turn into marriage. This is just for me to get experience before college.

The front door opens into a small kitchen, candles burning on the countertop and a bouquet of colorful peonies in the center of a two-person table.

Penn sets me down as I gaze around in wonder. "Did you do all of this?"

"Yeah." Penn swaggers over to the flowers and plucks out a coral-colored peony, handing it to me. "Lily and I had a deal. She planned everything from earlier tonight, and I got to plan all of this." He motions with his hands.

I bring the peony to my nose and inhale.

I knew Penn had a sweet side, but I didn't realize he had such a romantic side. He's put so much effort into this evening. It makes my heart full.

A rich and mellow piano melody I've never heard before plays from the stereo.

"Want a tour?" A relaxed smile crosses his face.

"Sure." I smell the peony one more time before setting it back in the vase on the table.

Penn points to the right side of the kitchen. "Bathroom is over there, as is the laundry."

I take a peek at the small bathroom, the floor is white mosaic tile, and a beautiful claw-foot bathtub sits in the corner, taking up most of the available space.

Penn wraps his hand with mine and takes me to the other side of the kitchen to a tiny room. There's a fireplace with more candles burning within, a two-person couch, and a small coffee table. A TV hangs on the wall. There are four windows on the two exterior walls, and the only light in the room comes from the moon and the candles in the fireplace.

This cottage is tiny but adorable. It's perfect for two people.

"Living room." Penn gestures with his hand, palm up and moving left to right. I laugh, thinking about how this room can't be any bigger than my closet back in the city, but I'm drawn to how charming it is.

"And over here"—Penn points to the left—"the bedroom." His eyes go deep as he looks at me.

That's the bed. The bed where I'm going to have sex for the first time. Tonight.

Oh my God, I'm going to have sex tonight.

I'm ready to just do it, but I'm way too scared to make the first move, so I decide to follow Penn's lead.

"This place is so cute." I look around, admiring the wainscoting and crown molding.

"I thought you'd like it. It's my friend's place, and they are away, so it's ours until tomorrow night."

"Tomorrow night?" I choke at the prospect of getting the rest of tonight and all day tomorrow with Penn.

"Yeah, think you'll be sick of me by then?" He cocks his head to the side and smirks.

No chance. If anything, I want even more time with him.

"Doubtful." My insides are already buzzing, and we haven't even touched.

Penn grabs me at the hips, pulling me into him.

The butterflies I get every time he touches me is overwhelming, in the best way. It's a feeling I've never experienced before, and I find myself craving it more and more.

This cottage, with the music, candles, flowers, and the fact that Penn and I are finally by ourselves, and not making out at his house or the Sundowner with other people always looming, pleases me.

"Dance with me." Penn doesn't wait for my answer before he pulls me in closer and wraps his arms around my lower back.

I let out a breath and place my hands on his shoulders, resting my head on his chest. My heart is racing, thinking about what will happen tonight.

Will it hurt? Will it feel good? Will I be any good?

The thought of sex is both thrilling and scary at the same time. Thrilling because I know how I feel when I kiss him and that the night at the lighthouse was heart-stopping. But also scary because I don't know what the hell I'm doing. He has so much experience, and I don't want to be a gigantic letdown.

"I made this mixed CD for you." He spins me around the little living room, stealing glances as he smirks.

No guy has ever made me a mixed CD—that seems like boyfriend territory, and nothing the teenage guys Lily and I hang out with at school would ever do.

"Thank you. So it's a bunch of heart songs all on one CD?" I gaze into his overcast gray eyes, feeling slightly dizzy with anticipation.

"Eighteen heart songs, to be exact. Same as your age." Penn leans down and gently kisses my lips. All the anxiousness I'd been holding in releases with a soft moan. My slight buzz from the Smirnoff Ice I had earlier has worn off. I'm one hundred percent present and here in the moment.

Penn moves his mouth to my ear. "Thank you."

I pull away from his face to look at him. I haven't done anything for him.

"Thank you? For what?"

"I didn't know I could ever feel like this." His voice shakes a little, and he holds me even tighter.

"Since my mom died, I've had difficulty opening up to people. I've never been in a real relationship, and honestly, it scares the shit out of me. But you waltzed in, or rather, fell in"—he smirks—"to my life just a little over a month ago, and you've completely changed me. The person I am when I'm with you isn't anyone I ever thought I could possibly be. And I like him. I want to be that guy for you."

His vulnerability surprises me.

I wish he'd see himself the way I see him.

Hardworking and dedicated to his job.

A loyal friend.

A charming sense of humor.

The hottest guy I've ever known.

I could keep going with the thoughts in my head, but instead I find the courage to reach up and place my palm on his face. "I like who I am when I'm with you too."

And I truly do. I'm more daring, more laid-back, somehow a little funnier—he does laugh at my jokes even when no one else does. I'm more confident in myself. I finally feel seen for me, not as Rhett Kellerman's niece, not as Lily Hart's best friend, or even Jed Cline's little sister. I'm just Raegan—well, to him, I'm Rae—and I don't want it any other way.

Penn releases his hold on me and takes my hands in his. "Today is also my mom's birthday." His eyes are red, and he looks like he's holding back tears. I want to tell him it's okay to cry, but I don't. I just let him talk. Relishing in the fact that his mom is my birthday-day twin.

"It's usually a day marked by sadness because it's just one more year without her, but as weird as it sounds, I feel like she sent you to me."

My heart flutters.

Penn looks down, appearing ashamed, his eyes red. "You make me feel so many different things at once. All I've thought about since we met has been you. I can't get you out of my head." He lets out a little chuckle before looking back at me.

And it's in that exact moment that I know. Penn Wells is not just some guy I met this summer to cross off a bunch of sexual activities with before I leave for college.

No. He's so much more.

I may only be eighteen, and he may be the first guy I'm going to be with, but at this moment, the future is clear.

It's got to be Raegan and Penn.

We were made for each other.

CHAPTER 24

Raegan

Penn's hand brushes a few strands of hair behind my ear, and his fingers trace down the side of my face, down my neck, above my shirt, stopping at my breast.

The want and desire between the two of us is powerful. It's shifting both our lives, and neither one of us can stop it.

We are the only crew on this ship, going full speed ahead. We may crash into land and sink, but neither one of us is capable of stopping it. Even if we were, I don't think we would.

Penn's lips crash onto mine. He doesn't need any permission. He knows I'm ready.

"I want you," I say into Penn's mouth between kisses.

"I'm yours." His words contain an intensity that fuels me.

"Couch. Now." I attempt to pull his muscular body toward the couch.

"Sweet Rae is getting demanding now that she's eighteen, huh?" Penn smiles before kissing me again.

Yes, demanding. I need him. All of him.

"I want this." I pause. "Please don't make me wait any longer." I don't even know who I am, speaking these words. I never talk like this, but I need him to be closer to me than ever before.

As soon as I say the words, he grabs my ass, lifting me off the ground and up to him. I wrap my legs around his torso.

Peppering me with kisses, Penn lays me down on the small couch and covers me with his body. His erection presses into me.

Knowing I can turn him on makes me heavy between my thighs.

The intensity of our mouths crashing into one another, our tongues seeking, is unlike any other time we've kissed.

Penn has been holding back on me.

He pulls me up so I sit on the edge of the couch as he kneels on the floor in front of me. I know where this is headed, and I'm anxious, but I feel safe with him. Penn lifts my arms and pulls my shirt off, throwing it on the floor, then pauses and looks at me. It's straight out of a movie, all in slow motion. He bites his bottom lip and shakes his head in appreciation of my new lacy, blush-colored bra, which Lily bought. She told me I could keep wearing T-shirts, but I needed to, in her words, "turn up the heat for things underneath." So into the donation pile went my plain cotton bra. Lily also bought me a matching thong, and as annoyed as I am by the intrusiveness of the scrap of material going up my butt crack, I can't wait to see Penn's face light up when he sees it.

I painstakingly undo each button on his shirt, not because I want to take my time and savor the moment, but because I can't keep my fingers from shaking. Penn covers my fingers with his large hands and brings them to his lips, kissing each before placing my hands back on his shirt to allow me to keep unbuttoning. Penn lets me do it in my time. He's patient and doesn't rush me.

I finally undo all the buttons and push his shirt off his smooth body. With the exception of a light patch of chest hair, he's not hairy. He's well groomed, and surprisingly, his skin is baby soft.

I run my fingers across his chest, wanting to memorize every inch. Penn lets out a small groan of pleasure. "Your touch feels so fucking good. Don't stop."

His reinforcing words give me the confidence to continue exploring. I run my hands up and down every part of his exposed skin before I move them to the button on his shorts. We're not kissing. We only stare into each other's eyes, breaths heavy, and when I touch the button, my fingers burn. I freeze, not sure if this is the next step. Should I wait for him to take my shorts off? I don't know the order of what to do.

Penn moves his hands to the button on my shorts, giving me a slight nod. Our hands mimic each other as we pull both of our buttons through the buttonholes and unzip the zippers. Penn runs his fingers across the fabric of my shorts, one hand on each hip. He tilts his head, asking me for permission to remove my shorts. I gulp a breath and nod back.

Yes, please.

Penn dips his fingers below the material of my shorts along with the elastic of my thong and slowly pulls them both down. I lean against the back of the couch and raise my hips to assist with the removal.

Penn goes slow, and each move is deliberate. So thought out and relaxed. He spies my thong inside my shorts and gives me a smirk of approval. I grin back at him.

I'm reclining against the back of the couch cushion in only my lacy bra, like a goddess, adored and beautiful, seen for the first time in my life.

I've never been this exposed, but Penn makes me feel comfortable, and this feels right.

I reach out for Penn's shorts, which I neglected to remove while he stripped me down. He places his hands over mine and helps me tug the shorts off. He's still on his knees, eye level with me on the couch.

I see his erection tenting in his boxers, begging me to set it free. I reach down but second-guess if this is what I'm supposed to do, and

Saltaire

I hesitate, freezing. I place my hands on my thighs, hoping I didn't just make things awkward. My eyes flick back to Penn, and he smiles before he reaches behind my back with one hand and unsnaps my bra. The straps fall down my shoulders, and Penn peels the bra off my chest.

I am now naked in front of Penn. Exposed but elated. I push my legs together to try to ease the pressure between them.

"You're fucking perfect."

Every insecurity I have about myself, from the size of my small boobs to my outie belly button and even the stretch marks on the inside of my thighs from my last growth spurt, go unseen at his words and the look of awe on his face.

I pause, absorbing Penn, his thick neck, his firm, broad chest, all the way down to his defined abs that disappear into his boxers. I take a mental picture that I can hold on to for the rest of my life. I reach my hand out and touch Penn's hardness over his boxers. I slowly begin to stroke, and after a few seconds Penn catches my hand with his, and I stiffen.

"I'm sorry. I don't know what I'm doing. Am I doing it wrong?" I shake my head, looking at Penn for guidance.

Penn's eyes go soft. "It felt *too* good. If you keep doing that, I won't last, and I'll be a huge disappointment for you." He smirks before leaning in and circling one of my nipples with his tongue. He gently bites and sucks while he pinches and twists my other nipple with his fingers.

Holy crap, the sensations stirring within me are unbelievable. This doesn't even compare to how Lily has described it.

I wrap my arms around Penn's neck and draw myself closer to him, pressing my hips up. Penn pulls away from my nipple and unlocks my hands, placing them on the couch with a gentle tap. He gives me a playful smile and hoists my legs over his shoulders as I lean back on the couch cushions. My ass is in the air as he pulls my intimate core to his mouth.

"This is going to feel fucking incredible. Just relax." He runs his fingers gingerly up and down my legs, and though I'm anything but cold, goose bumps take over my body. I ease myself into his touch and trust his words.

Penn settles between my thighs, running his hot tongue over, in, and on my swollen mound. I grow hot, and a fluttery sensation fills low in my abdomen. I no longer hear the music coming from the speakers. The only sound I hear is my heart beating against my chest.

I squirm when the hair on his head tickles against the inside of my thighs. He's methodical and self-assured as he travels up and down with a perfect amount of lapping, sucking, and blowing. He eats me up, focusing on my sensitive bud, and I'm washed with an overindulgent heaviness inside the bottom of my belly.

Penn's finger enters me, pushing in and out, while his other hand roams up and down my leg in unison with his tongue and mouth. It's all part of the composition he's creating, and it's overwhelming, but I crave even more.

I'm not sure how long Penn's masterpiece lasts because I'm not even present. I'm in some other dimension, trying to remember to breathe between my moans and whimpers.

And then, without any warning, I'm overcome with a need from deep within. I chase it until it hits me, and I let everything go, riding the surge of pleasure. Penn responds, lightening up on his sucking and licking at the exact right moment, until I peak.

My breathing is erratic, and I can't move, frozen on the couch, with my legs still draped over his shoulders. Penn pulls away from between my legs, his eyes smoldering, and the bottom part of his face glistening with ... *me* ...

My realization of what he just did breaks across my face in a smile. "That. Was. Incredible." I'm still trying to catch my breath.

"Told you." Penn playfully drags his teeth over his lower lip before wiping the back of his hand across his mouth. "And we're just getting started." He grabs my ankles and sets my feet flat on the ground, but I'm anything but stable.

That was already *so much.*

I sit up and move my body toward the edge of the couch, suddenly aware again that I'm naked. And I can't help but look down at Penn's boxers. I just need to know if he's still *excited.*

Oh, goodness. Yes. Yes, he is excited. Even more so than earlier.

I quickly look up, caught. Penn wraps his arms around me and lifts me off the couch. I place my arms around his neck and lock my legs around his torso, and he walks us to the bedroom. Penn lays me down at the foot of the bed, and I push my body up toward the headboard and pillows, our eyes never wavering from each other.

I'm feeling a little more confident than earlier, but it's not lost on me how much experience Penn has. I want this to be great for him, but I don't know if I'm living up to expectations.

Penn stands at the end of the bed, and God, is he a sight.

Disheveled hair falls into his eyes, curling up at the ends.

Deep gray eyes burn into my body.

His absolutely pristine set of abs on full display.

His tattooed arm.

He's enticing.

Penn eyes me as he pulls his boxers down. His gaze tells me that he is well aware of the effect he has on me.

My eyes must go big at the sight of him because Penn's face changes to concern as he pulls his boxers back up. "We can stop. We don't need to do anything more tonight." His voice is soft and caring as he holds his hand over his gigantic manhood that's *trying* to be set free from within his boxers.

I'm messing all this up. I still want to do more. That was just a little intense, and I had a momentary freak-out, but I'm already recovered. "No. It's okay. Sorry. I just. I don't know. I don't want you to stop. I just got a little scared." I give him a wry half smile, looking down. I shrug, embarrassed, feeling a flush creep across my cheeks.

I just needed a moment.

Penn walks to the side of the bed and sits on the edge, taking my hand in his. "We're only doing what you're comfortable with. I'm okay if we stop. I don't want you to feel pressure to do anything."

"I want to keep going," I whisper, pulling him into me, our lips reuniting.

Penn's tongue presses against my lips, asking gently for permission, which I willingly allow as the pressure begins to build again.

I lean back on a pillow as Penn crawls onto the bed, hovering above me, forearms on either side of my face. His hard-on presses lightly against my abdomen, through his boxers, as he moves, and I can tell he's trying to keep it away from me so I don't freak out again.

I push my hips toward Penn, wanting to feel just how hard he is and to let him know I'm searching for more.

His eyes flutter shut, then open, and for a split second he looks deep in thought and about to pull away, but he kisses my neck, and his heated breath against my skin tickles.

I run my fingernails down his back and earn a groan from Penn. I feel powerful, knowing my touch elicits such a reaction from him.

I push myself against him again, needing to feel him once more, and I'm rewarded with him pressing down onto me. My body pulses with electricity.

I capture the elastic of his boxers and begin to tug them down, suddenly needing all of him.

Penn touches my hand, not letting me pull the boxers down any farther. "You sure?"

"Yes. I'm sure. I want this. With you."

That's all he needs to hear. Penn moves his hand off mine and kicks his boxers off quickly.

His thickness is only inches away from making contact with me.

We are like two wild animals, carnal and hungry. I move my hands to his naked ass and pull him down onto me.

That's the only encouragement Penn needs. Something switches in his face, and he nips and bites at my neck, my nipples, my navel, my thighs. I run my hands everywhere over his hard body, sucking on his neck and chest, positive I'm leaving dark-purple brandings all over him.

His bare tip rubs at my slick entrance, and we both pause, chests rising and falling.

This is the moment.

Penn looks at me, and with his face asks if it's okay. I nod, unable to speak. He reaches for the bedside table and pulls a condom from the drawer. He tears open the foil and quickly rolls it on.

My heart is racing. It's coming. My head is filled with so many thoughts, but the thing most evident to me right now is how much I want this. How much I need this.

Penn leans into my ear. "I'm going to go slow. Tell me if I'm hurting you."

My chest tightens.

The orgasm from the couch has primed me, and Penn takes his time, but when he enters me a sharp pain shoots inside. I hold my breath. Penn doesn't take his eyes off me. He's reading my face, wanting to know how I'm doing. Slowly, little by little, Penn fills me, and the pain subsides, but not without a single tear falling from my eye. I'm not sure if the tear is because of the internal sting, or because I'm flooded by this deep ache within.

Penn captures my tear with his thumb and places soft kisses on my cheek.

"You are beautiful," he whispers into my ear before he slowly begins to thrust in and out of me. The stinging pain turns to a burn, but is quickly washed away by pleasure.

I press back into him with my hips, meeting his momentum as I tighten around his hardness.

"Fuck, Rae." Penn's words are a pant. He's just as lost and as far gone as I am.

I respond by pushing back harder as I build up again, chasing the high I know is coming. My eyes go dark, and I'm on the edge, toes curling into the mattress.

I cry out as my entire body trembles and fills with ecstasy.

Penn plunges into me a few more times and then finds his release, filling me. Penn lowers to me as I pant, breathless. A wave of exhaustion captures me. Penn lightly lies on me for a few minutes as he catches his breath before he pulls out and takes care of the condom.

Penn rolls us so we are facing each other. He softly places a kiss on my forehead and runs a finger through my hair. "Rae, you are the best thing to ever happen to me."

I'm breathing heavily and feeling delirious. I just lost my virginity, and now I get to stay the night with Penn. I don't ever want to wake from this dream.

As I lie with Penn, I run my fingers up his arm, tracing over my favorite tattoo, a colorful poppy flower with the initials *M.W.* Penn told me this was the first tattoo he got when he was sixteen. He found a guy in Bay Shore who did it for him, underage, in exchange for free ferry and water taxi fare all summer. The tattoo is for his mom, Mabel. Poppies were her favorite flowers, and he got the tattoo in her memory.

I lean into him and kiss the tattoo. Knowing his mom and I share the same birthday feels like a sign that we are meant to be more.

A new song begins to play over the speakers, and I tuck my head into his shoulder. I immediately recognize it's the song Penn played earlier tonight on the piano back at his house.

"Is this the song you wrote?"

"It is." He twirls a strand of my hair on his finger.

"You recorded it?" It sounds professional and high quality.

"Yeah, Theo has a friend in the city with studio space, and he hooked me up with a few hours to record a couple songs. I did it while you were in Saint Lucia."

My voice chokes with tears. "You wrote and recorded a song after we'd only kissed twice?"

"I did." He stares longingly at me before cupping my face with his hand. "I knew immediately that I wanted you."

I'm overcome with emotion, a feeling of gratitude, as a few happy tears fall down my cheek. Penn wipes away my tears.

Penn is so talented. His songs could be on the radio—they are that good.

"You should send those demos off to some labels."

"I can't do that. Who would run the ferry business when I hit it big?" He gives me a humble smile. "Dad needs me here." He runs his fingers up and down my arm. Goose bumps prickle my skin.

"That's not fair, Penn. You need to follow your dreams."

"Says the girl who's going to school to be a lawyer because her mom wants her to." He narrows his eyes on me. I have no leverage in this discussion.

"Ugh. Fair point." I cup his face with my hands. "Promise you'll always sing for me?"

"Always." Penn kisses me, sealing his promise.

My tummy flutters at the thought of *always* with Penn.

CHAPTER 25

Penn

Because I never stay the night after sex, I've never cuddled after sex either. I'm usually up and putting my pants back on before it gets awkward and the chick asks me to stay.

With Raegan, though, just as expected, everything feels different. My need and desire for her are unlike anything I've felt before. I don't want to miss one minute of being with her. I want to spoon and snuggle her. All the shit I used to think was stupid and annoying.

The sun is coming up, and I'm tangled in Raegan. Her silky-smooth legs wrap into mine under the sheets.

I hope Raegan's not too sore today. I worshipped the hell out of her last night. It was powerful, and I'm pretty sure *she's* broken *me* for anyone else. No other woman will ever compare to what I had with her last night.

I didn't fuck her. I made love to her—another thing I've never done before.

I could tell she was nervous and worried about whether her hands were in the right place, if she was moving her body the right way, and if the noises she was making were okay. She did all of it right. I ate up each bit of her shyness and caution. It was refreshing, every single hesitation and pause only amplified what we had. It was absolute perfection.

And that matching bra-and-panty set. Holy shit. I almost came right then.

I hope last night was everything she imagined it would be. I tried to be gentle. There were a few times when I was inside her that I wanted to go deeper and harder, but I held back, not wanting to hurt her.

My stomach growls, and as much as I want to go down on Raegan for breakfast, I need to give her a little rest. We do have all day.

I slip my arm out from under her and head to the kitchen to make us breakfast.

The bacon is crisping up and the eggs are cracked and ready to be cooked when I hear shuffling. Raegan is standing at the archway between the kitchen and living room in my button-up shirt, her hair sitting on top of her head in a messy bun, a little mascara under her eyes. She is by far the most exquisite thing I've ever seen.

I need to make her mine.

"Good morning. Thought we might need some breakfast after last night. Eggs and bacon are all I know how to make." I give her a wink as I flip a slice of bacon on the pan and splatter hot oil.

"Morning," Raegan replies, looking at the ground, almost embarrassed.

The last thing I want is for her to be uncomfortable or feel awkward.

"You okay?" I take a step toward her, tongs in hand.

"Mm-hmm." A small smile appears, and she looks up at me as she comes closer and wraps her arms around me. She runs her fingers along the waistband of my sweatpants. "Just thinking about last night."

My dick is thinking about it too. "There's that enchantress who came out to play last night. I thought I told you no more spells. Do you not want bacon for breakfast?"

I reach over to the stove and twist off the gas burner, and before Raegan can answer, I wrap my arms around her. She looks up at me with her mesmerizing green eyes, and I quickly imagine a life where we wake up like this every day. Sharing a home and loving one another till we are old, gray, and wrinkled.

What was that?

That's not a thought I've ever had before.

"I don't want bacon." Her eyes don't waver from mine.

"Be my girlfriend." The words come out, sincere and honest. I mean them. Absolutely, positively.

I need Raegan. I need her all-consuming energy and smile and laugh. Hell. I need all of her. I'm a selfish man.

"What?" She loosens her hold on me and steps back with a frightened look on her face.

Shit. I just took it too far, too fast.

"Or not. We can just be casual."

Casual? Fuck that. I don't want casual.

But Raegan's face doesn't show any expression. This is the first time I can't read her, and I'm panicking. Maybe I should have thought this through more. She just turned eighteen. We had sex for the first time last night, and she leaves for college in a month and a half. What am I doing complicating things by making this more than it should be?

This is just a summer thing, right?

No. It can't be. There's no way this ends in August. We'll figure it out when the time comes.

"I thought you didn't do girlfriends." Confusion marks her face.

I don't want to drag my past into the picture because I'm ready to be an unselfish lover and shower Raegan with my affection.

I take Raegan's hands in mine. Moving closer to her, I look deep into her eyes. "Rae, you're different. I have these insanely strong feelings for you that I've never felt before. You are all I can think about when I'm awake, and you consume my dreams when I sleep. Waking up next to you this morning is something I've never done before, and it felt right. So fucking right. It didn't feel scary or overwhelming. I'm nowhere near good enough for you, but tell me you feel it too?"

I pour it out, for the first time in my life, not to a piano or sheet music, but to a living person. I open up, allowing myself to be vulnerable.

Raegan remains still, and when I finish, she clears her throat, and the corner of her mouth turns up.

"You want to be my boyfriend?" She leans into my chest with her shoulder, resting her head on me. My heart is hammering and my knees feel weak.

I wrap my arms around her and bury my face in her hair. "Yeah, I want to be your boyfriend." I pull away and hold her hand, looking at her. "I want to buy you shit and take you out to dinner. I want to steal kisses on the beach. Play footsies at the Sundowner. I want us to have so many more firsts together."

She squeezes my hand three times.

Tell me that's a yes.

"What about Jed?"

And the moment comes crashing down. Fast.

Damn you, Jed.

"He and I have already talked. We're good." I told Jed I wouldn't hurt Raegan, and I absolutely intend to keep that promise.

"He told me you guys talked about you and me being casual. I don't know if he will be okay with the whole boyfriend-girlfriend thing." She tugs on my hand a little, a small, nervous tic I've picked up on.

"You're eighteen. You should be able to decide who you want to be with, not Jed. Plus, it's not like he didn't know we were spending last night together. Let me deal with him." I tuck a little piece of hair back into her bun.

I don't want to *deal* with Jed, but if it's what I need to do to make

Raegan say yes, then I'll do it. Jed's going to say yes anyway. I've come to find that he'll do anything to see his sister happy.

"Okay." Raegan nods.

"Okay, I can deal with Jed, or okay, you'll be my girlfriend?" I hold my breath as I wait for her answer.

"Both." She smiles up at me.

I wrap my arms around Raegan and lift her onto the island counter. I inhale her addictive scent and nuzzle my face back in her neck.

"Yellowcard, 'One Year, Six Months'—my heart song to you." I begin to nip at her neck.

Raegan giggles, pushing me away. "Don't try to give me a hickey!" Raegan swats at my arms.

"I need to mark you somehow," I tease as I go back to her neck.

"Jed will for sure kill you if you try to brand me."

"Then I better leave it in a place where he won't see it." I'm feeling fun and flirty, but I do want to mark her. I want every other guy on the island to know she is mine, and mine alone.

Raegan has no witty comeback. She only flashes a smile and her perfect teeth at me.

I crash my lips onto hers. The sparks between us outshine the fireworks from the beach and the sparklers on her birthday cake. It's bright and loud as her legs wrap around my waist. Her hands roam across my chest and down the front of my sweats. She confidently wraps her hand around my hard cock, and even through the sweatpants it's an incredible feeling. I'm glad she's more comfortable with the intimacy between us. I don't want her to be embarrassed or uneasy around me.

I pull my mouth off her and bury my face in her neck, sucking and kissing her skin as she continues to rub me through the sweats. My growl encourages her, and I slip my hand between her legs to find she's already wet, wanting.

She smiles into our kiss, knowing exactly what she's doing to me. I may come in my sweats, here in the kitchen, smelling like bacon, and I don't have one care in the world.

I grin into the nape of Raegan's neck as I lean her back on the island counter, spread her legs, and feast on my girlfriend for breakfast.

My girlfriend. That's a word I never thought I'd use.

The guys are going to give me so much shit for this, but I don't give a fuck. I've never been this content.

CHAPTER 26

Raegan

P enn and I have been together, as boyfriend and girlfriend, for seventeen days.

Yes, I'm counting.

Surprisingly, Jed was okay with Penn and me being together *officially.*

I'm not sure why Jed's so merry and easygoing these days because it sounds like work has been an absolute mess. He's still traveling back to Manhattan a few days a week to clean up some disaster, so I've seen him around even less than before.

But with Jed being gone, it has been much easier for me to stay the night at Penn's place. Uncle Rhett thinks Lily and I are staying over at our school friend's house in Kismet. When in reality I'm at Boys of Summer, and Lily is off meeting up with people and staying the night at who knows where. She's happy for me and Penn and doesn't mind doing her own thing, which is what she's doing today. She met some guy a few days ago, and he's leaving in a couple of days, so she's spending time with him—uncomplicated and super casual, just the way Lily likes it. I enjoy something deeper and more meaningful with Penn, but if just a few nights works for Lily, then I'm happy for her.

It's late morning on a beautiful sunny day as I walk from Uncle

Rhett's to the Ocean Beach dock to meet Penn. I don't quite know what he has planned for us today, but he told me to wear a swimsuit. So I decided on a tank top and shorts over my bikini.

Penn and I have spent as much of the last two weeks together as possible. Penn still has to work, and I join him on the water taxis during the evenings. Otherwise, my days are spent with Lily, or by myself reading on the beach. It's been fun and relaxing—a perfect last summer before college.

Uncle Rhett informed me yesterday that a letter from UC Berkeley arrived at the townhouse in the city. The letter included my dorm assignment and confirmed Lily and I would be roommates, just as requested. The letter also had a full itinerary for Welcome Week, with back-to-back activities for us to meet other incoming freshmen. I should be focusing on my upcoming college departure, only three weeks until I'm supposed to leave, but every time I try, I cannot get interested. I know I should be eager to go, but I'm not. My chest feels heavy when I think about college.

Beyond my better judgment and what I know is right, ignoring my perfectly planned future, I've decided that I don't want to go to college. I want to take a year off and figure out what I want to do. I've never had time just for myself. I've always done things for other people—well, primarily for my mother. My deep-seated need for her approval has dictated my life since childhood, and the thought of having a year off to figure myself out and find what I want to do ignites me, turning the heaviness in my chest to lightness.

I've kept these thoughts to myself, knowing this will not fly with Uncle Rhett, Jed, Lily, and especially my mother. My future has been planned and determined for years now. A lawyer is what I'm supposed to be. I'll work hard and make money, just like my mother. But I don't want to be a lawyer, not even a little, and especially not a divorce lawyer. The idea of dissolving marriages and fighting for property isn't something that I have any desire to do. But since I have no clue what I'd rather do instead, I guess that's why I've always just moved forward toward my mother's goals.

A water taxi filled to capacity with people pulls up alongside the dock just as I arrive. Penn is behind the helm, looking sexy as always in his signature work attire, an unbuttoned shirt, cargo shorts, and a backward hat. He maneuvers the taxi against the dock with ease, and Eamon throws out the lines and fenders to tie up on the pier.

Eamon assists passengers off, and a few women approach Penn. I'm jealous and intimidated at the same time. One of the women, wearing a ridiculously expensive-looking dress, with teardrop diamond earrings and a Chanel handbag dangling from her forearm, strokes Penn's arm and laughs like he just said the funniest thing in the world. My heart drops. Penn hasn't yet noticed me on the dock. At the touch of the woman's hand, Penn leans away, looking uncomfortable, and my jealousy fades slightly, though I'm still very apprehensive. Penn shuts down the engines, and the rumbling hum dissipates as he gestures for the woman to move onto the dock. As they get closer, I overhear their exchange.

"Thank you so much for the ride today, Penn." Her voice is high. I've been around enough of Uncle Rhett and Finn's friends to know a rich, obnoxious tone when I hear it. It's annoying.

"Just doing my job," Penn says flatly. He appears inattentive to the conversation, and warmth radiates in my body, knowing he isn't giving her the time of day.

"I think we both know that your job includes some extracurricular activities." She leans in and clutches his biceps, and I want to scream, "Hands off, lady!"

This woman is not quite my mother's age, but she's not quite

Penn's age, either. Maybe ten years older than him? I immediately feel inadequate in this woman's presence. She's sophisticated and poised, and I'm over here in cutoff jean shorts after polishing off a bowl of Lucky Charms for breakfast.

I'm a child in comparison.

"Not this season, Brenda." Penn removes her hand from his arm.

"Is Penn 'The Stallion' Wells finally settling down? I never thought this day would come."

The Stallion? What is this? A porno?

I want to slap the old cougar.

Fine, she's not *old*, but she *is* a cougar. Preying on younger men and all.

"Yeah, I actually think I am." He smiles.

"Well, whoever she is, she's one lucky woman. You always know where you can find me if things don't work out."

Brenda winks and I want to barf.

She's got to be pushing forty, hitting on a twenty-three-year-old—that's just gross.

Penn looks over and sees me on the dock. I give him a quick half-circle wave and tight-lipped smile. He's looking at me, eyes big.

Brenda makes a show of getting off the boat and even reaches out for Eamon's hand to help her.

I hold back my eye roll, which is good because Brenda looks at me, then back to Penn, realizing I've been watching him. She leans over and whispers, "Oh, sweetie, you're far too young for a man like that. Maybe one day you'll find out about the mind-blowing sex and what a good time he is, but Lord, that man is impossible to break. I've been working on it a few years now, and he only does hookups ... with experienced women." She bugs her eyes out, which only adds to her patronizing tone.

I'm speechless, consumed by old insecurities.

Penn jumps off the water taxi and ushers Brenda away from me as fast as he can. "Thank you, Brenda. We'll see you on Islander Ferry again soon."

He seems tense, and rightfully so. One of his hookups is here, and even though she's a class-act bitch, she's gorgeous, and so put together.

Penn comes to my side and wraps a hand around my waist. "You ready?" Quickly squashing my self-doubt, he makes me feel like I'm the only other person on this island.

I smile to myself.

Brenda couldn't break Penn, but I did.

He's my boyfriend, and somehow, I am enough. And you know what, *Brenda*, I do know about the mind-blowing sex.

"I don't know, Stallion," I half sneer, half chuckle. "Am I going to meet any more of your previous lovers today?"

"First of all, don't call me *Stallion*." He pauses and smiles. "That just makes me feel like a horse. And second of all, I don't have any previous lovers. You know I've never done relationships before you. Those were all just women I'd hook up with. And you already know none of that has happened since I laid eyes on you, bloody and barfing Cheetos on my ferry. It was at that exact moment I knew I needed you in my life." Penn's grip on my hip tightens, and he tilts his head down to be closer to mine. He smiles widely, swaying me around on the dock, like it's just him and me.

I laugh, my jealousy replaced with fondness for Penn. "So you're a man slut?" I mockingly pat Penn's chest with my hand. I don't know why I'm startled by his solid pecs. It's not like I don't feel them every time we have sex, but I keep my hand there and look up at him.

Penn takes my hand, removes it from his chest, and whispers into my ear. "I once was a man slut, but those days are gone. I only have eyes for you now—I promise."

"Mm-hmm, sure. You're gonna have to prove that to me," I taunt.

"I will." Penn's gaze holds on my eyes, and I swear he reaches into my heart and pulls it out through my throat with his stare. He's not joking or trying to be playful. He's serious, and I wish he wasn't because it makes the thought of leaving for college even harder.

"I see you wore your swimsuit. That's good." Penn tugs on the bikini string tied around my neck before he pulls his pager out and looks at it. "Time to go." Penn locks his fingers into mine and looks at Eamon. "Got it from here, man?"

"You know I do. Captain Gus is walking down the dock as we speak, so we are good." Eamon nods.

"Fucking Gus. Thank God he's showing up to do his job." Penn laughs as we walk down the dock toward the sailboats in the marina.

"No band T-shirt today?" Penn asks.

I look down at my shirt, a plain heather purple tank. "No, not today. Why? You miss them?"

"I have a difficult time reading your emotions when you don't wear them on your shirt." Penn looks down and smiles. I stop mid-stride, intrigued by his answer.

"I never thought people noticed my band tees." My voice rises as I talk, and a tentative smile builds.

Penn presses two fingers against my smiling lips. "I notice everything about you."

I reach up and cover his fingers with my hand, then place a soft kiss on his palm. My heart is full.

Penn takes my hand, and we make our way to the end of the dock until we are standing in front of a clean and very white sailboat. Across the back of the boat, in fancy cursive, is the name *Rocket Fuel*.

"Is this boat named after an alcoholic drink?" I laugh.

"Sure is. Fire Island's finest." Penn chuckles. "I finally get to take you sailing. When's the last time you went?" Penn questions as he gracefully jumps on board.

"Uncle Rhett has a sailboat. We used to go out on it often, but not so much these past few years. When we'd go out, it would be fully crewed, so I have no clue how to sail."

Penn extends his hand. "I'm going to teach you how to sail today. You don't get seasick, do you?"

"Hasn't happened yet." I smile back at Penn, hoping today isn't the day I become seasick. I place my hand in his, and he pulls me on board. "Is this your boat?"

"Well, technically, it's owned by the Islander Ferry company. But seeing as my dad owns the company, it is pretty much mine." He grins. "We rent it out to visitors and do charter sunset cruises in the summer. It just so happens it's not in use today, so I thought we could head out for a sail."

Penn shows me around the thirty-two-foot sailboat, which is slowly rocking back and forth against the water. This boat is smaller than Uncle Rhett's, but just as clean and obviously very well taken care of. Penn explains that this boat could be used for racing or mindless, relaxing sails. It doesn't have too many extra frills, like teak and massive seating areas like Uncle Rhett's boat, but it's no less impressive.

Penn explains what a boom is and the differences between a sheet and a halyard, port versus starboard. He hoists the mainsail using the main halyard, and it flaps lightly in the soft wind.

"So you're ready," Penn says as a statement, not a question.

"Um. No. Nothing you just taught me qualifies me to sail." My heart starts to beat faster, and my stomach tightens as I swallow the thoughts of trying to sail this boat with Penn.

"Well, I guess it's a good thing I can sail this boat single-handed."

He sheepishly grins. "Sit down and watch the master."

I press my palms into my eyes. "Cocky much?" I give him a good eye roll after removing my palms, and a sense of relief washes over me, knowing I don't have to do much to keep the boat afloat.

Penn smirks and shakes his head at me. "You have no idea."

I'm pretty sure there was sexual innuendo in there, but it went over my head.

Penn tells me that our sex is incredible. I know I'm getting better at it, but I'm still a little shy and timid once we are both naked.

I push my thoughts of inadequacy out of my head and sit next to him at the helm. He pulls and tugs on different sheets ... or halyards ... I can't remember which is which anymore. He's so natural and comfortable working his way around the boat.

"How long have you been sailing?"

"Sailing with my parents and Chase are some of my first memories. We sailed everywhere when I was younger, especially during the off-season. I was on a competitive sailing team throughout high school, and that's when I became a competent sailor." He smiles.

Penn tightens the lines on the boom and leads us out of Ocean Beach harbor and into the Great South Bay. I'm mesmerized, watching his expert hands grind the wench and steer the boat.

"Where are we going?"

"Can't tell you. It's a surprise." Penn lifts his eyebrows.

I shake my head, playfully annoyed at not knowing. "Everything's a surprise with you."

"Okay, fine. I thought we could take a little cruise out east and then see where the wind takes us."

I smirk. He gives in so quickly.

With one hand on the tiller, Penn grins like a child with a triple scoop of ice cream, as a carefree spirit taking over his usual tense persona.

I lean back in my seat, taking in the sight of Penn. "Sounds perfect."

CHAPTER 27

Penn

Today on the water with Raegan has been better than I could have imagined.

The wind is cooperative and the temperature ideal.

I take the boat slow, savoring every moment we head east. I use the light wind and calm waters to teach Raegan how to sail. I have her crank the winch to trim the jib and even let her operate the tiller.

Her hair is windblown, her summer tan deeper and darker than when she first arrived, and I'm a complete goner when she takes off her tank top and shorts and sails with me in just her black bikini.

She's exquisite.

I talk to her about everything and nothing at the same time. This is what I enjoy most about Raegan. It's easy being with her, even when we talk about heavy stuff, like my mom, or her self-consumed mom—now that woman's a piece of work.

Raegan has a pure heart, always thinking about others and wanting to figure out how to make this world a better place. She's different from any other *socialite* I've ever met. I don't like to call her that because she is anything but a socialite.

Raegan is the first girl I've ever brought on the boat. No other has even come close to getting on board. It's clear I've fallen fast for

Raegan. I want her to know everything about me, and I want to know everything about her.

I dock the boat at Watch Hill Marina. Then I go below deck to grab the cooler with the picnic I packed, a blanket, a towel, and my backpack, while Raegan puts her clothes back on over her bikini.

"Let's go." I take Raegan's hand and lead her off the dock toward the beach on the ocean side of the island.

"Have you ever been this far east?" I ask, because not many people from our side of the island come this way. It's too far and doesn't have quite as many amenities.

"I haven't."

"I like it out here. It's a little more isolated, and quiet."

I'm hoping for some isolated and quiet moments for the two of us on the beach later.

"I'm actually not supposed to go past Sunken Forest," she tells me, embarrassed.

Welp. Another Uncle Rhett rule that we're breaking—though, technically, her uncle's been easing up on both Raegan and Lily, so I'm not too worried about Raegan getting in trouble. I have been trying to be somewhat respectful of her uncle's rules, but some of them are just ridiculous.

"Let's just not tell your uncle about this trip." She nods and smiles. "Where does your uncle think you are today, anyway?"

"Lily and I told him that we are spending the day in Kismet with some friends from school. Obviously, I'm here with you, and Lily is actually on the beach somewhere with a guy she met a few nights ago."

"I'm so glad you are here with me." I squeeze Raegan's hand three times, something my mom used to do to me when I was a little kid, and it's now become a thing I do with Raegan. Our unspoken words of comfort.

"Me too." Raegan smiles back.

When we reach the sandy beach, I remove my sandals and take Raegan's, too, putting both pairs in my backpack. I walk with her farther east, the soft warm sand pressing against my bare feet.

I have not seen another person in a good twenty minutes or so, and eventually we are the only two people on the beach. I lay the blanket down and take the snacks I packed this morning out of the cooler. I've never made a picnic before—another first for me.

I can't believe the things I've been doing as Raegan's boyfriend, but it all seems to come naturally. I don't feel like I'm doing it just to impress her. I wholeheartedly want to do this and show her just how much I care about her.

I pull out grapes, Ritz crackers, Cracker Barrel cheese, and chocolate chip cookies Maddie and Raegan baked last night at Boys of Summer while the guys and I played poker.

"Quite the spread. I'm overwhelmed." Raegan smiles before letting out a little laugh, and I know exactly why. She's probably used to picnics with foie gras and caviar, not cheap crackers and processed cheese, but this is why I enjoy being with her. She doesn't flaunt all she has. I looked her uncle up on the Internet because I was curious what he was worth, and it's a cool one billion. You'd never know Raegan comes from that much money—she's too down to earth, and too fucking good for me.

I pull Raegan down onto the blanket, and she plucks a grape off the bunch and pops it in her mouth, chewing slowly, eyes glued to me.

Turning me on just by eating a grape.

"Only the best for you." I run my finger over her bottom lip.

Two can play this game.

"And we can't forget the most important part of enjoying cheese and crackers." I grin and reach into the backpack.

"And what's that?" Raegan inquires and pops another grape into her mouth.

"Wine." I pull the bottle out of my backpack, followed by a plastic cup.

Raegan scrunches her face.

Crap. I've never actually seen her drink wine, only beer, Smirnoff Ice, and mixed drinks.

"You don't like wine?"

"I've only tried it once, last Thanksgiving. I was not a fan. I don't drink too much. I don't like feeling out of control, and I'm usually the one taking care of Lily when she's had too much. When I do drink, I prefer sweet and fruity. I guess I'm just not as refined as you." She giggles, knowing I'm far from refined.

I had to ask Margot, the old lady who works at the market, which wine she recommends, and it was this one, some red from the Napa Valley. Set me back fifty-five bucks. It better be luxurious on my tongue for that price.

"Ah, yes. I forgot. You have the palate of an eighteen-year-old. I should have thought that through." I mock her in good fun, and she swats at me.

Even though we can barely keep our hands off each other when we are together, I still can't get used to how her touch stimulates everything within me. I keep expecting the passion to stop, but sometimes it feels even more substantial than the last. Like a thunderbolt striking the tallest tree on the mountaintop—completely scorched.

I'm determined to drink this posh red wine today—it's part of the picnic, after all. "Do you want to try some?"

"Sure. I'll give it a try." She smiles.

"Living large." I smile back.

I take the wine opener from the backpack, pop the cork, and pour one plastic cup for us to share. I don't want her to feel pressure to drink any more than she wants.

I place the cup in the sand. "You need to pair the wine with some crackers and cheese—that's what Margot told me."

Raegan laughs. She likes to pop into the market and talk with Margot about books they are reading, and they often swap their copies back and forth. Raegan may be eighteen, but she has a little old soul in there, making friends with people of all ages.

I lean over and place a cheese wedge between two Ritz crackers. I move my hand to Raegan's mouth, and she opens it to take a bite. The crackers begin to crumble, and Raegan places her hands under her jaw in an attempt to catch the falling crumbs. The majority of cracker crumbs fall on the blanket, and Raegan is left with half a piece of cheese in her mouth. She lets out a little laugh, and dry cracker crumbs fly out of her mouth and onto me.

She covers her mouth with her hands, blushing, and all I want to do is wrap her up in my arms and hold her even closer. I'm enamored by Raegan. She's captivating. Even when her mouth is full of food, she's desirable.

I don't know what she sees in a guy like me. I literally have nothing going for me. I'll be on this small island for the rest of my life, and when I'm not working, I'll be locked away, writing music that no one will ever hear.

She's far too good for me.

I push the thoughts out of my mind. "Thirsty?"

She shakes her head up and down, her cheeks still rosy from covering me in her mouth-cracker crumbs. She's gorgeous and doesn't even know it.

I place the cup in her hand and move it up to her perfectly plump lips. Raegan looks in my eyes while sipping the red wine, her green eyes piercing deep into my soul. I watch her lips wrap around the cup and envision those same lips wrapped around my cock.

"Mmm," she moans, and my dick twitches. "That pairs well." She lifts her hand into the air with her pinkie out, pretending to be pretentious, something she'd have to try very hard to be. Her humor is infectious. I stare back at her, emotionless, but with a million fantasies running through my mind.

"What?" Her eyes go big and she smiles.

"Heart song: Mae, 'Suspension.'" I tuck a strand of windblown hair behind her ear. Then, with no inhibition, I crash my mouth onto hers.

I wrap my arms around her lithe frame, pulling her into me and lifting her up to straddle my hips. Raegan wraps her arms around my neck, opens her mouth, and accepts my invading tongue. I kiss her neck, and her sweet coconut lotion intoxicates every part of me. My dick is pressed hard against my board shorts, begging to be set free.

"Penn," she breathlessly says between kisses, "I need you."

I exhale. "I need you more than I've needed anything in my life." In every way.

I need her.

I want her.

She is becoming my everything.

CHAPTER 28

Penn

I glide my hand under her tank top, and my fingers drag up her torso. I quickly pull her top off in one motion. Her impeccable breasts are right at eye level. Not too big, not too small. Just enough to fill my palms.

Raegan reaches her hands down and pulls my board shorts off just enough to expose my cock. Raegan has become more self-assured over the past few weeks, vocalizing what she likes when we are intimate and taking the lead in being assertive. But she still gets uncertain sometimes and looks to me for guidance on what to do next, and today I'm going to encourage her to just do what feels good.

"Don't overthink it," I whisper, and tug the strings at the end of her bikini top. Her breasts fall free. I lie back on the blanket, pulling Raegan down above me. I take one nipple in my mouth, sucking and licking, using the combination that I know drives her wild. My thumb and pointer are on her other nipple, rolling and pinching.

I'm not too worried about getting seen or caught by anyone else out here. We are far enough east from the last community and tucked up near the dunes that we have privacy for messing around—though the thought of getting caught in broad daylight is a total turn-on.

"Penn ..." she moans and throws her head back, unashamed that we

are on a public beach—though, granted, it's empty.

I'm always turned on by how quickly Raegan responds to my touch. She's a constant inferno ready to burst, and it's been thrilling figuring out the best ways to make her detonate.

Our passionate, make-out foreplay session continues with reckless abandon. I silently laugh away the thought that I look like a horny teenager getting his first taste of ass.

Raegan peels her shorts off and is in only her bikini bottom as she straddles me again, moving her hips slowly back and forth over my dick. The sensation is unreal. I shiver from pleasure, and my hands ache with a need to explore and touch more of Raegan's body. Tiny spots overtake my vision. Raegan removes my shirt and draws her slim fingers over the outlines of the tattoo on my right arm. She slips her hand down and grabs my dick, not overthinking it. She strokes me in rhythm with my sucks and tugs on her nipples.

My skin tightens, and I want to flip her over and fuck her brains out, but with one last roll of my fingers, the fire that's been building inside Raegan ignites, and she lets go.

I watch her, eyes closed, riding out the ripples that course through her body. I don't stop or remove my hands from her chest until she opens her eyes and gifts me with her beautiful smile.

"Holy. Crap." She breathes hard as she looks down at me. "I didn't know I could orgasm that way."

"What way?" I ask with a sheepish grin, wanting her to say the words aloud.

"You know." Getting uncomfortable and shy now that we aren't lost in the moment of passion, she motions with her hands in a circular motion around her naked chest. "With just these."

I let out a deep laugh. "Oh, Rae, we still have so much more to learn." I slowly run my hand down her leg toward her knee before I reach behind her neck and pull her in for a kiss. Her damp swimsuit bottom presses against me. I deepen the kiss, stroking my tongue against hers. My dick is stiff and throbbing.

Raegan is a fucking temptress.

She reaches down and begins to pump me. Her strokes feel divine, and her tits are bobbing right in front of my face, swollen and slightly red from my previous attentions.

I take a moment to appreciate everything she has going on. She is slim but fit, and her sun-kissed skin has not one blemish on it. She is toned, and I cannot find one flaw.

I roll Raegan under me, lying her down on the blanket. I remove my board shorts and hover above her.

I reach for my backpack to get a condom. I check every zipper and pocket, tugging them open, and I can't find one. I could have sworn I threw a couple in there the other day.

Did we really use them all already?

I take a deep breath and hold it in, hoping to release some of my tension when I exhale. "I don't have a condom," I grumble. She's not on the pill, and I'm not willing to risk her getting pregnant by pulling out. I flick my gaze upward toward the sky and groan.

"It's okay. I could use my hand."

I look down, and Raegan's giving me a blushing smirk. Always finding the cup half-full.

Yet another quality of hers I'm consumed by.

Before I respond, Raegan grips my shaft and methodically runs her hand up and down my length. Her hands are like magic. My hand alone has never felt quite like this. Raegan's other hand wanders to my balls, and she palms them. A tightness pulses in my dick, and it seems I am a teenager, because that's all I need to be quickly pushed over the edge.

I release myself onto Raegan's belly and chest.

"Rae ..." I can't even finish my thought. I bury my face into her neck, careful not to let my body touch her seeded chest.

I pull back, and Raegan giggles. She looks down at my load covering her, then gazes back at me with those emerald doe eyes. She bites her lower lip, and I'm high off the fact that she's turned on by this situation.

"Wanna go in the ocean and clean off?" I point my thumb over my shoulder toward the water. The swells are low today, and it's relatively calm.

"Um, sure." Raegan sits up and tries to cover herself in embarrassment.

Reaching out, I pull her hands down. "You don't need to hide from me." The words roll off my tongue, but they are sincere. Everything I say to her is from the heart.

"Mm-hmm. Sure. Stallion," she teases back at me before breaking out in laughter. She stands up and looks at me in only her bikini bottoms.

My lips part as I reach behind and rub my neck. "Oh, you think you're so funny!" I move to catch her, but she steps out of the way.

"Race you to the water," she yells as she covers her breasts and runs toward the ocean.

I jump to my feet, grab my board shorts, and pull them up as I run to catch up to Raegan. I don't even want to know what fine we'd get for public indecency, but right now, I don't give a shit. I'll pay whatever the cost is to see Raegan running into the Atlantic topless.

I catch up to her and take her by the waist, easily throwing her over my shoulder before walking farther into the ocean. I don't care that I'm now covered in my bodily fluids because I've got my girl in my arms.

I quickly look around and confirm I can't see anyone in either direction before I walk us farther out in the water, closer to the breaking waves. I slide Raegan down my chest and slowly set her down. The water comes to her hips, her breasts on full display, and my semen is dripping down her abdomen. Her teeth chatter from the initial shock of the cold. I cup some ocean water in my hands and gently let it splash on her chest and stomach. I continue to clean her, touching her lightly every so often, watching the goose bumps rise on her arms, belly, and breasts.

Raegan bends down and cups the salty water in her hands, then tosses it toward me, splashing me right in my face.

I wipe the water out of my eyes. "Oh! So that's how you want to play?"

She squeals as she tries to move deeper into the ocean.

I catch her, locking my fingers into hers. Raegan is so much shorter than me, the water is already to her chest, and my hips are barely submerged.

We bob under an incoming swell and pop up on the other side; her wet hair sticking to her back and seawater falling off her eyelashes. We're now far enough away from the shore that we don't need to worry about the waves crashing into us. I can stand with my head out of the water, and instead of treading water, Raegan wraps her legs around my torso, interlocking her fingers behind my neck. I let the current push and pull us back and forth for a few minutes, until Raegan's teeth begin to clink together.

"Let's get you back on land and dry off." I kiss a droplet of saltwater off the tip of her nose.

"Soundssss gooooood," the words chatter out of her mouth.

I carry her on my back toward shore, walking sideways so I can keep watch of the waves behind me. Once we reach the beach, I run as fast as I can to our blanket. Sand flies everywhere. We are sticky from the saltwater, and now covered in thousands of tiny pieces of ground-up earth.

I lie Raegan on the blanket and hand her the towel I brought. She pats herself dry as I tie her bikini top back on, sad to see those sweet tits go back into hiding.

I sit on the blanket, allowing the sun to dry me. We polish off the bottle of red wine and *refined* snacks as we talk. Raegan is tipsy, maybe even borderline drunk, which shouldn't surprise me because she doesn't drink that often. She's lowering her inhibitions, and it's adorable. She's rapidly tapping her lips with her fingers and then suddenly stops.

"What's up?" I reach out for her hand and gently pull it away from her lips.

"So, I've been thinking. I don't know if I want to go to college," Raegan blurts out, then reaches for the wine cup and finishes the last sip.

What? Shit.

"I want to stay on Fire Island and not go to Berkeley. Would that be stupid?" Her words slur a bit.

My shoulders tense, and I pinch the bridge of my nose. Thinking. Stalling.

Stupid? Yes.

Would I love it more than anything? Another yes.

Should she stay? No.

How did I not see this coming?

Fire Island doesn't have anything to offer someone like Raegan. For her, Fire Island is a vacation spot, not a place to live her *real* life. When vacation is over, she needs something more to do than just be here with me. I can't let her throw away her future.

How did I let it get this far?

I attempt to muster up some courage, and the heaviness in my stomach drops even lower when I grab Raegan's hand, knowing what I have to tell her. "You ..." I hesitate, wanting to pick each word as carefully as I can. "You can't stay. You have so much ahead for you at Berkeley, and you're going with Lily. You've been looking forward to it all summer." My chest caves as she tilts her face down and frowns.

Withdrawing her hand from mine, she clutches herself, gripping her elbows. "But I've never been this happy." She tucks into herself further.

I pull her into my arms and hold her tight—breathe her in. I don't want to push her away, but I need to step lightly through this discussion.

"I wish I had the opportunity to go to college, to move away and do something I'm passionate about. Sure, I love working for Islander Ferry. One day it will be mine, but if I had a choice when I was younger, I would have gone to college and majored in something to do with the music business."

I can't mourn my past; it is what it is, but Raegan shouldn't give up a full-ride scholarship. "There is so much that *you* still need to experience. You need to live on your own, stay out all night, and eat crappy cafeteria food. You can't give it all up to stay here." I rub my hand down her arm, attempting to comfort her.

"But I don't want to. I want to stay here and figure out what I want to do and who I want to be. And I don't want to be away from you."

Jed's words echo in my mind ... *Don't fucking break my sister's heart* ... well, shit.

Raegan stares at me with a glazed-over look.

I know I'm going to have to break this off, but I can't, not yet.

I'm too selfish.

I need her.

Fuck. I'm screwed.

"I want to be with you too." I kiss her forehead. "We still have three more weeks of summer. Let's just wait and see how things go." It's a pussy answer. If I were a real man, I would end things now and .

not drag it out.

She replies with only a meek, "Okay."

Trying to end the conversation, but not be an asshole, I stand up and help Raegan off the blanket. She sways, the wine rushing through her veins.

I hold her hand as we walk back to the marina, the blanket and my backpack stuffed under my other arm. I stare at my feet in the sand as I walk, annoyed at myself that I didn't realize how much wine she had and for the fact that I didn't bring any water bottles to the beach.

I get us on the boat and have Raegan drink a bottle of water before I lie her in the small cabin to sleep the wine off. I hope the boat's sway against the current will put her to sleep and not make her sick.

I climb to the deck and prepare the boat to sail back to Ocean Beach. I'm in the zone, going through the steps to get the boat out of the marina and into the bay.

On the sail back, I'm alone with my thoughts, and it's a scary place. I'm still not sure exactly how Raegan and I got this serious.

I'd love nothing more than to come home to Raegan every day. We could have a simple life, but I don't know if I could ever be enough for her. She deserves the fucking world. There is nothing out here for someone like her. She's destined to make an impact in her wake and do something that brings meaning to her life. I know she doesn't want to be a lawyer, but if she goes to college, she can figure out other opportunities and still make a difference.

It takes a little over two hours until I steer the boat into the Ocean Beach marina. Raegan is still knocked out downstairs. I've made a note not to give her wine again. I should probably be responsible and not let her drink alcohol at all, since she's not even twenty-one, but, truthfully, I can be only so good at any one time.

After I tie the boat up, cover the sails, and hose off the deck, I go below and admire Raegan. Her salty hair has dried in a beautiful mess of curls, and her cheeks are pink from neglecting to add sunscreen throughout the day.

Against my better judgment, I crawl into bed next to her and wrap her tight in my arms. I know I shouldn't continue with this relationship, but I can't stop.

I wake up to the sounds of Raegan stirring. I'm not sure what time it is, but it's dark outside, so I know it's late.

"Hey." I reach for Raegan in the shadow of the cabin and brush her shoulder.

"Hey. Did I fall asleep?" She yawns and turns to face me on the mattress.

"You did. You enjoyed the red wine and then took a little nap." I chuckle, wanting to add "lightweight," but I hesitate, unsure if she will remember our discussion from the beach.

"I did. Oh my gosh, I'm so sorry. Did I throw up?" She cups her hand in front of her mouth and blows her breath into it. Seriously, could she be any cuter?

I laugh again. "Nope. No throw up."

You did throw up some words about your feelings of not wanting to go to college, but I'm hoping you've forgotten about them since you haven't mentioned it.

I sit up and see the digital clock in the galley from my spot, it reads 23:47. "It's almost midnight. Is your uncle expecting you home tonight?"

Raegan pushes herself up off the mattress and climbs out of the cabin. "I told him that Lily and I were sleeping at a friend's house and would be back tomorrow morning. So I'm good to stay the night, if you want me to."

My pulse deepens, knowing I'll get to be with her all night, and relief washes over me because she does not seem to remember the conversation, and things appear normal. I move to the end of the cabin and sit on the edge of the bed, pulling Raegan by her hips between my legs. "I'd love for you to stay the night. Do you want to sleep on the boat?" I've never done that with a girl before.

Another first ...

"Sure. But would I be able to rinse off in the shower? My hair is sticky, and there's sand all over me."

"Of course." I kiss her and hold her tight, wanting to savor tonight.

I show Raegan the tiny shower in the head. Since we rent the boat out, we keep shampoo, conditioner, and soap stocked so she can clean up.

While Raegan's in the shower, I clean the sand off the bed and lay fresh linens out.

After Raegan finishes with her shower, I jump in quickly, and sand fills the bottom of the drain as I wash away the day.

I grab a towel and wrap it around my waist. I find Raegan standing next to the small table in the kitchen area, hair down and half-wet, still wrapped in her towel. I guess we are both sleeping naked tonight because we don't have any clean clothes. I take her hand and lead her back to our cabin bed. We both drop our towels before we crawl in and settle under the silky sheets.

I'm exhausted from sailing half the day in the hot sun, and Raegan's in that post-drunk, half-awake haze, so I'm perfectly agreeable when she cuddles up next to me and asks, "Are you okay if we just go to sleep?"

I drag my fingers through her damp hair and place a kiss on her head. "Of course."

I'm grateful for the darkness of the boat. If I had to look into Raegan's eyes tonight, I might completely fall apart.

I need to pull back, but slowly. Not just for her, but for myself.

The thought of letting Raegan go tears me apart.

CHAPTER 29

Raegan

"Hey, hey, hey!" Lily's voice pulls me from my thoughts of the past week and a half.

"Lily!" I jump off my bed as she skips her way over to me. "I wasn't expecting you back until tomorrow." I give her a long hug, and she picks me up off the ground and spins me around.

Lily's been in Manhattan for the past few days because her parents were visiting from Turkey and requested to see her. Literally *requested*. She got a phone call here on the island from her Manhattan penthouse butler, notifying her of her parents' arrival and the need of her presence back in the city.

She was basically summoned to her yearly visit with them.

Lily sets me down on the ground. "My parents left last night; their plans changed, so I got on the first ferry this morning."

I'm so glad she's back. I'm not a great actress, and I feel like a sneaky liar, but somehow, I made Penn believe I was a little more intoxicated than I really was when I vulnerably told him I want to stay on the island and not go to college. Sure, I was a little tipsy from the red wine, but I was present and clearheaded when the words came out of me. It wasn't until I saw the look on his face, and he told me I should go to college, that I shrunk down in embarrassment and decided the best way to play it off was to pretend to be drunk.

I laid awake the entire sail back to Ocean Beach, too humiliated to bring myself up to the deck and face Penn. So I stewed with my thoughts, alone, and decided not to bring it up again.

Now I'm pretty sure I've scared Penn because he's been working a lot since that day, picking up extra shifts, and I can't figure out if it's because of what I said, or if they truly are extra busy.

I've been keeping all my thoughts to myself, but I need to talk with Lily about all of it and get her advice. I've never kept something big from Lily before, and it's eating away at me.

I'm sure she needs to talk too. Every time she sees her parents or has a conversation with them on the phone, she needs to decompress.

"I'm meeting up with Penn and the guys at the Sundowner tonight. It's eighties night. You coming?"

Every Tuesday evening, the Sundowner hosts a themed party. So far this summer I've been to *Jaws* night, where everyone wore their swimsuits with fake blood dripping off different appendages; Greek night, where it was a sea of men's naked chests and sheets wrapped around women as togas; and perhaps my favorite night thus far, Western night, because I got to see Penn wear a cowboy hat and extremely tight jeans with a huge belt buckle. Cowboy Penn may be my new fantasy.

"Uh, duh. I've been looking forward to eighties night all summer. I was so thrilled when my parents told me they couldn't stay one more day, 'cause I was legit sad thinking I'd miss eighties night. I stopped at that funky boutique in the village when I was in the city and grabbed us some awesome outfits." Lily holds up a few bags and flashes me a big grin. The contents will either be fun and mild, or over the top and hideous.

"So do you have any plans during the day, until eighties night?"

Even though Penn's been working, or maybe avoiding me, I've still been hanging out with him as often as I can. I stay the night at Boys of Summer frequently. But Penn is hanging with his dad and brother all day, and he said he'll be at the Sundowner later tonight, after he does his thing with them. I hope Lily doesn't have plans so she and I can do something together.

"Nope, no plans." She tosses the bags from the store on the ground.

"*Us* day?" we both ask at the same time.

Laughter erupts between us as we channel our inner BFF twin telepathy.

I love *Us* days because Lily and I get each other's full attention, because it's, well ... just us.

She will not be pleased once I tell her about Berkeley because it's been our dream since the ninth grade to go to college together.

"Beach?" Lily inquires as she reaches into the dresser and pulls out her red bikini.

I shake off the college thoughts. "Of course." I walk to the closet and pull out my brown-and-yellow bikini and begin to change. I apply a layer of sunscreen, put on my favorite Von Dutch trucker hat, and throw my swimsuit cover-up on.

"Ready?" I poke my head into the bathroom where Lily is brushing her teeth.

"Two minutes." Lily spits in the sink.

When she moves her head away from the sink, her hair swings to the side, and I notice a huge hickey on her neck.

"Lil! Who's been sucking on you?" I ask with amusement. I know for a fact she did not have that hickey before she left for Manhattan. Lily's hand immediately grips her neck to cover the evidence. She slowly turns toward me and smiles.

"Someone . . ." She grins, lost in thought.

"Does this someone have a name?" I pull her hand off her neck as she turns back to the mirror, stifling a laugh.

"He doesn't have a name because you don't know him." Our eyes meet in the mirror, and I glare at her in the way a best friend does when they want more information.

"I don't know any of the guys you've been with this summer, other than Theo. You've been so secretive. Running off all the time." I fold my arms across my chest.

Secret Lily isn't anything new, but this is a different type of Secret Lily.

"I promise. I'll tell you when I'm ready. I'm just not there yet."

Fine. I'll drop it and be respectful.

"Okay." I walk back into the bedroom with this unsolved mystery playing in my head and grab the book I'm currently reading from the side table, and throw it into my beach bag.

Ten minutes later, we are on the beach, laying out our towels on an open strip of sand.

"Okay. *Us* day. What do you want to talk about first? And not my hickey—that's off-limits. For today. Maybe I'll talk about it tomorrow." Lily smirks.

I dig around in my beach bag, looking for nothing in particular, just trying to keep my hands busy because I need to tell Lily. I need her input and thoughts about everything. My stomach churns, and my head goes to worst-case scenarios.

I gather my thoughts and start. "Okay. So you know how Penn took me on his boat last week?"

"Um, duh. That's the day he jizzed all over your naked chest. How on earth could I forget my little Rae-Rae becoming such a porn star exhibitionist on the beach." She roars in laughter.

I can't help the smile that crosses my face. Only Lily could turn that intensely charged moment with Penn into something funny.

"Yes, that day." I roll my eyes.

"Everything still going good?" she asks while applying sun oil to her legs.

"Yeah. Things are good. Being with Penn is easy and just feels right." I clutch on to the book I pulled out of the beach bag, running my fingers up and down the spine.

"And the sex? Still fucking awesome?" Lily raises her brows as she rubs the sun oil on her shoulders and arms.

The sex is unreal. I never knew this was what sex is like. Absolutely mind-blowing. Beyond anything I ever expected. Penn knows exactly what to do to make my body writhe with an orgasm.

Enough of the naughty sex thoughts, Raegan. Get to the point.

"Yes, the sex is still amazing. But about the day on the boat, I—"

I chicken out.

I'm not ready to tell Lily. She will be heartbroken if I don't go to Berkeley with her. I'm also slightly disappointed with myself. I should have figured these feelings out a year or more ago, not a week before we leave.

"You what?" She's invested and eager for the information I'm about to share.

I can't do it.

"I almost got stung by a jellyfish." I hide my trembling hand behind the book.

Oh my God, that's a pathetic lie.

"Um, okay." She's confused and is going to start asking questions if I don't fill in the blanks for her.

"Yeah, it was a red jelly, not one of those clear ones that don't sting. But it reminded me of when you got stung last summer and the lifeguard had to carry you off the beach."

"Oh my God. Yes. I was totally crushing on him all day, and then he was the one who came to my rescue and took me back to the lifeguard hut to wrap my leg and give me first aid. I wish I needed CPR because I wanted those lips on mine." She stares off at the ocean. "Remember I asked him out on a date, and he told me he was married?" Lily throws her head back and laughs.

I hysterically laugh, too, because I do remember.

"And then we saw him at Shipwreck a few nights later, and you approached him, but this time he was with his wife. That was freaking hilarious. You almost got your ass kicked by a thirty-something-year-old woman."

Lily's laugh radiates through the beach. "Ah, yes. That is a great story."

The jellyfish conversation turns into a full-on reminiscing session about the years past, and all the fun we've had together here on Fire Island and back in the city.

I think about the memories I will miss with Lily when I don't go to Berkeley—themed parties, late-night study cramming sessions, new restaurants, concerts, co-ed showers, public transit—there's so much. Lily and I have had so many experiences together, spanning since first grade. I'm about to change her entire world, and for a slight moment I think maybe I'll just go, for her, but I can't.

I decide that for the rest of the afternoon, I just need to relax and have fun with Lily. All the difficult conversations can come later.

—

"We should probably head back to the house now so we have enough time to get ready," I suggest to Lily as I start packing my beach bag.

"Yup. Sounds good. I'm gonna need extra time because I'm going to poof the shit out of my hair and may use an entire bottle of hair spray to hold it in place."

Lily may have been born in the wrong decade. The eighties are her jam.

I walk side by side with Lily up the beach to the street until we reach Uncle Rhett's place.

Penn has been ping-ponging in my mind today too. I'm looking forward to seeing him at the Sundowner later, since we didn't get to see each other yesterday.

Walking around the side of the house, Lily and I stop at the dual-head outside shower to wash the sand off before going inside. I leave my bikini on and let the warm water rinse the ocean and sand off my body. Lily jumps under the second nozzle and runs her fingers through her long blond hair, trying to get all the knots out.

I'm again trying to find the courage to talk about Berkeley. I don't want to continue letting fear stand in the way. Once we get to the room, I'll do it. I have to.

I reach for the clean towels Finn keeps stocked next to the shower and pass one to Lily before wrapping one around my waist.

Lily and I walk out of the shower, ready to head inside. "Hey!"

I turn toward the pool and see Jed in the water, resting his arms on the edge.

I walk closer to him. "What are you doing here? I thought you were in Manhattan until the end of this week?"

"Yeah. We were able to wrap things up quicker than anticipated. So I decided to come back to the island. It is eighties night tonight, and I don't want to miss that." He smiles weirdly at me, and then at Lily, as he lifts himself out of the pool. He walks to a lounge chair and grabs a towel to dry his face. "Can I invite myself to go with you two to the Sundowner tonight?"

"Sure. We're going to head to the dock at seven o'clock to catch a water taxi."

"Sounds good. I'll meet you downstairs at seven." Jed dives back in and begins doing breaststrokes down the length of the pool.

Lily shrugs and walks toward the French door. I follow behind her and we go upstairs to begin the transformation into eighties queens.

CHAPTER 30

Raegan

After we enter the room, Lily pulls out the bag of goodies she bought in the city and holds up a hot-green, zebra-printed leotard. The neck scoops so low it looks like half the leotard is missing.

"Hell no. I'm not wearing that." I'm serious. It's hideous.

"Duh. I know. This is for me. I'm gonna wear this strapless shirt underneath." She holds up a little half shirt of fabric.

If anyone can pull it off, it's Lily. Her long torso and legs will rock that leotard till sun up.

Lily then reveals a baggy pair of acid-washed jeans. "These are for you."

I laugh, relieved. "Thank you. And what do I get for the top?"

Please don't say a leotard. Please don't say a leotard.

"I went to a retro store and found this Beastie Boys *Licensed to Ill* shirt—they're eighties, right? If not, close enough. But they only had a size large, and it's way too big for you, but I thought we could make it super cute and cut the shirt so it fits you a little better." She tosses it over the bed to me, and holds up a pair of scissors.

Lily gets me. She knows that this outfit makes me comfortable, and that's another reason why she's my best friend. I hold the shirt up to my

body. "I love it."

"Let's get to work. I bought a crimper and some bright makeup too." She pulls the crimper out of the package and clicks the paddles together like cooking tongs.

Lily takes a shower first, while I get us some food from the kitchen and bring it up to the room so we can eat as we get ready.

When I get in the shower, Lily starts to talk above the sound of the water spray. "So I was thinking we should go shopping when we get to Berkeley and find matching bedspreads and decorations for our dorm room. What do you think about light blue and white floral? Kind of an airy vibe? We need our space to be welcoming and relaxed—laid-back. We also need to get a mini fridge for our Smirnoff Ice. And I need to find a cute carrier to take all my hair products to and from the bathroom."

I hesitate before I respond. Now would be a perfect time, but I don't bring it up. I'm a coward because my mind is made up, and I know I don't want to go. I just don't know how to tell Lily. I wash the conditioner out of my hair, "Sounds good." I cringe as I lie to Lily.

Through the foggy glass shower door, I see Lily give a little clap of excitement before walking out of the bathroom.

After getting dressed and blowing out my hair, I crimp and tease it to perfect the poof, but not too big. I'll leave the extra-big poof to Lily. I sit in my vanity chair in the bathroom, pick up the makeup brush, and begin to cover my eyes in bright-blue shadow.

"Oh! I forgot to tell you." Lily stops applying pink eyeliner from her vanity chair next to me. "We're basically in at Tri Delta. We still have to do all the rush activities, so it doesn't look like favoritism, but Jessica called me yesterday and told me that we're both in, no matter what."

Tri Delta, Lily's dream sorority. It's the sisterhood her mom was a part of, and though she doesn't even have a close relationship with her mom, she wants to continue the tradition.

Jessica was a senior at our prep school when we were freshmen. She was on the cheerleading squad with Lily that year, and they bonded over all things short skirts and high ponytails. Jessica attends Berkeley and will be the Tri Delta president this upcoming school year. Lily has kept in touch with her throughout the years, and she even hosted us when we visited Berkeley back in the spring. I've never been into the whole sorority thing, but it means so much to Lily, I told her I'd rush with her.

This is the perfect pivot. I have to do it now. It may ruin tonight, but we're supposed to leave for California in a week, and I can't wait any longer.

I set down the makeup brush and clasp my hands together. My knee bounces as I look at myself in the mirror, unable to make eye contact with Lily. "Can we talk?" I speak into the mirror but glance at her.

Lily pauses and turns her body toward me. "You look serious. Why are you serious? What's going on? Are you pregnant? Oh shit, you're pregnant. It's okay. We can figure this out." She reaches for my hand. "Does Penn know? Have you been drinking? Oh my God, what will your mom think? I can't believe—"

"Lil." I cut her off. "I'm not pregnant."

"Oh, thank God. I mean, a little baby Raegan would be adorable, but that would really put a damper on our whole college experience."

I give Lily a weak smile. There is no use in waiting any longer. I face her, push down my fears, and quickly rip the Band-Aid off.

"I want to stay on the island and not go to Berkeley." I blurt it out and raise my clasped hands to my face. I take a calming breath as I wait for Lily's reaction.

I held it in for so long because I've been afraid of hurting Lily—

that's the last thing I want to do.

Lily's processing what I just said. I'm half expecting her to turn on the dramatic part of her personality, but her face is frozen. I have caused her to become speechless. This is a first.

She stares off toward the shower, like she's unsure how to respond.

"Lily?" I move my chair next to her and take her hand, trying to pull her out of her trance.

Lily slowly turns to me. She frowns and sniffles, then wipes her nose.

"You don't want to go to Berkeley?" Her voice squeaks.

"Of course I want to be with you. But I've finally figured out that I don't want to move to California. I know you are looking forward to college, Tri Delta, and everything else that will be there. But I've been lying to myself when I look at why I'm going. I'm not going for myself. I'm going for you. Of course, you're my best friend, and I want to do college with you, but my heart hasn't been in it for a while. And you already know that I don't want to be a lawyer. That's my mother's dream for me, or really for herself. Like she feels it's her obligation to make sure I have the ability to crush a man with my words and skills in a courtroom, so he won't be like my dad and take everything when he leaves his family with absolutely nothing. I don't know what I want to do, so I've been thinking, why not take a year or two and stay here to figure it out?"

She eyes me, slowly removes her hand from mine, and pats my leg. I know she's letting me know she loves me but needs a little space. "Are you sure this change of heart has nothing to do with a certain guy who has shaggy hair and a liking for not clasping all the buttons on his shirt?"

It has a lot to do with that certain someone, but I can't admit that to Lily. She'll freak out. I haven't known him long enough for him to be the only reason I stay.

Right?

But I can't say I haven't taken Penn into consideration in all of this.

"Fire Island is my favorite place in the world, so why leave? Penn is perfect. He makes me feel appreciated. He cares about me and treats me like I'm the most important person in his life. Lily, I've never felt this way before, and I'm not staying just for him, but what if we are meant to be? What if he's my lobster?" I ask, referring to Rachel and Ross from *Friends*. "Penn living here is the bonus, the cherry on top."

She opens then closes her mouth without saying anything. I wait, and she begins to talk. "What will you do? How are you going to make money?" she shoots back. Her tone isn't angry as much as it is sad, or disappointed, or both. I can't tell.

I've thought about this a lot already, so I'm prepared with my response. "I was thinking I could work at Islander Ferry, pick up calls or take tickets or something. Or maybe I could waitress at the Sundowner. Chase is the general manager. I'm sure he'd hire me without experience and teach me on the job."

"So you're going to work a minimum-wage job, live paycheck to paycheck, and eat Top Ramen every day? You're going to end up shopping at thrift stores because you can't afford new clothes. Your lifestyle will totally change." Her voice is quieter, less animated, but she finally looks at me.

I could live on minimum wage and tips. I don't need a big expensive townhouse in the city and a driver and personal chef. I can do simple and understated. I'm sure I could find a reasonably priced rental in the off-season in Kismet so I could still be close to Penn. I'm not assuming that we'll live together.

"I know I can find a job, and I'll enjoy it, as long as it means I get to do something for myself for once in my life. And I don't want to live here forever, maybe just a year or two. Everything has always been handed to me, and it's time for me to figure things out on my own." I rub the middle of my forehead and close my eyes.

Not at Berkeley with Uncle Rhett's credit card.

Not at Berkeley with Lily introducing me to new friends.

And not at Berkeley with Abril sending me care packages.

Lily blows her cheeks out, then takes another deep breath. "You can't throw your future away for a guy."

Great. All of a sudden, Lily's a feminist.

"I'm not throwing away my future, and he's not just any guy." My voice chokes, and tears fill my eyes. I have to tell her. She's my best friend, but I haven't even admitted this to myself yet. "I think I may love him." My voice quakes.

Lily shakes her head repeatedly and gives me a glassy stare. "I *know* you love him." Lily doesn't miss a beat when she responds, like she's known my feelings for Penn long before I've even confessed them to myself. "He's been a great summer guy. Your *first* guy. But he's not going to be your long-term boyfriend or future husband. You shouldn't throw away everything just because you want to stay with him." She reaches out to me, taking my hand. "Neither of you have ever been in a relationship. The odds of this being true love are close to zero. I just don't want you to get hurt. You're my bestie, forever, no matter what." She moves her hands over her chest, and her lip quivers.

My heart breaks a little at her words. Penn's attentive, and kind, and sweet, and fun. Sure, he used to sleep around, but I don't see why we couldn't work. I'm not looking to marry him next week, but I do want to see how a future with him could unfold, especially now that I've decided I'm not going to Berkeley.

"Lily. He looks at me with passion, like I'm his reason for breathing. I know it sounds ridiculous, and I've only known him for a short time, but he's the one. I'm afraid if I leave it's going to change everything, and we're going to fall apart. And Berkeley, and law, has never been my dream." My voice is soft, and I rub my palm with my thumb.

A sense of relief washes over me to have this off my chest. I didn't expect Lily to support this plan, and I know we'll work through it. We always do.

"Have you considered what your mom and Uncle Rhett are going to say? They're going to be livid." She offers a flash of a smile that doesn't quite reach her eyes, but it's a step in the right direction.

"Oh, they're going to crap their pants and freak out." I laugh. I know that's exactly what they'll do. "Then they're probably going to cut me off. I already know what's coming, but you told me when we were at the dock before we left for Saint Lucia all about 'butterflies and twisting feelings in your stomach.' Then you went on to say, 'when it's your person, it feels right.' Well, Penn is my right person. He's my reason for butterflies. And total tangent, but I've been meaning to ask you how you even know about this *right person* business? You've never given a guy more than five days of your time. Theo is your longest relationship."

"Theo wasn't a relationship. We had a mutual understanding. We used each other for the other person's benefit. I've never been *in* love, but I know I'm capable *of* love." Lily's face strains as she talks. The impact of our conversation is taking a toll on her, and I feel guilty about it.

I clutch my chest. "When the day comes and you find the person you want to be *in* love with, you'll understand part of the reason I need to stay here."

At this moment, I guess I'm also admitting that a part of me wants to stay here for Penn. It feels and sounds that way, but it isn't my only reasoning.

Lily sits and continues to watch me as she picks at her cuticle. Her wheels are turning, but I continue, "I want to stay here. Berkeley is not where I want to be. I need time to figure out who I am, and not who everyone else wants me to be. I know this is crazy. But you know I don't make these types of decisions without thought. I've thought this through over and over. I can't go." I clasp my hands in prayer, pressing fingers to my lips.

Lily reaches over, wraps my hands in hers, and pulls them between us. A sense of calm fills the bathroom. "You have to go to Berkeley, but don't go for me, or your mom, or Uncle Rhett, but for yourself. Take it semester by semester. Get through to Christmas, and if you still feel the same as you do now, and want to be on Fire Island, then don't go back to Berkeley after winter break. But don't not come to Berkeley next week because you are scared of the unknown. You owe it to yourself to give it an honest try."

She squeezes my hand. It's hard to take her seriously in the scrappy bright leotard and the pink eyeliner.

"I love you, but I think you've lost your mind a little." She pulls me into a side hug.

I laugh into her arms, then pull away from the hug, and she blows me a kiss that I capture in the air and place on my cheek, just like we've done since we were kids. I know everything is going to be okay between us no matter what happens.

I hold my hands out, weighing the options.

Do I stay or do I go?

I stay. But I'm not telling Lily. Not yet, at least. So I lie, again, and I feel horrible. "I'll think about the one-semester thing, but no promises."

Lily holds her arms up in a victory V, tips her head back, and yelps. "Good. But make the decision for yourself, nobody else."

I nod so I don't give her another verbal lie.

"Okay. But right now you need to call your mom and tell her you don't want to be a lawyer."

Um, absolutely not.

Telling my mother I don't want to be a lawyer will be like stripping down naked and streaking across Times Square in the middle of winter. Cold and awkward.

"No way. I can't do that." I glance at Lily and shake my head in fear.

"Yes, you can. You need to finally stand up to her. You don't have to tell her about not wanting to go to Berkeley, but at least take the first step and tell her you don't want to be a lawyer." Lily stands and moves to the bedroom, pacing back and forth.

I follow her out of the bathroom and sit on the edge of my bed. "I'm scared to tell her. She's going to be all *Elenore* and make me feel like a piece of crap. Then she'll end up being disappointed in me for veering off the path of my preplanned future." I tap my heel on the floor, unable to remain still. I feel physically ill thinking about telling her.

"So what if she is? You'll never know if you don't call. Plus, doing this over the phone will be much easier than in person."

Neither phone nor in person are good options, but I understand where Lily is coming from. If I can't even tell my mother that I don't want to be a lawyer, how will I tell her that I don't want to go to college?

"Okay. Fine. I'll do it." I shift from foot to foot and rub the cotton material of my Beastie Boys T-shirt.

Lily jumps up. "Let me get the phone." She runs out of the room and rushes down the stairs. She returns a minute later with the cordless phone from the kitchen in her hand. I'm still in the same place where she left me.

Last I heard, she was in Florida, so I hope she's still there now, and in the same time zone. I find her cell phone number in my address book and punch it into the phone keypad.

It rings once, twice.

"Elenore Cline." My mother's voice is stiff.

"Hi, Mom. It's Raegan." My voice, on the other hand, is shaky and riddled with trepidation.

"What's wrong? Why are you calling? Is Rhett okay? Something wrong with Jed?"

I guess her surprised reaction is valid. I can count on one hand the number of times I've called my mother while she's traveling. It's not lost on me how she doesn't inquire about me; it automatically must be about Uncle Rhett or Jed.

"Everything is fine. Or, I guess it will be. I just wanted to call to tell you something."

"Oh, for fuck's sake, Raegan. Are you pregnant?"

What? Why is this her first conclusion too?

"No. I'm not pregnant."

Lily holds back a laugh from her spot on the bed. She gestures for me to proceed, but I choke on my words again.

"I'm a busy woman, Raegan. I've got a lot to do tonight and don't have time for small talk. If you need more than three minutes, I can pencil you in for later next week."

Because that's what every daughter wants to hear from the person who birthed them into the world. I'm tempted to just hang up the phone. She doesn't deserve to hear what I have to say, but I'm done with her making demands and trying to run my life from the sideline. It's time to prove to myself that I'm both capable and worthy of making my own decisions, and my mother can accept it or not. I'm done submitting to her every expectation.

"Actually, Mom," I say, adding a little bite when I say her name, "I wanted to let you know that I'm not going to be a lawyer. I've never wanted to be one, and I'm going to find something else to do as a career."

I spit the words out as fast as I can.

I wait.

And wait.

My mother is silent. Knowing her, she's planning each word to her response, perfectly calculated.

"Are you still there?" I brace myself for the onslaught of her opinion.

"Yes, Raegan. I'm here." She clears her throat. "If that's your prerogative, then fine. It's your life."

I don't respond. I wait patiently for the rest of her judgment.

But nothing more comes.

"Raegan? Did you hear me?" Her voice is blunt.

"Um. Yeah. I did." I cover my mouth with my palm. This is not at all what I expected. I thought there'd be a fight and an entire doctoral dissertation on her point of view.

"Okay. Then it's settled. You won't be a lawyer. I must get back to what I was working on. We can talk more another time."

What? She's okay with it?

Well, maybe she's not okay, she's passive-aggressive, but whatever. I'll take it.

"Okay. Thanks, Mom. I appreciate your understanding."

If that's what I can call it?

Did I just stand up to her, or is she playing a game with my mind?

"Mm-hmm. Oh, I forgot to tell you. I won't be able to join you next week when you fly to Berkeley. Something's come up with one of Rhett's estates, and I'll be leaving for Ireland in a few days. But I'll stop by for a visit sometime in October when I'm in California for work. I'll let you know when my schedule is firmer. Bye, honey."

She doesn't even wait for me to respond before she hangs up.

Bye.

"You did it! I'm so proud of you." Lily pulls me into a hug, lifting me off the ground.

I wrap my arms around Lily's neck. "That was bizarre." I laugh. "Thank you for making me do that. It was much easier than I expected." I squeeze tight to Lily.

If I told my mother that, I know I can tell her that I'm not going to Berkeley too.

Lily squeezes me back and pecks my cheek before putting my feet back on the floor. "Let's forget about all of this for the rest of the night and go get a little drunk and have a kick-ass time at the Sundowner. I can't let this awesome Spandex go to waste. You've still got time. Don't make a firm Berkeley decision tonight." She grabs the leotard straps by her shoulders and snaps them against her skin before she looks in her compact mirror and paints on a layer of bubblegum-pink lipstick.

Lily is right. Standing up, if that's what I can call it, to my mother felt good. Now I just need to go and have fun tonight.

Next up is Penn. I need to tell him everything—and not be fake drunk this time.

CHAPTER 31

Penn

Today is a day I hate more than anything. I'm usually on edge and irritable in the days leading up to today, and the guys know to give me space.

It's been ten years since my mom's last breath. Ten years of missed memories and moments. I'd give anything to have just one more day with her.

I miss her so much.

I wonder what she'd think of the man I've become. I haven't been too proud of him these past few years, but this summer has been different, and I know exactly why.

Rae.

Dad likes to do this "remembrance of Mom" ritual every year where we spend the anniversary of her death in the Ocean Beach house I grew up in, talking about Mom. He and Mom bought this house in the late seventies, and he's slowly made updates throughout the years, but he's always been careful to maintain things that have Mom's memory. Like this hideous avocado-green and burnt-orange floral wallpaper in the kitchen nook. She loved it, and he can't even bear the thought of removing it. So it stayed even when new kitchen cabinets and countertops were installed a few years ago.

We're sitting at the kitchen table, eating an early dinner of chicken enchiladas, Mom's favorite, while we continue sharing stories of her. Chase, my dad, and I have already shared some of our most memorable memories, and Dad always tells us the story of when they first met on Coney Island, as high schoolers.

Each year, Dad tells Chase and me a new story that he's never shared before. Today it's the story of when, and how, Chase was conceived. My dad is about halfway through the story, and I'm thinking this is something I could go my entire life without ever needing to know details of, but my dad is beaming just thinking back to that night. I can't hurt his feelings and tell him to stop. My parents had more love for each other than any other couple I've ever known.

Between laughs, silent moments of reflection, and some red eyes, we finish eating, clean up the dishes, and walk to the bayside beach to watch the sunset, another yearly tradition.

I sit on the sand between my dad and Chase, and the conversation changes from memories of Mom to Islander Ferry and how business is doing this season. Things are going well for Dad and the company these days. He's been trying to expand our services, and this past season he purchased a new water taxi to allow for more scheduled transits across the island. It's been paying off. Visitors are happy not waiting upward of an hour to get a water taxi. I know Dad has been putting a lot of time and effort into making Islander Ferry successful, so when we do the transfer of ownership, I'll be able to step right in and take over.

Our conversation moves from Islander Ferry to that of Chase and the Sundowner. Chase has been in the process of purchasing the Sundowner for a few months now, and he expects it to close shortly after summer. So he's not planning to go south to fish this off-season. He'll be here on the island doing a huge overhaul of the restaurant and bar, so next season it's fresh and new. I can't wait to see how it's going to look. Eamon will do most of the construction work since remodeling homes on the island is what he does in the off-season anyway.

We watch the sun set over the horizon as the sky takes on the pastel colors of spring.

Dad stands up and looks down at Chase and me. "Well, boys, I'm off. Thank you for today. You know it means so much to me." His eyes are puffy and his voice sincere.

I do know how much it means to him.

It means the world.

I'm not surprised my dad is leaving right after sunset. Each year he ends the night earlier than the year prior. He likes to have some time to himself and thoughts of Mom before the day ends.

I stand up and embrace my dad, thinking about how hard it must be to wake up every day without Mom by his side. Raegan is still alive, but even the thought of her going off to college in a week is torture, and I can't imagine how my dad wakes up every day and continues to live without Mom.

I let go of my dad as Chase comes in for his hug. "Good night, Dad."

Chase and I watch Dad walk up the beach toward our childhood house.

I expect Chase to follow behind him, but he stays put next to me.

"What's up?" I glance at Chase and see him staring at me, shaking his head.

"You tell me. You've been quiet and distant lately. The piano in your room hasn't been getting much play time. What's going on? Raegan issues?" He gives me a small smile.

I'm shocked he's this perceptive, or have I just been that obvious?

I don't usually have important information to confide in any of the guys, and when I do, I typically go to Eamon. But Chase is the one who's here, so he's going to get the story.

I exhale. "Yeah. She told me she doesn't want to go to college and that she wants to stay here." I stare at the sky, watching the sunset colors change, as darkness begins to take over. "Look around. Do you think I can provide the kind of life she's used to? The kind of life she deserves? She deserves to go off to college and experience life. She sure as fuck deserves so much better than me. She deserves so much more than anything I could ever give her out here." It feels good to finally let it out. I've been brewing on it since the day on the sailboat.

Chase pauses before he responds. "Remember Emily? These things fade."

"I haven't forgotten about Emily."

She was Chase's summer fling two summers ago, similar backstory and upbringing as Raegan. Daughter of a wealthy New York City businessman. She hooked up with Chase that summer, and they became inseparable, even talked about marriage and kids.

At the end of the summer season she stayed, renting a house close to ours in Kismet, and she got a part-time job at the market. She lasted only six months, couldn't handle the isolation and solitude of the island during the off-season. She eventually came to resent Chase and moved back to the city, breaking his heart as she left.

"Dude, I don't even like being here during off-season. I hate feeling landlocked and get antsy because there's nothing to do. Why do you think I head south to fish?"

I nod. "I'm not crazy about it, either, but I don't have a choice. Someone needs to run the ferries and water taxis." I don't mean it as a jab to Chase, it's the truth.

"Raegan is a city girl at heart. She doesn't understand the slow island life we live, the service side, especially during off-season. I've come to like Raegan, and I know she isn't exactly like Emily, but she grew up with privileges we can't even imagine. Her mom can just show up and whisk her away to the Caribbean without a second thought. She grew up with expensive things, her own driver, people who cook every meal and clean up after her. She attends galas and has unlimited cash flow. Guys like you and I make a living serving people like her and her family. She'll never fit into your world, and you'll never entirely fit into hers. Better to cut your losses now and let her go."

Chase is right about most of it, but not all. Yes, Raegan grew up privileged, but she doesn't act like it. She is down-to-earth and unpretentious, but life on the island is different from what she's used to. Fire Island is fun for the summer, but for real life, when the snow comes in and everything shuts down and we lose power and can't get to the store—that shit sucks. Unless you've been raised out here, as a true Fire Islander, it's a hard life to adjust to. I don't want to admit it to Chase, but I know he's right. Eventually Raegan would end up leaving, and that would be even harder to deal with than if she left now.

Why delay the inevitable?

"Or, dude, look, maybe you don't have to cut your losses. Why don't you go with her to Berkeley? You sure as hell don't have to stay on the island."

"I can't do that. You and I both know I can't leave Dad and the business. It's expected that I take over the company so he can retire. God knows he's worked hard enough all these years. He's entitled to it. No matter how much I want to be with Raegan, I need to think about Dad and how much he gave up to give us a home and a comfortable life. I can't leave him high and dry."

My dad almost lost Islander Ferry the summer my mom was sick. He was so committed to being by her side that he neglected everything else. Luckily, one of his captains and good friends stepped in and helped keep everything running. That was when I knew that I'd need to be there for Dad and Islander Ferry as I got older, and that's part of the reason I can't leave Fire Island and follow Raegan to college. I've thought about it so much, and I've tried to figure out how to make her and me work, but I can't, no matter how I run options. The only one that works is me staying here and taking over the company. It's time for my dad to finally live, and for me to step up and do what I'm supposed to.

"I'm sure he'd understand. He was young and in love once before." Chase claps back.

"Even if I did walk away from Dad and the company, Raegan's young and needs to be single and have fun. Make mistakes and have regrets."

She needs to hook up with strangers and have one-night stands. Though I'll never openly say this to Chase because that's the last thing I want to admit out loud. The thought of Raegan with another guy rips my heart apart.

"Why can't she have regrets with you? I would." He chuckles and I punch him in his side.

"I have never felt for anyone the way I feel for Raegan. She was not some conquest or some quick fuck. It will destroy me to let her go, but she can't stay here. And I'm not going to follow her to college. That's not fair either."

"Fuck what's fair. Follow your heart. Figure out how to make long distance work. There's the phone and email. Her uncle has enough money. He could fly her back here any time she wants, and soon enough it will be off-season, and you can fly out there to visit, and maybe after a year or two you move out there." My brother has become a fairy-tale narrator with the shit he's feeding me right now.

I've watched Eamon and Maddie do off-season long distance for the past three years, while Maddie finishes college at Yale. There is no way I can do it. And she's not clear across the country, just a ferry and car drive away. Their love is fierce and deep, and somehow, they've persevered, but not without their own trust and jealousy issues. Fights over the phone and tears every time one of them has to leave the other after a visit.

The thought of being with Raegan but not being able to touch her and hold her everyday sounds like absolute torture. I'm not sure if that torture is worse than not being together at all. But I just don't know if long distance will work for us, talking on the phone and seeing each other in person every few months, when our schedules align.

Am I not trying hard enough?

Dammit. I can't think straight. I can't focus. My chest burns, like I have acid reflux. "It's a no, man. Can we just not talk about it anymore?"

All I know is I want to be with Raegan, and I can't fathom the idea of letting her go, but I can't allow her to stay here. I don't know how I'm going to get her to leave, but I need to find a way.

Chase raises his hands in the air. "Fine. Your loss. I'm just trying to help. You heading to the Sundowner tonight? It's eighties night."

"Yeah, I'm going. Raegan will be there." I gaze out toward the water as thoughts of my childhood consume me, alongside those of Raegan.

"All right, man. I'm gonna catch a taxi and head home before going. I finally have a night off, so I get to hang out with everyone. But listen, man, we're all here for you if you need us." He grips my shoulder and squeezes.

"Thanks, Chase. I'm going to go for a bike ride. When you see Raegan at the Sundowner, will you tell her I'll still be there tonight? I just need a little time by myself right now."

"Absolutely, man. Do what you need to do."

Chase and I walk toward the houses, and he continues to the dock while I hop on my beach cruiser and pedal west.

The air is surprisingly cold for this part of summer, and I make it to the lighthouse without seeing anyone I know, which I appreciate. I'm not in the mood to talk to people right now.

I take out my key to the lighthouse, unlock the door, and climb the steps up to the observation deck.

The last time I was here was when I brought Raegan and we messed around. I smile, thinking about that night and how much has happened since then.

She and I were meant to be an uncomplicated summer thing, not a full-blown relationship.

I'm an idiot. With only days before she leaves for college, I'm finding myself at this impossible crossroads.

I wish my mom were here and I could talk to her. She'd know exactly what I should do. I reach for my poppy tattoo and rub it with my thumb, longing for it to be a magic lamp and for a genie to appear and grant me three wishes.

Dad, Chase, and I were by Mom's side when it happened. She and my dad decided early on that she would pass at home and not at the hospital. They had a special bed brought into our home, and the hospice nurses took shifts to care for her twenty-four seven.

I still remember her last day vividly.

Summer was in full swing. As a thirteen-year-old boy, I was more focused on spending time with my friends on the beach and trying to get the attention of girls, that I didn't realize how little time she had left.

A part of me didn't want to admit just how sick she was. Her body was frail and tiny, as she withered away in bed, barely eating, morphine drip constantly running into her veins to keep the pain at bay.

That morning, my dad came into the bedroom I shared with Chase, his eyes bloodshot and swollen from lack of sleep. He woke us up early and told us we weren't allowed to leave the house that day. We had to stay home and be together as a family. I was a shithead and threw a fit, pissed that I'd miss out on the plans I'd made with friends. Thinking back on that summer now, I'd change everything. I'd never have left her side, not once. I would have asked her to recount as many stories from my youth as she could. I'd have asked about her parents and childhood, about when she knew Dad was the one. I'd hug her, kiss her, and hold her hand once more before she was so delirious and cancer-ridden that she couldn't even recognize me.

I still remember the feel of the wooden kitchen chair I sat in all day, next to Mom's bed. Chase sat on the other side and Dad paced, walking around in a constant daze. My mom slept most of the day, but Dad asked us to tell stories and memories from when we were kids.

We never traveled for vacation and only went to New York City a handful of times. Due to the nature of Dad owning Islander Ferry and him needing to be around, even in the off-season, as he was crucial to supplying goods and food to the island, along with getting people back and forth. So we made the most of the time we spent here on the island. This was our home and our vacation.

Almost every story we shared that day included a boat of some sort, the beach, or a body of water. We also shared stories of the off-season. How Mom would somehow always get us to school on time in the freezing snow with no car, or how she'd let us build these wild forts throughout the house to occupy our time when everything was shut down and it was too cold to play outside.

We had a magical childhood, even if it was all spent on this small island.

Occasionally, throughout her last day, Mom would open her eyes, and we could feel her presence, but when she'd try to talk, she'd be incoherent and ramble. Nothing she said made sense, but we knew she heard our stories because she'd smile, even when her eyes were closed.

For some reason, it's those moments I remember most about my mom. Not the amazing ones when she was healthy and laughing and smiling, but the excruciating, sad moments of her last day. Her cheekbones hollow, skin pale and translucent, her body weak and fragile.

The doctors told us chemotherapy wouldn't help because her cancer was so progressed, and I remember thinking how lucky she was that she'd die with her golden-brown hair. It was an ignorant thought to have, but for some reason it gave me hope to know she wouldn't meet her end bald. On that last day, though, her hair was pulled back into a braid after not being able to shower for over a week. It was the best the hospice nurses could do to help ease the burden of Dad brushing her hair.

My mom was never more beautiful than on the day she died. At the end, she opened her eyes with a sense of peace and comfort, then looked at Dad, then Chase, then me, and when she met my eyes, she said, "I love you." And that was it. She closed her eyes, and her head fell slightly to the side. Her spirit immediately departed from her body. She never took another breath.

Dad let out a mournful scream and grabbed her in his arms, holding her with tears falling down his face, making promises to her that he's still kept to this day. Chase sat in the chair and watched, tears falling down his face. And I ran. I ran as fast and as far as I could, and that's when I ended up at the lighthouse, until my dad found me and took me home.

Every anniversary, I come here to be close to her.

I usually stay all night, sometimes until the sun comes up. But this year it feels different. I may have finally found some peace with her death, and I know it's because of a short and breathtaking girl who has stolen my heart.

I finally have someone I care about more than myself.

I know my mom is watching and hopefully smiling, proud of the man I've become, but it's time for me to go and enjoy tonight with Raegan. The right thing to do is end everything with her, and tonight will be the last time I'll have her.

"Embrace the present," as my mom would always say.

CHAPTER 32

Penn

I climb down the lighthouse stairs, lock everything up, and get on my bike. It only takes me five minutes until I'm walking into the Sundowner where Whitney Houston's "I Wanna Dance with Somebody" blasts from the DJ's speakers.

I scan the crowd and smile when I spot Raegan with Lily and Maddie. All three are dancing on top of one of the booth tables in the back corner, dressed like they are in the eighties. The guys—Chase, Eamon, and Jed—stand in front of the booth, drinking beer, assuming the role of protecting the girls from onlookers and any other guys who try to get too close. Theo is there, too, with his arm around a girl I've seen around the house a few times this past week.

Lily's wearing a lime-green, animal-looking scrap of material that scoops down to her belly button, with a black strapless bra-like shirt. She has on black leggings with neon-green leg warmers. The top is bright. So bright.

Maddie is decked out in a gray sweatshirt dress that falls mid-thigh, with a pair of black high heels.

And Raegan is making sexy look so effortless, in an oversized T-shirt, cut short exposing her tight tummy, with a pair of baggy jeans and her Chucks. She's in the least revealing outfit, and yet I find her to be the most attractive of any woman in here.

The chorus hits, and all three girls sing at the top of their lungs into their makeshift beer bottle microphones, while they jump up and down on the booth to the beat, consumed in their world of fun. I make my way closer through the crowded bar and laugh at how carefree they are when they are drunk.

Raegan sees me as I approach. She smiles and jumps off the booth, right into my arms. Her legs wrap around my waist, arms around my neck. Her beer bottle collides with Eamon's shoulder, and she giggles as she apologizes. She's probably had a few beers already, and I hold her tight, savoring the feel of her face on my neck as she kisses me. Her body is warm and slightly sweaty. She's feisty tonight, and I'm all for it after the somber day I've had thinking about my mom and the realization that I need to break up with her.

"I missed you," Raegan purrs into my ear.

"I missed you more." I kiss Raegan's lips, knowing each and every moment may be our last. I set her on the ground as Whitney belts out the final few notes of the song.

Lily and Maddie jump off the booth and drag us all outside for some fresh air and another round of drinks.

The hum and bass of the music rattles the dock, but I'm just glad we're able to talk and not have to shout.

"You girls look nice tonight. Very authentic eighties outfits," I tell them and spend an extra moment checking Raegan out.

"Can you believe Lily paid full price for half a leotard?" Jed looks around at us guys and chuckles.

"You looovvvve it." Lily dramatically smirks back at Jed before finishing her beer.

I wrap my arm around Raegan and pull her close. "Have you ever seen the Beastie Boys?"

Raegan shakes her head. "I like their music, but haven't seen them in concert."

"I saw them with Chase and Eamon at Madison Square Garden back in ninety-eight. I was seventeen. That was the first concert our parents let us go to that wasn't at Jones Beach. We thought we were such hot shit that night, going into the city on our own. We ended up getting so stoned that we missed the last train out of Penn Station, but we met some college girls on the street who went to NYU, and they invited us back to their dorm rooms and I—" I stop the story. Raegan wouldn't want to know the rest of it anyway. It's not a story I'm particularly proud of.

"And you what?" Raegan pokes my side.

"Naw, you don't want to know. We were young and stupid and so fucking high." I wave off the story with my hand.

"He lost his virginity and didn't even last a minute!" Eamon shouts from across the table.

"Thank you for telling the entire dock, you dick." I flip him off as laughter erupts from our group.

Eamon shrugs, laughs, and turns back to Maddie, Theo, and Theo's chick.

I lean into Raegan's ear. "Like I said, not a story I'm particularly proud of. I don't smoke weed anymore, either—Coast Guard regulations and all."

Raegan smiles and sways a little, undeniably buzzed, but Eamon's comment doesn't seem to faze her. "Did you have a good day, with your dad and Chase? I mean, as good of a day as you can. Ugh, I mean. Sorry. I don't know what to say."

"It's okay. I know what you're asking. Yeah, I did. I thought this year was going to be rough because it's ten years and all, but it's actually been the easiest one yet." I smile at Raegan. I want to tell her it's because of her, but I don't. Because I know I'm about to break her into a million pieces, and I don't need her to have any extra part of me to hold on to.

"I want you to know that I'm here for you." She reaches for my hand and squeezes it three times.

I'm not sure what I've done to be worthy of a girl like Raegan, but I squeeze three times back, and give her a smile before pressing a light kiss to her lips.

I pull away and brush a frizzy piece of her eighties hair behind her ear. "Thank you for being here for me."

I'm honest and so fucking confused.

I shouldn't have come tonight.

"I could be here forever, if you want me. I'll always support you. You support me just the same." Raegan pulls away slightly and tugs my arm, pulling me over to an empty table. I catch Jed staring at me as I sit down next to Raegan. His stare is intense, but I can't figure out if he's pissed or just drunk and in a daze.

"I wanted to talk to you about something. I know you think I was drunk that day on the boat. But I wasn't." She looks down at her feet, ashamed.

So she does remember that conversation.

"I told you I want to stay here on Fire Island. I'll admit, when I said it that day, it was impulsive, and I hadn't thought it through completely. But I've thought about it a lot since then, and I don't want to leave." She runs her fingers through her hair, her eyes seeking mine for a response.

The conflict in my head tugs in two opposite directions.

"I don't want you to leave either. But there's so much for you to experience at college. You're meant for more than a summer island." I reach for her waist, pull her closer, and wrap her in my arms. "I don't have to work tomorrow. How about we meet at the docks, and we'll go for a sail. We can talk more then, when we are both sober."

I can't do this here and now, but tomorrow I have to. Pain radiates throughout my chest. I need to lie down.

Raegan wraps her arms around me. "Okay."

I look toward our group of friends and quickly thank God I'm getting saved from having to come up with anything more because Lily is approaching, her eyes glued to Raegan.

I wonder if Lily knows?

"Hey! You two. We're going back inside, and you're coming with us." Lily pulls Raegan's arm away from my embrace and doesn't even give her a chance to decline.

Raegan gives me a small smile and follows Lily. I can tell she's not pleased that our conversation is ending without resolution.

How am I going to do this?

I grab my beer and walk back inside behind the two of them.

The girls dance the rest of the night, while the guys and I drink beers, talk shit about the tourists, and say hi to the people we know. I plaster on a fake smile so nobody questions my mood.

It's almost closing time, and I'm drained. The emotions from everything with my dad and Chase today have left me with nothing, and I'm trying to process everything with Raegan; plus, I'm a little buzzed from drinking.

I'm a fucking mess. I have so many emotions and feelings rushing through me.

"Hey, man. You okay?" Chase sits across from me and pushes a glass of water my way.

"Yeah, I'm good. I'm just ready to crash." I run my palms across my face in an attempt to wake up, then take a few gulps of the water.

"Did you and Raegan talk?"

"Sort of. I don't know how to handle all of this. I want her to stay, but she needs to go. I don't know what to do. I feel like I'm a woman, all emotional and vulnerable." I laugh because I am absolutely becoming a woman with all these feelings.

"It's all going to work out how it's supposed to. Hang in there." Chase pats my back, grabs my empty beer, and walks behind the bar. Even though he has tonight off, he's been helping his team out because the crowd is so large.

Raegan walks over to me and sits on my lap, wrapping her arms around my neck. I soak in the feel of her on me and her smell around me.

Suddenly I'm awake. I'm ready to take Raegan home and worship her until the sun rises up from the Atlantic. I selfishly need this one last night before I break her heart, and I know she needs it too.

"Hey, so I know I usually stay at your place on late nights when we are in Kismet, but tonight Lily and I are gonna both stay at Uncle Rhett's. Not sure if you saw those hickeys on her neck, but she wants to tell me how she got them. Are we still on for tomorrow?" She looks at me with her captivating eyes.

A sudden weakness overtakes my limbs, and I swallow the lump in my throat. My heart hurts, knowing that I won't get one last night with her.

I try not to let Raegan see how upset I am that she won't be staying the night at my place.

How am I ever going to let her go?

"Of course. I'll meet you at Ocean Beach dock at eleven." Unable to keep my hands to myself, I rub my thumbs across her waist and down to her thighs. I never want to forget the way she feels or how her breathing hitches when I touch her.

Raegan leans in, bites my ear, then whispers, "I wish Lily didn't want to tell me all this stuff. I'd much rather stay with you tonight."

"Me too." I pull her face toward mine and kiss her.

I pour myself into the kiss, and try to use it to tell her everything that I'm unable to speak.

"Heart song: Dashboard Confessional, 'The Brilliant Dance,'" I whisper into her ear. I know she knows the song along with the lyrics, and confusion crosses her face. It's not a *love* heart song; it's a *conflicted* heart song.

"Raegan," Lily calls from the other booth and points to an imaginary watch on her wrist. "Jed's ready to go."

Raegan's torn, wanting to stay and understand the heart song I just gave her, but also wanting to support Lily, so she tells me, "I need to go. I'll see you at eleven, and we can talk about everything." She kisses my cheek and walks out the door with Lily.

I manage to grab Jed's attention before he walks out. "Hey, man. Can you stop by tomorrow morning? I need to talk with you."

Jed looks around. "Sure. Is this about my sister?" He narrows his eyes to me.

"Yeah. Think you could come around nine, and keep this between us?" I hate the secrecy, but I need to talk to him before I see Raegan.

"I'll be there." He nods.

Jed leaves to catch up with Lily and Raegan, and I wait until I can't see them before I get on my bike and ride the two blocks home.

I crawl into my empty bed, but sleep doesn't come. I almost ride back to the lighthouse, but I don't. I push play on my boom box and a song by The Starting Line fills the room. I lie in bed and stare at the ceiling, trying to figure out how I can break Raegan's heart, and I don't fucking know how ... let alone want to.

CHAPTER 33

Penn

A knock on my bedroom door wakes me from sleep. I glance at my clock. It's 9:15 in the morning.

I finally fell asleep close to 6:00 a.m. I'm not going to be functioning well today.

"Penn. Jed's at the front door." It's Eamon.

"Tell him I'll be right there." I roll out of bed and throw a clean black shirt on, then grab a pair of gym shorts off my floor and pull them up and over my boxers before I unlock and open my door.

I take a quick stop to piss and brush my teeth, then walk into the living room, where Jed sits on the couch.

Eamon has disappeared to his room, I suppose.

"Thanks for coming over. You want a coffee?" I head into the kitchen and pour a mug for myself from the pot Eamon must have already brewed this morning. I have no energy and need something to wake me up.

"I'm good." Jed nods and waits on the couch for me to return.

I decide to get right to the point. My mood is bleak, and I don't want to drag this out any more than necessary. "So, at the beginning of summer, I made you a promise. I told you I wouldn't hurt Raegan. But I never expected to fall for her. I know there's going to be no easy way

to end this. I have to break her heart so she'll go to college. It's for her own good, for her future. I know you know that."

Jed is quiet for a moment. "I do understand. I never predicted how good you two would be for each other. I see how much you've changed, and I've watched my little sister grow into an independent woman. She's not the same girl who came here in May, and I know it has a lot to do with you. I know she wants to stay on the island, and she's hinted that you are pushing her to go, and I appreciate that."

My chest tightens as thoughts of Raegan fill my head, and I know exactly what I have to do.

"This is going to kill me, but I know I have to end it. Today. Completely. It will be over." My voice cracks and I'm about to fucking cry. "I'm meeting her at the dock at eleven. Maybe you could let Lily know?" My emotions shut down. I sound like a robot, my insides tear apart, and I'm losing every ounce of control I possess.

Jed nods. "I'll talk to Lily and make sure she's there to pick up the pieces. Thank you, Wells."

"I didn't mean for it to get this serious. But I want you to know that your sister means the world to me. I care about her more than anything. I promise now to walk away, but I need you to promise that you'll make sure she doesn't end up with a complete asshole."

"I admire you, man. I promise." He offers me a sad smile.

I draw my breath in and try to regulate my heartbeat.

"See you around." Jed extends his hand.

We've done a lot of hand shaking this summer. But this is by far the worst one because this handshake is filled with sorrow and regret. Without another word I walk him out, head straight for my bedroom, and close the door.

"Fuck!" I punch my fist into the drywall.

How the hell am I actually going to end this?

I can't do it. I can't look her in her eyes and break her heart, and mine. Why can't I let her go?

I'm sure I look as shitty as I feel, so I head to the bathroom to shower.

I stand under the spray until the water runs cold, and when I get back into my bedroom, I stop at my dresser, open the top drawer, and pull out a velvet pouch. It's a gift I bought Raegan when she was in Saint Lucia, before we even slept together. Before we were anything. I've been planning on giving it to her, but I haven't been able to find the appropriate time.

I stuff the velvet pouch in my pocket, not sure if gift giving when you break up with someone is acceptable, but I'll have it with me in case I do have an opportunity to give it to her.

—

I arrive at the Ocean Beach dock with the velvet pouch in my pocket and pace. Back and forth. Back and forth. I'm going to wear down the wooden boards with how excessive my steps are. My heart beats uncontrollably. The words in my head start to jumble, and I can't remember what I intend to say.

I glance toward the main dock, and Raegan's coming my way in her signature outfit of T-shirt and cutoffs. I don't know what band she has on the shirt today because she's too far away, but I hold my breath as I wait for her.

The breeze carries her fruity hair into my nose before she comes in for a hug. The feeling of her small hands wrapping around my waist crushes me. The wind is knocked out of me, and I can't breathe.

I wrap my arms around her. Never wanting this moment to end. This is the last time I will get to touch her, and I don't want to forget anything about her and how she fits in my arms like a nesting doll, how her sweet smell infiltrates my senses and overpowers my system. I don't want to forget her beautiful smile or her infectious laugh. I want to lock every single thing about her away in my head. I'll throw the key into the Atlantic so I can never unlock it. I'll torture my soul for the rest of my life.

"You look tired." Raegan pulls away from the hug, seeking my eyes, and I'm immediately cold.

"Yeah, I didn't get much sleep last night." I cast my face down toward the dock. I can't even look her in her eyes. I don't know how I do it, but I let go of Raegan.

"Everything okay?" Raegan's face fills with concern and a flash of innocence. She doesn't know what's coming, and that makes me feel even worse about what I need to do.

I take a step away. I can't be this close to her as I end it.

Raegan becomes immediately aware that something is off. Her posture straightens as she looks at me.

"Penn, what's going on?" Her voice cracks with confusion.

"You are far too good for me, and you deserve so much more than I can give." My hands are sweating, and I may have a heart attack.

"What are you doing? Penn? Don't do this." Her head is shaking. She now knows exactly where this is going.

I watch her eyes fill with tears, and my heart aches at the pain I'm causing her. But I know I have to push her away. She needs to go to college, and I cannot give her any hope of holding on to this—to us.

"Rae, this summer has been the best of my life. I've never felt so alive and complete. I knew from the very moment I first saw you on the ferry that I wouldn't be able to stay away from you." I'm speaking from my heart, and I'm on edge, about to collapse.

"You transformed me, our worlds colliding hard, and even with everything stacked against us, I wouldn't change one moment of it."

A tear rolls down Raegan's cheek, and I reach out to capture it, but she pulls away before I can touch her. I stare down at my empty hands as the world spins around me.

She's hurt ... because of me.

"You have your whole life ahead of you, so much you can do beyond here. You will accomplish so much. I'm sure of it." Another tear falls, but this one doesn't even touch her cheek, it hits the dock with a splatter. "We come from different worlds. You're Rose and I'm Jack. They didn't get a happily ever after, and neither will we. Our ship sinks in the end. There are too many obstacles that will prevent us from being together."

"No!" Raegan is shaking. "There aren't too many obstacles. We can make this work. I'll go to college, just please let's try long distance."

We can't do long distance. It will only prolong the inevitable.

I force myself to stay where I am and try not to touch or comfort her.

"I'll never be enough for you. You'll figure it out one day, and I can't let you throw every other experience that you deserve away. I need you to promise that once you get to college, you'll let me go, allow yourself to have fun, go to parties, meet people, maybe even fall in love. If you promise me that, I promise you that I will always look back on our time together and remember every single detail." A tear swells in my eye, and I can't hide it anymore. One blink and the lone tear rolls down my face.

"You've helped me heal from the demons that hid the light in my life, and as much as I want to keep you here all to myself, I'm never going to be able to leave this island. This is all I have to offer. There are so many people out there whose lives will be transformed by what you will accomplish, and I can't hold you back."

Even though I want to.

I pause, waiting to see if Raegan will say anything, but she doesn't. Her eyes are puffy as she folds her arms across her chest, protecting her heart from the words I'm breaking her with.

"Rae. This is the hardest thing I've ever had to do, but I know that

I need to walk away, and we both need to let each other go." She covers her eyes. I should stop talking, but I need to say just a few more things. I can't regret not getting it all out.

"Everything, and I mean fucking everything, that we've experienced together will sit in a special place in my heart forever. I know that you will make some man very lucky to have you as a wife one day." I choke on the word *wife*. The thought of Raegan with anyone but me crushes my soul.

"I love you, Raegan." I say it. The words I've held close to my heart since my mom died. Words I don't throw around or use lightly. Words that I've never spoken to another woman, ever.

I'm completely empty, having now said it all.

Raegan covers her mouth with one hand and uses the other to reach down and slowly lower herself to the dock. She pulls her knees into her chest and wraps her arms around them.

She sobs.

Broken. Completely wrecked.

She doesn't say *I love you* back, and I don't expect her to. I'm not worthy of it.

I want to wrap her in my arms and take back everything I just unloaded. I'm a monster, and I stand frozen, unable to do anything to remedy this.

I look up and see Lily running down the dock toward us. Coming to save her best friend.

I crouch down, taking Raegan's hand in mine, and squeeze three times. "Thank you for healing me. I'll never forget this summer. Something Corporate. 'Konstantine.'"

I don't need to tell her this is my heart song—she knows. This was the song the band played when we saw them together at Jones Beach, when I first got to wrap my arm around her.

Raegan pulls her hand away and doesn't squeeze my hand back. She doesn't look at me.

Lily slows as she approaches. Raegan's back is to her, so she doesn't know she's here. Lily frowns at me, feeling the pain of her friend.

I take a few steps toward Lily. "I'm so sorry. Please take care of her." I use a hushed voice, surprised I can even talk.

"I will." Lily gives me a hug, and it startles me. I was not expecting a hug from her after I just broke her best friend. "I know this was just as hard on you." She pulls away, and one more tear falls down my face.

I walk down the dock toward the Sundowner and put my hand into my pocket, feeling the velvet pouch.

So much for the gift.

It wouldn't have been right to give it to her today. I take my hand out of my pocket, knowing it will never be given to anyone else, ever.

As I approach the Sundowner, I see Jed sitting on a bench outside. His face rests in his hands, knowing his little sister's heart is now broken on the dock. He must have come down here with Lily.

"It's done," I tell him as I pass, continuing to walk toward Boys of Summer. I have no more energy to devote to anyone or anything at this moment.

"Wells!" Jed calls after me. I stop but don't turn around. I can't face him right now. I'm too emotional and scattered.

"You're a better man than I am."

"Please, make sure she ends up happy."

I flinch when Jed's hand touches my shoulder. "I will."

I walk away with trembling hands.

Once I'm inside the house and have confirmed that none of the other guys are here, I grab a beer, walk into my room, sit down at the piano, and force all my feelings onto the hammers and strings.

CHAPTER 34

Raegan

Thursday:

I can't think, can't talk, can't eat.

I'm barely breathing, barely surviving.

Yesterday my heart was shattered.

We come from different worlds. You're Rose and I'm Jack.

Lily and Jed brought me back to Uncle Rhett's, and I told them I just wanted to be by myself. I've been under my bedsheets with the lights out since.

The only thing I asked Lily and Jed to do was promise they wouldn't say anything to Uncle Rhett or Finn. I don't want them to know what happened and what a stupid, *stupid* girl I am.

Rain pelts against the bay window.

You are far too good for me, and you deserve so much more than I can give.

What are you doing? Penn? Don't do this.

Rae, this summer has been the best of my life. I've never felt so alive and complete. I knew from the very moment I first saw you on the ferry that I wouldn't be able to stay away from you.

The weather outside is just as dreary as my insides, and it seems fitting. I pull the comforter over my face, roll to the side, and curl

against my extra pillow. I beg my eyes to close so I can sleep and forget yesterday ever happened.

Forget Penn Wells even exists.

Friday:

I barely slept last night. Lightning and thunder rattled the house throughout the night, the weather an accomplice to my dark mood. But now the sun is shining through the balcony door and bay window, warming my legs despite the cold breeze from the AC.

It's too bright and merry for how I'm feeling.

No band T-shirt today?

No, not today. Why? You miss them?

I have a difficult time reading your emotions when you don't wear them on your shirt.

A knock at the door pulls me from my thoughts. I open my mouth to tell whoever it is to enter, but nothing comes out. My voice is nowhere to be found.

The door cracks open. "Hey, you." Lily walks in. "I brought some breakfast. Coffee and bagels." She smiles at me and sits at the edge of my bed. "You need to eat." Lily hasn't been back to our room since she and Jed left me here on Wednesday. I know she's been giving me the space I asked for, but I'm ready for her presence. I'm glad she's here.

"I'm not hungry." I'll surely barf if I even try. My insides are a mess.

"Just one small bite, please." She looks at me with concerned eyes.

"Fine." I take the bagel and lift it to my lips, taking a tiny bite, chewing it slowly between my molars and forcing it down my throat.

"I thought we could binge some *Dawson's Creek* today." She holds up a massive pack of DVDs, and it looks like all the seasons. In a strange, roundabout way, watching the *Dawson's Creek* crew struggle with adolescence and heartbreak just may help me.

"Okay," is all I can manage to say.

Saturday:

Lily and I spent all of yesterday watching episode after episode of *Dawson's Creek*, until we finished season one.

Lily would go down to the kitchen and come back with snacks and water every so often. We barely talked. It was the quietest she's ever been, but she let me cry in her arms when my emotions would overtake me.

Right now, we are snuggled in my twin bed. It's dinnertime, and we just finished season two.

"Let me go downstairs and grab some dinner, and we can start season three." Lily smiles and jumps off the bed, heading for the door.

I smile but don't respond. If it weren't for Lily, I would surely be prisoner to an even deeper, darker place.

Fuck. Rae. You're gonna be the death of me.

Nobody calls me Rae.

May I call you Rae?

Yes ...

Lily returns ten minutes later with Finn's homemade chicken pot pie. More comfort food. Finn must know I'm heartbroken up here, but I don't ask Lily to confirm.

My appetite is slowly returning, and I try to enjoy the food as we continue with our *Dawson's* marathon well into the middle of the night.

Sunday:

"Raegan. Wake up." I'm pulled out of my dream-like state by Lily shaking my shoulder.

I grumble some words, too tired to open my eyes. "Too early," I groggily say.

"It's eleven. And we're leaving this room today. As much as I want to continue with our *Dawson's* binge, we need sun, fresh air, and a long hot shower for you. You smell. We are going to the beach."

"I don't want to go to the beach. What if ..." I can't finish my words.

"What if you see Penn?" Of course, Lily reads my mind.

"Yeah. Him." I can't even say his name. "I can't see him. I'm finally feeling like I'm coming to grips with it all." I nervously pick at my nail bed.

"*If* you see him, you sit up tall and strong and don't let him know the power or effect he has on you." I wish I had Lily's self-esteem.

"Yeah, sure. I'll work on that." I lift my thumb to the corner of my mouth to bite at the cuticle.

Lily slaps my hand away from my mouth. "Don't bite and don't pick. You don't need to worry about Penn. I've already done my homework, and I've been informed that he's working today and tomorrow and won't be anywhere near the beach. We just need to avoid the dock."

I know I need to get out of this room, out of this bed, and see the outside world. If Lily says I won't see Penn, then I'll go.

"Okay." I force my body out of bed to shower and get ready for the beach.

—

Lily is right. The sun and saltwater are doing wonders to my headspace. Jed meets up with us and doesn't push or prod, but I smile for the first time in days. I even laugh at Lily's mischief on the beach a few times.

This is exactly what I need.

It's normal and relaxed.

A little hope fills within.

Perhaps I will be able to mend my heart, slowly, piece by piece.

Monday:

Lily and I are almost finished with season three of *Dawson's Creek*. This is most definitely the most TV I've ever watched at one time. Though it makes no sense, I'm exhausted, yet I've done nothing physical for the past four-and-a-half days, except for the excursion to the beach yesterday.

I grab the remote and turn down the volume of the TV. Lily looks over to me from her bed as she places a kernel of popcorn in her mouth.

"You never told me about the hickey the other night, since we both passed out when we got home. So. Who is it?"

"Really? You finally want to talk, but it's about my little hickey?" She tenderly touches her neck, almost as if she's reflecting on the moment it was branded on her. "It was just some guy I know in the city. We ended up seeing each other when I was there visiting my parents, and we hooked up that night. It's no biggie." She shrugs.

"What's his name?" I push mute and silence takes over the room.

"Jeremey. You don't know him." I don't believe her. She delayed in coming up with the name, but I shake my head in acknowledgment and don't follow up with any more questions.

"Do you want to talk about Penn?"

No. I don't want to talk about him.

Not at all.

But I know I should. I need closure before I leave for Berkeley, and Lily has been patient with me locked up in here. I need to start talking.

I've decided that I will go to Berkeley for one semester. I'll give it a try as Lily suggested, and if it's not for me, then I'll go somewhere else, just not back here.

I shouldn't hold it in anymore.

I swallow, knowing Lily will give me all the love and support I need.

"I feel like I'm being immature and acting like a needy child." I puff the words out quickly. Admitting this makes me feel like I'm twelve. Lily is quiet, letting me continue. "I'm not sure why his rejection hurts as bad as it does. He told me all the reasons we can't be together and why we have to end it, but he also told me that he loves me. Lily, he said 'I love you,' and I can't stop thinking about that. Because I love him too." My eyes swell with tears and emptiness takes over.

Lily walks over to my bed and curls under the covers next to me. "Did you tell him that?"

"No. I fell to the ground and cried. Then you found me, and you know how the rest has gone."

Lily doesn't respond again. I'm not sure how she became a therapist in the last three minutes, but my mind finally settles, and I want to tell her every little thought running through my head.

She grabs my hand and holds it.

"Then before he walked away, he gave me a heart song to ruin all heart songs. He's now tainted my favorite song. I'm broken. I gave him everything, every piece of my heart and body, and he's left me with nothing but a memory."

A memory that I know I'll carry with me forever. No matter how much I'm going to try to forget it, I'll never be able to.

"You are fucking amazing. Look at me." Lily sits up and pulls me with her. "This is your first heartbreak. I know it hurts, but I also know that there's no way you won't find those same feelings again. You're a catch, a full-on fifteen out of ten. I'm not telling you that you have to forget Penn exists, or that it will be easy, but you're gonna survive. You're gonna move on, and life will continue. You are strong, and your heart will become whole again. I promise." She wraps her arms around me and holds me as I let the last of my tears out.

"Let's go away to college together, live our lives, and have fun. We can settle down, get jobs, and be adults later. Right now, it's about you and me having the best time we can.

Lily is right. I need to move on, and I will—maybe not quite yet, but I have to. I can't live in this unsettled state forever.

I will survive this. I have to.

Tuesday:

"You sure you don't want to come to the party tonight?" Lily pops into the bathroom as I'm washing my face.

"Yes. Absolutely. I'm sure Penn will be there, and I don't want to see him. I'm finally feeling better since we talked yesterday, and if I see him, I'm going to go back to the *dark place.*"

"Do you want me to skip the party and stay in with you? I'd do that in a heartbeat. You just have to say the word."

"No. You should go. It's our last night here. Go find one last hookup." I laugh and grab a cloth to rinse off my facial cleanser.

Lily leaves the bathroom and replies from what sounds like the closet. "I can't believe how fast this summer went."

"Yeah, me too."

Lily and I leave tomorrow to head back to New York City to pack the rest of our personal things. Then Lily, Abril, and I will head to Berkeley to move into the dorms. Abril has been there for all my significant life events. It makes sense that she is the adult taking me to college.

I know this is all part of growing up.

Things change, people change, and life changes.

All I can do is learn to adapt.

I look in the bathroom mirror, taking in how much I've changed this summer. On the outside, my skin is now a deep olive, and my hair has lightened from the sun. I turn a bit and look into the full-length body mirror on the wall. My butt and legs are leaner and more muscular since I have been riding my bike and walking everywhere. On the outside, I've changed and look healthy, maybe even older, but on the inside, I'm a fragile mess. Barely holding on, my pieces mended together with thin string that will snap with one more tug.

I know I need to go to Berkeley, and I'll figure the rest out, like what I want to major in and if I want to join Tri Delta when I get there.

I know it's time for me to do things for myself and take my future into my own hands.

Lily pops her head into the bathroom again. "If you're sure you're good and don't want to come, then I'm going to head out and grab a bite to eat before the party." She pauses, catching me as I look at myself in the mirror. "Are you checking out your ass?"

"I was just thinking about how much stronger I've gotten this summer. Physically," I clarify.

"Your ass looks great, and you've gotten stronger emotionally too. Not just physically." She leans in and hugs me. "If you change your mind, the party is in Kismet, on the beach." I wrap my arms around her and hug her back.

I do not know what I'd do without Lily, but I've got my own plans tonight, plans that don't involve anyone but myself.

"I won't be here when you get back tonight, if you come back." Knowing Lily, she'll probably meet some guy and end up in his bed until morning.

Lily pulls away from the hug.

"Wait, are you going out without me? Where are you going?"

"There is a meteor shower tonight." I know this only because Penn told me about it at the beginning of the summer, and it's stuck in my mind because I knew it would be my last night here on the island. I envisioned it as some romantic event with Penn, not as a sad affair with me piecing together my broken heart.

"Oh, more stars." Lily laughs at my newfound enjoyment of the night sky, because growing up in Manhattan never allowed for much stargazing due to light pollution.

"Yes. More stars." I laugh. "The newspaper says there can be forty to sixty meteors per hour, with the peak right in the middle of the night around two a.m. If you're still up, and not busy in bed, you should go outside and see if you can find any. It's going to be pretty cool."

"Mm-hmm. Super cool." Lily loves to make fun of me for nerding out about the balls of gas shining in the night sky.

CHAPTER 35

Raegan

I pre-cleared my evening with Uncle Rhett since I plan to stay up as late as my body can do to watch. He didn't have any problem with me leaving the house in the middle of the night, and even with the vague time of when I'd be back. He mostly just seemed glad to see me going out.

Lily leaves for her party, and I spend the next few hours finishing packing up my clothes and toiletries, and I even take a small nap so I won't fall asleep on the beach later. I wake up around 10:00 p.m. and head to the kitchen to find something to eat. I read for a while in bed, and at eleven I pack my new iPod, a blanket, and the two Smirnoff Ice bottles I smuggled out of the refrigerator. Then I walk down to the beach.

Once my feet touch the sand, I take off my flip-flops and head east to escape from the Ocean Beach lights and the few large groups of people partying on the beach.

I walk for about ten minutes until I'm far enough away from the lights and other people. It's perfect, up near the dunes, on a small hill, next to the beach grass. I lay the blanket down and push play on my iPod. Taking Back Sunday's "You're So Last Summer" begins to play in

my headphones—some good angry music, just what I need.

I reach into the backpack, take out a Smirnoff Ice, and twist off the cap.

Memories of the summer, all the moments spent with Penn, flood my brain. I can't hold back the dam anymore—they powerfully cascade in and overtake every little bit of free space. The good and the ugly.

What's left of my heart tears into even smaller pieces.

You are absolutely breathtaking tonight. Eighteen looks good on you.

I finally settle and recline back, looking out to the horizon. I try to smile at the impressive show of shooting stars. They fall every few minutes, and sometimes I'm lucky enough to see two or three per minute.

I'm lost in my music and the solitude of the evening when something moves out of the corner of my eye. I shriek and wrap my arms around my legs, pulling them to my chest.

The shadow gets closer, and I rip my headphones off. I'm about to pick up my stuff and start running when a familiar voice fills my ears. "Rae, hey. It's me."

Even though I can't see him clearly in the darkness, I know it's Penn. His voice is unmistakable, and only he calls me Rae.

"You scared me." My heart is racing, not only because someone approached me in the dark, but because that someone is Penn.

I don't know why he's here. This is supposed to be my last night, and I can't deal with seeing him.

"I'm sorry. I was walking and saw someone looking at the stars. I figured it was you. I didn't mean to interrupt." He takes a step away from me. "Do you want me to leave?"

Yes. "No. It's okay." Why does my brain betray my heart? I didn't even hesitate. So much for standing my ground. I'm weak in his presence.

Penn holds up a blanket and chokes out a shallow breath before looking up to the sky, then back to me. "Could I maybe join you?"

He came prepared to stay.

He knew I'd be here. I can't even begin to try to figure out what that means.

No. "Sure." Again, my brain commits treason.

Penn lays his large blanket next to mine, not too close, but not too far away.

From the corner of my eye, I watch him sit down and pull out a few beers from his backpack.

"I brought provisions." He shows me a beer.

I'm not sure how he can be so casual at this moment. I'm barely remembering to breathe.

"No, thanks." I hold up my drink from the opposite side of Penn.

"Smirnoff, huh? You partying by yourself, Rae?" His small smile fades when I look over to him with a straight face.

I'm numb. This is not a party for me.

"Not partying. I'm watching stars fall." I take my eyes off him and look up just in time to see another shoot through the sky.

We sit in silence, staring out into the night. Stars envelop us, falling at every corner, but neither of us moves or says a word.

Penn's words swirl inside my head. Adding to the confusion and ache in my heart.

I need you. I need you more than I've needed anything in my life.

Be my girlfriend.

You are all I can think about when I'm awake, and you consume my dreams when I sleep.

Even if I could talk, I don't know what I would say.

Penn cracks open another beer, and I look at him. His face carries pain. He opens his mouth, looking like he wants to say something, but all I see are his heavy breaths in and out.

I can't talk to him. I'm filled with too many emotions. More time passes, and my neck is starting to hurt from the angle with which I'm looking up at the sky. I'm intense and focused. I don't know how I've sat here for this long with Penn right next to me. Every breeze carries his smell, and it's torture.

You're a storm, Raegan. A hurricane. I want to rush into the center of it, completely unprepared. You make me want to do all these things I don't normally do. I want to play a song for you.

Penn turns, so his entire body faces mine, but I continue to ignore him, willing another star to fall. "I want to be honest with you." I turn my head his way, trying to keep my emotions in check but knowing I can't resist what he has to say.

"I know this is your last night on the island, and I came to the beach hoping I'd find you. I knew you'd be here. I thought maybe Lily or Jed would be with you, but I didn't expect to find you on the beach alone. I don't know why I couldn't just turn around and walk away, or why I had to let you know I was here. I'm drawn to you. Like a moth to the flame."

If anyone's the moth, it's me. I've been torched, completely incinerated, and dead on the ground. The only reason I know I'm still alive right now is because my heart is beating like it may push out of my chest.

"I want to apologize for everything that happened this summer. I never expected to fall for you, but I did, and I just want you to know how sorry I am for letting it go that far."

Eighteen heart songs, to be exact. Same as your age.

"I forgive you." I have so much more I want to say, but all the mean and angry things I had planned to throw at him, that I've stewed over and thought about for the past week, are nowhere to be found.

All I feel in this moment is a deep and burning forgiveness.

I know there is a part of me that will never fully be able to let him go.

I want to keep seeing you, and I want to be the only one seeing you when you turn eighteen.

I turn more toward Penn, exposing myself to his presence. "I understand why you think I should go to college, and I want you to know that I am going to go, and I'm not just going because you broke up with me. I'm going to try it for a semester and see if I like it."

He smiles, seemingly relieved by my words. "I think you're going to love college."

I don't know about love, but I need to stay firm in my decision.

"I think so too." I will myself not to cry. I've made it this far. I can do it.

"I don't want you to leave tomorrow thinking you aren't enough. You are more than enough and far more than I'm worthy of having."

I move to Penn's blanket, reach out, and grab his hand. I don't know how or why I do, but I need it.

You want to be my boyfriend?

Yeah, I want to be your boyfriend. I want to buy you shit and take you out to dinner. I want to steal kisses on the beach. Play footsies at the Sundowner. I want us to have so many more firsts together.

The current running through us is electrifying. It feels like the first time he touched me at the bottom of the stairs on the ferry. Pins and needles prick me all over.

Penn wraps his fingers into mine, pulling me close. He's also unable to ignore the gravitational force between us. I welcome his warmth and body and bury my face in his chest while his head rests on top of mine.

"I love you."

There, I said it.

I've known for a while that I love Penn, but I've been too scared to say it, and then when he told me on the dock that he loves me, I didn't have the strength to say it back.

The first guy I've ever loved. He's right here and I can't have him.

"I love you too," Penn whispers into my hair. "All I want to do right this second is kiss away all the pain I've caused you."

"So do it. If I can't have you forever, at least give me tonight." I push myself up into Penn's lap, straddling him. Wrapping my arms around his neck, no longer the chaste girl who stepped foot on the island two-and-a-half months ago.

Penn's arms stay planted on the blanket, but he lets out a deep exhale. "We really shouldn't."

Penn is conflicted. His words say one thing, but his slack mouth, rapid breathing, and the bulge in his pants tell me he wants this.

"I know we shouldn't, but we both need it." I press down on him, and he lets out a moan that sounds more like a growl. He's trying to be the bigger person, the responsible one. I push down once again, and his hands wrap around my waist. I'm relieved he's not rejecting me. His fingers tighten, and I let out a whimper, begging him for more. He looks at me, hesitation filling his eyes. I'm not sure what comes over me, but I tug the hair at the bottom of his neck and say into his ear, "I want you to fuck me."

I've never spoken to him like that before. It feels salacious and wrong, but I need him. I need all of him before I can walk away and never look back.

Penn slams his mouth over mine. We are hungry for each other. Sloppy and needy. The kiss is urgent and demanding. Penn tugs and bites at my lower lip before pressing his tongue into my mouth. His hands grip me tighter than ever, sure to leave bruises, but I don't care.

I want him to mark me, scar me on the outside to match the cuts and bruises on the inside.

Penn flips me over on my back. The stars fill my eyes, and I feel the sand crunch underneath me.

Dance with me. I made this mixed CD for you.

Penn hovers above, rubbing his hardness against my center. He teases kisses along my jaw and neck, down to my belly button, where he's pulled my shirt up. His hands quickly unbutton my shorts, and in an instant, they are off.

I savor the moment. Even with the bits of sand all over the blanket, I don't care.

He darts his face back toward mine, his breathing uneven.

I thought you didn't do girlfriends.

Rae, you're different.

You're fucking perfect.

I lower my hands to unbutton Penn's shorts. He kicks them down to his ankles, reaches over to my blanket, shakes out some sand, and creates a pillow for my head.

Sand finds its way all over us as we unforgivingly punish and ruthlessly take hold and steal from each other what the other needs.

Penn reaches for his shorts, grabs his wallet, and pulls out a condom. He quickly wraps his erection, almost as if he's afraid I'll come to my senses and tell him to stop if he takes too long.

There is no priming as Penn fills me completely. He's rougher than he's ever been, and I need more.

I wrap my hands around his muscular waist and push him farther into me as I force my hips back against him.

I have these insanely strong feelings for you that I've never felt before.

Penn's pounding is relentless, driving in and out, going deeper and harder each time. It's painful and arousing all at once, but I push against him and meet each thrust.

Waking up next to you this morning is something I've never done before, and it felt right. So fucking right. It didn't feel scary or overwhelming.

I keep my eyes closed, afraid if I open them, I'll never leave. It isn't until the familiar build reaches my limit, the euphoria of pending release, that I weakly open my eyes, needing to see him in this moment. His eyes are wide open, focused on me. I see pain deep within—his usual spark has vanished.

"Let it go, Rae," he breathes into my ear.

I love you, Raegan.

I combust and feel Penn stiffen above me as he finds his release.

Penn collapses on top of me, breathless and spent, but holding most of his weight on his forearms.

After a few minutes, our breathing regulates, and he slowly pulls out of me and rolls off, a wave of guilt seeming to plague him.

We quietly and slowly find our clothes scattered on the sand and put them back on. I expected this moment to feel more awkward, but it doesn't.

Penn sits down and pulls me between his legs, my back to his chest. He wraps his arms around me, our fingers lock within each other's, and we watch the falling stars over the horizon of the Atlantic. Lyra shines even brighter tonight, taunting me with memories of the night Penn and I went up to the lighthouse. I wish Lyra would fall out of the sky so I never have to look at it again.

We sit in silence for what feels like hours, having used our bodies to say goodbye, and there is nothing more to say or do.

My body may physically leave Fire Island, but my heart is staying here. It will be here forever with Penn. But I'm going to try college, for myself, and no one else.

At half-past two, Penn breaks the silence. "I need to go. I have to be at the dock for work at five, and I need a shower and to get a little sleep." His voice is low and quiet in my ear.

I hold tight to him one last time before letting go.

Penn stands and helps me up. He wraps me into his embrace, and I don't move, not wanting the end of *us* to happen.

Penn places his hands on my shoulders and gently leans me back, looking into my eyes. "Rae, you came into my life like a storm and broke down all my walls, then rebuilt me into a different person. You are everything to me, but I know you need to go and live your life."

A single tear falls from my eye before I look up to Penn. "I'll never forget you."

Penn presses a gentle kiss to my forehead and runs his hands down my arms, taking my hands into his. He squeezes three times, barely making eye contact with me, but I notice his eyes are red and teary.

I squeeze back. I shouldn't. But I do. He means too much to me not to.

The saddest smile I've ever seen appears on Penn's face. With shaky hands, he releases me and turns away.

Without another word or glance, Penn walks up the beach toward town, and as loud as the screaming is in my head, begging him to turn around and run back to me, he doesn't. My life isn't a movie, and he doesn't change his mind. He's not coming back.

I'm a mess, emotionally and physically. My hair is a disaster, my clothes are wet and damp from ocean spray, and I have sand in all the places sand shouldn't be. Once I no longer see Penn, I gather my things through the tears that won't stop and slowly start the walk back to Uncle Rhett's.

When I'm almost off the beach, I wipe away the tears just long enough to look up to the sky, desperate for the universe to give me a sign. I see one last star fall through the atmosphere, and my heart beats deep within my chest, as the slightest sliver of hope emerges. I know somehow, someway, this can't be it. This isn't where our story ends.

—

Want to know how Penn and Raegan's story ends? Answers will come in book two of the Fire Island Series, *Return to Saltaire.*

THANK YOU!

If you enjoyed *Saltaire* would you please consider leaving a review on the platform(s) of your choice? Reviews help other readers find my book and I appreciate it more than you know.

ACKNOWLEDGMENTS

This has been a long time in the making, and I never thought it would amount to anything more than a story that was stuck in my head. The path to get here was long and exhausting. So many times, I wanted to give up and quit, but I kept pushing because of the love and support from so many. I offer my thanks and gratitude to the following amazing people.

Dawn—My coach and cheerleader. Thank you for taking a chance on me and guiding me every step, especially through those first few drafts. Your honesty and feedback were critical to the unfolding and telling of this story. Even though it took at least six separate times for you to remind me that Penn couldn't have random lines like a character from the 1800s—I finally got there. LOL.

James—Working with you has been an absolute dream. Your edits are meticulous and thoughtful, and your kind words always lift me up. I appreciate everything you've done to help me along the way.

Elaine—Thank you for your helpful comments and edits beyond the proofread. It was a pleasure working with you.

Marla—You have an eagle eye for details, and I'm so grateful you were the final proofreader on the manuscript. Thank you for all the English and grammar lessons along the way. I'm still unsure when to use blonde or blond, but knowing you do is all that matters.

Mary—Thank you for taking my mess of thoughts and creating a stunning cover and beautiful formatting. The entire book, from front to back, is absolutely gorgeous. Your work is amazing, and I can't wait to work with you on the next one.

Nancy—Thank you for your help. You have such a talent, and I look forward to working with you again.

To the Grey's Promotions team—Thank you for holding my hand

through all the promotion and launch activities. You are a fantastic group!

My beta readers and dear friends—Kaitlin, Erin, Joslyn, Julie, Joanie, and Kristin. This book wouldn't be what it is without your thoughtful feedback and encouragement from the very beginning. Thank you for letting me text, call, and steal evenings so I could obsess over Penn and Raegan. You ladies are the absolute best; without you, this never would have happened.

Kristi—I'm so grateful to have you along on this journey. Thank you for all your help.

Mom, Dad, and brother—Your support means everything, and should you ever read this book, just go ahead and skip the parts that make you feel uncomfortable [... insert emoji face with wide open eyes followed by the grimacing emoji face...]

To all my friends and family who have supported me along this journey—especially my Joyful Noise girls and my beautiful sisters-in-law—thank you for always being there and loving on me. I don't take for granted how lucky I am to have so many wonderful people in my life.

N—words can't express my gratitude for your support and encouragement. Thank you for letting me lock myself away nightly and on weekends to get this story out of my head. I don't think either of us realized that this is only getting started, so thank you for the future nights and weekends to come.

M—my sweet girl. I love you more than applesauce (special thanks to Jack Prelutsky for our favorite poem, and Ms. S for teaching it to us).

A huge thank you to the Bookstagrammers, bloggers, podcasters, and everyone else in the bookish community who read advanced copies, posted on social media, left reviews, and supported promotional efforts. You are the reason I can dream this into reality.

To the music that saves us—Every song on the playlist has carried me through a time in my life (happy, sad, complicated ... the list goes on and on), and I hope just one song here can mean something to you.

Finally, to you, the readers—Thank you for taking a chance on me. Without you, this entire thing would mean nothing.

ABOUT THE AUTHOR

Hazel Jacks is fueled by boba tea, pop punk/emo music, the beach, and sour candy. She lives on the West Coast with her husband and daughter.

Printed in Great Britain
by Amazon